# ANONYMOUS
# FOOTSTEPS

# ANONYMOUS FOOTSTEPS

JOHN M. O'CONNOR

COACHWHIP PUBLICATIONS
Greenville, Ohio

# TO PHILIPPA

*Anonymous Footsteps*, by John M. O'Connor
© 2017 Coachwhip Publications
Introduction © 2017 Curtis Evans

Title published 1932
No claims made on public domain material.
Cover image: Snowflakes © Alexey Kljatov

CoachwhipBooks.com

ISBN 1-61646-406-2
ISBN-13 978-1-61646-406-6

# INTRODUCTION
## Curtis Evans

### TRACKING A MYSTERY WRITER'S ELUSIVE TRAIL
#### John Marshall O'Connor (1909-1975)
#### and *Anonymous Footsteps* (1932)

Among the personal estate of Elinor Colby (Mahoney) Smith at her death in January 2003 at the age of 93 was seemingly a quite incidental thing, at least to non-bibliophiles: a copy of a 71-year-old mystery novel, *Anonymous Footsteps*, published by a long defunct New York firm, Cheshire House. Elinor Smith evidently had been rather interested in the author of the novel, John M. O'Connor, for inside the book she had pasted not only his photograph as a very young man (captioned "John Marshall O'Connor January 1927"), but additionally a couple of obituary notices and a sheet of information which she apparently had researched and compiled about the author in her own hand. Without this information it seems likely that John M. O'Connor would have remained as anonymous as the titular footsteps of his novel. With this information the author of this introduction has been able to piece together the story of an interesting man—an actor, teacher, and author of an accomplished detective novel—and his unique publisher, Walter P. Chrysler, Jr.

John Marshall O'Connor was born on September 4, 1909, in Manchester, New Hampshire, the son of a doctor, John Christopher O'Connor, and Helen Jackson Raymond. The new arrival was named for his mother's father, John Marshall Raymond, an attorney, banker and one-time mayor of Salem, Massachusetts. (John's only sibling, a younger brother named Raymond, was also named in honor of their prominent maternal grandfather.) Dr. O'Connor was a 1902 graduate of Dartmouth, where he was a noted member of the football team. After graduation he coached college football for five years, including two at his alma mater, where he compiled a record of 14-1-2. During the First World War he served in Europe as a major in the Medical Corps, afterward returning to Manchester, where he met an untimely death from a heart attack at the age of 43 in 1922, when John was but twelve years old. The doctor's widow relocated with their two boys to a three story brick colonial home in her home town of Salem. Later that year John was sent to Phillips Academy in Andover, Massachusetts, from which he graduated in 1926. Following in his football hero father's footsteps, he matriculated the next year at Dartmouth, though he does not seem to have taken up sports, like his parent. Rather, he became, before his graduation from Dartmouth in 1931, extremely active in collegiate acting, creative writing, and debate. (According to newspaper accounts "he was a member of the victorious debating team that toured England and defeated the teams from Oxford and Cambridge Universities.") All in all, according to later book promotional material, John had been "one of the best liked men on the campus."

Like his slightly older contemporary, the great locked room mystery writer John Dickson Carr, whose first detective novel, the superbly creepy *It Walks by Night*, had just been published in 1930, John Marshall O'Connor decided upon his graduation from college to try his hand at a career that was precarious even during the bountiful period known as the Golden Age of detective fiction: mystery writing. An additional potential model (indeed a very likely one) for John O'Connor would have been the decade older Clifford Orr, who, several years after his own graduation from Dartmouth, published two detective novels, *The Dartmouth Murders*, 1929, and *The Wailing Rock Murders*, 1932, the former receiving a great deal of attention at his alma mater at the time John was in attendance there. (Both of Orr's novels have been reprinted by Coachwhip.) In any event, the year after his graduation from Dartmouth, John published a detective novel with the new firm of Cheshire House, started in 1930 by a twenty-one-year-old Dartmouth classmate, Walter Percy Chrysler, son of the wealthy automotive executive of the same name. At Dartmouth John and Walter Chrysler had edited *The Arts Quarterly*, to which John had contributed plays, short stories, and novelettes. (While still a student Chrysler later founded the college magazine *Five Arts*, which he co-edited with yet another Dartmouth classmate: Nelson Rockefeller, future vice-president of the United States.)

From offices on the fifty-seventh floor of the Chrysler Building, young Walter Chrysler directed his nascent publishing enterprise, which issued a dozen books in 1931, all lavishly produced limited editions of classic literature, such as *The Rime of the Ancient Mariner*, *The Fall of the House of Usher*, *The Legend of Sleepy Hollow*, *The Scarlet Letter*, *Aesop's Fables*, and *Through the Looking-Glass*, at $10 a volume. Subscribers to the ambitious project, which in 1931 netted Cheshire House three places (the maximum allowable) in the Fifty Best Books of the Year as ranked by the Institute of Graphic Arts, included Nelson Rockefeller; Mrs. E. F. Hutton (aka Marjorie Merriweather Post); Anne Morgan, daughter of the late J. P. Morgan; boxer Gene Tunney; and a much-touted postal clerk in Vermont making merely $60 a month. However, after fourteen months and the reported loss of $38,000 on an edition of Dante's *Inferno* illustrated with seven William Blake engravings, Chrysler decided to enter the fray of "general trade" with, what else, a line of mystery fiction, priced at the market rate of $2 a book. Chrysler divulged to the *New York Times* that he had spent a substantial amount of time over those fourteen months "trying to find what he considered a well-written mystery story." The young publisher pronounced to the *Times* that "most detective stories are not at all well-written. . . . From any literary standpoint Edgar Wallace [then the world's bestselling crime writer] is no good . . . I don't want to publish a book that I can't believe is well-written."

Happily, Chrysler considered his Dartmouth pal John O'Connor's *Anonymous Footsteps* well-written indeed, enjoying the book so much that he scouted Hollywood executives in an attempt (unfortunately unsuccessful) to get a film adaptation of the novel made. Some carping newspapers noted an incongruity in the hoity-toity Cheshire House publishing a murder story concerning "a handful of characters on a remote Adirondack island who murder each other with reckless abandon," but mystery fans, a devoted breed, did not complain about being presented with what the mystery critic for the *New York Times Book Review* called "an entertaining and absorbing yarn." The superbly-produced volume included in the front matter three floor plans of the murder mansion.

In style *Anonymous Footsteps* bears similarity to John Dickson Carr's aforementioned shocker *It Walks by Night* and Mignon Eberhart's old dark house mystery *While the Patient Slept*, both published in 1930, though the structure of the novel resembles S. S. Van Dine's bestselling family elimination mystery, *The Greene Murder Case* (1928), filmed under the same title in 1929, with William Powell playing gentleman amateur detective Philo Vance; and it also anticipates *And Then There Were None* (1939), Agatha Christie's famous mystery novel about people stranded on an island being bumped off one by one by a remorseless murderer. The notice of the novel in the *New York Times* provides a good description of its plot: "No matter whom you may suspect of the murder with which this story opens, the odds are that he or she will be dead before the end of the book. One after another the members of the Lanard household die violent deaths in their island home in the Adirondacks. No police are at hand to ferret out the murderer, for a wintry gale has cut off all communication with the mainland."

On hand in the house of death are focal character Ethel (Baines) Trevor, a nurse brought by her secret husband, Dr. Alfred Trevor, to the Lanard mansion to care for the dying head of the family, Henry Lanard; Lanard's fickle wife, Frieda; his calculating attorney brother Courtney; his bitter spinster sister, Janet; his handsome black sheep son, Neville; and his servants, African-American couple Sophie and Cowpers Freedly, respectively the cook and butler, and Hodges, the rather uppish chauffeur. Hovering like a specter over the household is the late Elizabeth Lanard, the youngest child in the Lanard clan, whose arresting portrait still hangs in the house. Additionally, in classic tradition an unexpected guest will make an arrival in the midst of the murder maelstrom that soon engulfs the mansion. Whether this person ultimately proves friend or foe I will leave the reader to determine for herself.

*Anonymous Footsteps* was well-received upon its publication, but, unfortunately for the neophyte mystery writer, his patron's publishing firm Cheshire House was about to fall. For his general trade market young Walter Chrysler had decided not to publish merely mystery fiction,

Original cover
(courtesy Curtis Evans)

but true crime as well. Toward that end, reports Walter Chrysler, Sr. biographer Vincent Curcio, "he hired a detective and a novelist to work on a book about a sensational rape and murder case in Hawaii that was then making big headlines." Doubtlessly this was what was known as the Massie Affair, the trial of socialite Grace Hubbard (Bell) Fortescue and several accomplices for the murder of local prizefighter Joseph Kahahawai, whom Fortescue believed had participated in the gang rape of her daughter Thalia (Fortescue) Massie. The titillating combination of sex, social position and race naturally made the scandalous affair major newspaper fodder. As advance sales for the Cheshire House book mounted and Walter, Hollywood stars again in his youthful eyes, hopefully planned yet another movie deal, Walter's father, mortified that his son would have truck with such unsavory matters, pulled the rug out from under Cheshire House, effectively shutting down the firm. ("If it's the last thing I do in my life," Curcio quotes the elder Chrysler as righteously avowing, "I'm going to see to it that this book is not published.")[1]

With the once glittering Cheshire House now permanently shuttered, John O'Connor found himself seeking other career options. At Dartmouth John had been heavily involved with the Experimental Theatre and the Dartmouth Players, serving as president of the latter organization during his senior year and for several seasons taking the lead in its stage productions. (In this respect John again resembled his Dartmouth predecessor Clifford Orr, who had written musicals for the Players in the early Twenties and likewise served as president of the organization.)[2] Even before his writing career had come to a sudden

---

[1] Vincent Curcio, *Chrysler: The Life and Times of an Automotive Genius* (Oxford and New York: Oxford University Press, 2000), 624.

[2] As I relate in "'A Bad, Bad Past: Rufus King, Clifford Orr, College Drag and Detective Fiction," an essay in *Murder in the Closet: Essays on Queer Clues in Crime Fiction Before Stonewall* (McFarland, 2017), the Dartmouth Players became embroiled in scandal in 1925, when actors in the group became suspected by the university administration of engaging in less than clandestine homosexual activity. Clifford Orr was himself gay and a friend of many of the people involved in the so-called "Beaver Meadow" affair, but he was not directly implicated in it. One consequence of the scandal was the gradual elimination of men in drag playing female roles on stage; by

halt, John was acting professionally upon the stage. In 1932 he had joined the Clare Tree Major Players, perhaps the most prominent children's theatre group in America. Over the next several years he performed roles in several northeastern states in such plays as *Alice in Wonderland* (the White King as well as the stage manager), *The Secret Garden* (Dickon Sowerby), *Aladdin* (the Magician) and *Huckleberry Finn* (Jim). Notices of John's "Jim," a character all too often referred to, most lamentably, as "Nigger Jim," were uniformly positive, a Reading, Pennsylvania, reviewer writing, for example, that, "as played by John M. O'Connor," Jim "not only won the childish audience with his first sneeze, but gave them more to laugh at with his dancing, his snoring and—his acting. He won, too, the adults of the audience."[3]

In January 1933 John wed another member of his acting troupe, native English actress Philippa Bevans (1913-1968), to whom he had dedicated *Anonymous Footsteps* the previous year. After leaving children's theatre the couple continued acting on the stage, appearing, for example, at the Westport Country Playhouse in Connecticut, John in Lynn Riggs' *Green Grow the Lilacs* (later adapted as the beloved musical *Oklahoma!*) and Philippa in George Bernard Shaw's *The Millionairess*. Unfortunately, the couple was growing apart—"marital troubles!" notes Elinor Smith—and they divorced in 1941. Philippa would later go on to enjoy a successful career on stage, film and television, her best known role being that of Henry Higgins' landlady Mrs. Pearce in the original stage production of the enduringly popular musical *My Fair Lady*. (Her voice can be heard on the original cast recording on such prominent numbers as "I Could Have Danced All Night," where she supports Julie Andrews.) Bevans, whose figure significantly rounded in her later years, most often seems to have played matronly women of

---

1929, when John O'Connor had become active in the Players, men in drag had been banished entirely from the Dartmouth stage, with women being imported to take the female roles. Although the twice-married Walter P. Chrysler was, like Clifford Orr, gay, I have seen no suggestion that John, who also wed twice (see below), was so inclined.

[3] Despite continued controversy over the novel's racial dimension, *Huckleberry Finn* remains a staple of children's theater. However, the portrayal of Jim by a white actor obviously would raise a multitude of objections today.

## CHILDREN'S PLAY SCENE

**"DICKON" and "MARY LENNOX"**

"Dickon" presents "Mary Lennox" with a hoe to work in the secret garden, in a scene from the play, "The Secret Garden," to be presented in the auditorium of William Penn High School, Monday afternoon at 3.45 o'clock.

The play will open, as the book does, with a scene in an English railway carriage as little Mary Lennox concludes her journey from India to Yorkshire, England. Ben Weatherstaff, the gardener at Misslethwaite Hall, Mary's new home, helps to teach her about England, which seems very different from India where she has spent her early years.

John M. O'Connor, who plays the part of Dickon, is a graduate of Dartmouth College, and his theatrical career has included important roles in support of Helen Hayes and Osgood Perkins. He has been a favorite with child audiences during the four years he has been with the Children's Theater.

The part of Mary Lennox will be played by Dorothy Major, while Philippa Bevans and Dorothy Fox Slaytor will play Martha and Mrs. Medlock, respectively. Miss Bevans will be remembered as the White Queen in "Alice in Wonderland," while Miss Slaytor, who has been a favorite member of the company for a number of years, returns at this time after a half a season's absence for radio work.

Harrisburg, PA, *Telegraph*, April 9, 1936

middle years, including not only in *My Fair Lady* but in 1962 episodes of *Alfred Hitchcock Presents* and *The Twilight Zone* and the Sixties films *The Notorious Landlady* (with Jack Lemmon and Kim Novak), *The World of Henry Orient* (with Peter Sellers), *The Group* (with Candice Bergen) and *Madigan* (with Richard Widmark and Henry Fonda).

While Philippa Bevans' career was waxing John's was waning. Philippa performed in seventeen Broadway plays over the course of her life, but John did so just twice, in 1938 and 1946, appearing both times in minor parts. For a time during the Second World War John served as a private in the US army, but Elinor Smith records that during the war John had a nervous breakdown. ("Nerv. Breakd. during War," she writes.) After the war John married again, to one Jacqueline Paige, and enrolled at Columbia University, where he obtained an MA and PhD; and he later taught classes for eleven years at Rockland Community College in New York. Sadly, John's health declined precipitously when he reached his early sixties, with the author and actor turned teacher becoming afflicted simultaneously with leukemia, diabetes, and degenerative arthritis. On July 26, 1975, John succumbed to a heart attack at the age of 65 and was interred in a small veterans' cemetery on the grounds of Rockland College, under the view of his old office.

Walter Percy Chrysler, Jr. passed away thirteen years later in 1988, at the age of 79, after a long career of art patronage, though he never revived Cheshire House, the once-promising publishing enterprise and plaything of his youth. Elinor Smith outlived both John M. O'Connor and Walter P. Chrysler, lasting to see the appearance of a new century. What, the reader of this introduction may wonder, was her own connection to John O'Connor, about whom in her later years she had gathered personal memorabilia and research notes into the still pristine white pages of her copy of *Anonymous Footsteps*?

Elinor Colby (Mahoney) Smith was born in 1909 in Salem, Massachusetts, where John O'Connor moved in 1922, when he was 12. In Salem the two young people lived less than half a mile apart from each other, he at 8 Chestnut Street and she at 39 Warren Street. At the same time John was attending Phillips Academy in Andover, Massachusetts, Elinor, a pretty brunette with a permanent wave, was attending Abbot Academy, Phillips' equivalent in Andover for girls. Elinor later graduated from Wellesley College and earned an MA in English literature

from Radcliffe College in 1934. After her marriage to Boston architect
Philip Horton Smith, she and her husband settled in Salem, where they
became active in the city's amateur theatricals group, The Privateers.
An obvious kindred spirit with John, Elinor made certain in her copy
of *Anonymous Footsteps* to preserve what currently is our best photo-
graphic image of John M. O'Connor: a young man laughing in the
Salem (?) snow, seemingly looking confidently ahead to a life burgeon-
ing with promise.

John Marshell O'Connor
Jan. 1927

Elinor Colby Smith
and the photo of
John M. O'Connor
saved in her copy of
*Anonymous Footsteps*

# ANONYMOUS FOOTSTEPS

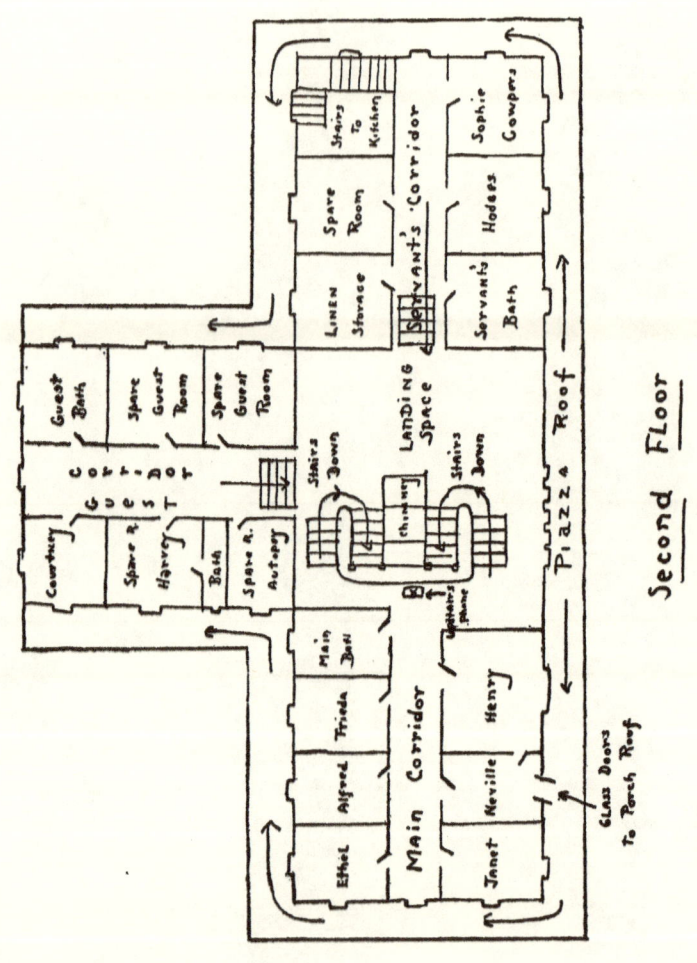

Second Floor

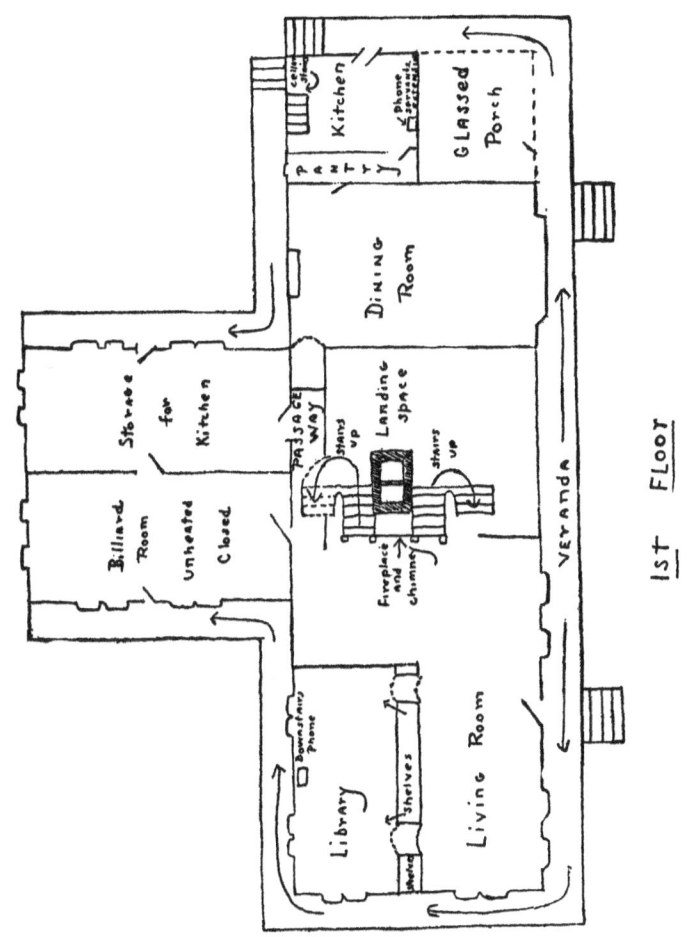

1st Floor

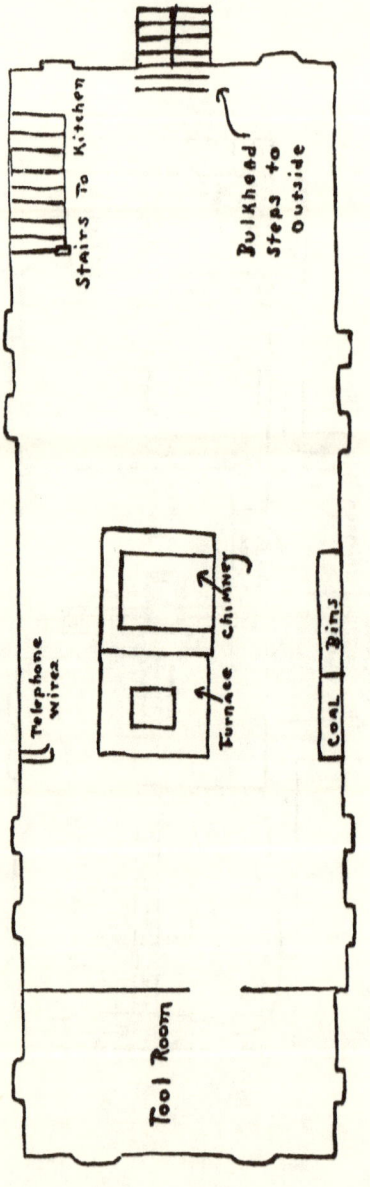

Cellar

# CHAPTER I

Ethel thought the buzzer must have rung at least three times before she sat up in the bed, switched on a light, and tried to cover herself in the ample woolen of a dark blue kimono. She slipped a wrist watch over her hand, and while fastening the clasp saw that the dial said twelve minutes after one, which meant that Mr. Larnard had been asleep for nearly three-quarters of an hour. He was probably worse, or he'd have slept the night through, after the medicine he'd been given. She brushed an edging of snow from the window sill. She could see nothing outside but the light from behind her piercing weakly into the infinite grey blur of the blizzard. The wind came savagely across the lake and nearly pulled the casement from her hands as she closed it.

She gathered the kimono more tightly about the chilly starched white of her uniform and tried to make her stiffened fingers tie the cord around her waist. For a few seconds she let her hands rest on the luke-warmth of the small radiator, quietly cursing the senile caprices of Henry Larnard, the deliberate patriarch, in contracting pneumonia at his summer home and thereby keeping a household of people in the wintry Adirondacks until the middle of November, especially with radiators that did little more than smell frightfully of steam. She renewed her bitterness against the whole selfish family—all but Neville; against Frieda Larnard, so obviously playing the solicitous young wife of the bronchial husband and becoming insultingly younger and more blithe as her husband's vitality waned into helplessness; against the legal blandness of Courtney, her patient's younger brother, so arrogantly aware that his soot-black hair was becomingly streaked with grey and that bachelorhood left him a constant prey to enticements.

Courtney had apparently stayed at the island to give a lawyer's sanction to the daily changes in Henry Larnard's will. But now that Henry was too weak to bother much about changes, Courtney continued to remain. Although he frequently avowed during breakfast that he must get back to New York, that the "firm" expected him to do three times as much work at fifty as it had at twenty-five, and that he really didn't know how he could excuse himself for idling away week after week in the wilderness, Ethel was perfectly sure that his connection with the world of affairs amounted to no more than an endless series of dinner engagements. He was staying, she felt sure, to see that no changes left *him* out of the inheritance. It was quite apparent to everyone but Henry, and at times he must have suspected, that Courtney and Frieda were pleasantly engrossed with each other and would marry the minute pneumonia had definitely overcome Henry. The most satisfying bit of cynicism which occurred to Ethel was that they would be perfectly suited to each other.

She resented Janet, the Larnard sister, as she resented the truth; because Janet was old at fifty-two, older than many centenarians, and she herself would soon be as old as Janet at thirty. Janet seemed always to be grimly present whenever you made a mistake. She gave the impression of never *entering* a room or leaving it; she was always there from the start—and stayed till everyone else had gone. Ethel resented Janet's resolute bitterness because she realized that she herself could never be resolutely anything, and the idea piqued her. Most of all, she loathed the pelican nose on Janet. This nose had been broken thirty years previous when Elizabeth, the youngest and the favorite Larnard, had flung Janet from a veranda roof. Everyone excepting Janet had thought it an accident. But for Ethel the nose was not so much part of Janet as it was a memento of Elizabeth. It never allowed her to forget that Elizabeth, although now dead, had been Alfred's first wife, and that Dr. Alfred Trevor had only married Ethel after Elizabeth's death two years ago, but so soon after the demise that he was still ashamed to let the Larnards know he was married again. At least, so he said, "out of consideration of their feelings."

Ethel knew very well that Alfred's consideration was for no more than his own chance of coming off well in Henry's will, a chance which would diminish out of sight if Henry ever discovered that Dr. Alfred

had belittled Elizabeth's memory by marrying again so abruptly. The
Larnards had always been inseparably, bitterly close to one another.
Alfred and Elizabeth had always spent their summers on Henry Larnard's island in the secluded waste of the Adirondack lake. Even after
Ethel had become his wife, Alfred had been there in the summer-
time. He had discreetly packed Ethel off to a healthy shore place in
Maine—not, she knew, without sharp misgivings. His love for her was
a strong and inquisitive series of possessions that left him disturbingly
alone when she was out of sight. She knew that Alfred never had any
awareness of her except through his eyes, ears, and hands, his sense of
mastery and excitement. He was divided between his zest for assuring
himself a portion of the Larnard fortune and his inordinate need of
securing her as a constant factor in his scheme of living. She realized
that with almost no effort she could have forced the choice, made him
renounce the Larnards, their feelings and their money, and care for
nothing but herself. But as he was already noxiously devoted to her and
she was more than tranquil when away from him, she had never made
the slightest effort to finesse.

When a telegram from him had brought her from Maine early in
October to nurse Henry Larnard's obvious decline, Ethel had presumed
that Alfred was at last making a clean confession to the Larnards and
staking his chances on being a faithful physician to Henry. But when
Alfred had explained to her during the long drive from the depot to the
lake that she was to appear in the household merely as a nurse and to
keep back the fact of being his wife, and had expected her to be pleased
with his adroitness, she almost balked. As it was too late to withdraw
gracefully, she had gracefully accepted, taken Alfred at his word, and
made it almost impossible for him to even see her during the subse-
quent month and a half.

She had begun flirting with Neville to plague her husband, to an-
noy him with the truth that he could not have his cake and eat it, or his
wife. Neville, being fond of gallant gestures and rather bored, was not
difficult to flirt with. He was the only child that Frieda had ever seen fit
to be begotten with, and Neville was hardly out of the bassinet before
he began to make Frieda regret her one compassion. He had inherited
a perfected form of her own brilliantly-dark good looks and a precoc-
ity from his father that far outdistanced Frieda's mere gushy vivacity.

His disposition alternated between a sharp surliness that echoed his mother's hauteur, and a lolling, debonair jollity that might once have been Henry with more spirit and fewer worries. Frieda supposed that Neville would be looked on as *her child*, but she rapidly found out that everyone, including Henry, looked on her merely as Neville's mother, and this was complete chagrin.

Ethel began flirting with him perfectly sure of herself and her excellent excuse to Alfred, but soon found that she was forgetting herself, the excuse, and Alfred completely. Neville's mildly fascinated attentions implied thousands of things to her, but among all the pleasant implications there was never the slightest hint that Neville would ever really love her or anyone else, or rather that he had loved, and would love, so many that one more or less made little difference. This was not very flattering for her, but she found by the beginning of November that she was caring for Neville not because he would, or wouldn't, care for her—but because of himself; his brief, trenchant flashes of charm when anyone really amused him; his storming descent on the breakfast table clad in a deep-red silk dressing gown, his black hair curling angrily back from a high forehead; his strong, slender weather-tanned face undershot with color, and the straight, keen nose; the full, frequently-swearing lips, with the ridiculous fringe of a moustache just above the upper one, which gave his mouth the pertness of a whiskered tomcat, and would have seemed silly and effete had it been any larger; his filthy tempers during the days when he was painting raw-colored pictures to sell for magazine advertisements, contrasted with the feverish pleasure that bubbled through him when he was slapping off water-colors for his first exhibit scheduled for February in New York; his rankled evenings of whiskey-drinking, when he insulted everyone, particularly Courtney and his mother; and his quiet, droll evenings, when he drank beer and exasperated Janet beyond all control by beating her easily and steadily at rummy.

Neville continued to rant, paint, and drink heavily even as Henry Larnard continued to expire. Neville had been promised an even half of the fortune if he would take up his father's interest in a woolen business, but Neville laughed uproariously at that. Larnard had pettishly remonstrated that he would cut him off entirely if the drinking didn't cease. Ethel had overheard Neville's answer:

"You know very well, old boy, that if I wouldn't stop while you were alive to please you, it'd be damned mean of me to stop when you died just to grab the money. I don't want your money anyway. I can get along. All I want is this place on the island, and nobody else wants it—so what's the quarrel?"

Even the servants in the Larnard household annoyed her. Sophie and Cowpers Freedly, the colored cook and butler, seemed agreed that Ethel should not be accepted in a status with the rest of the family, and that they should be silently affronted if she dared to make a request. If Ethel ordered a broth or a tumbler of hot water for Mr. Larnard's medicine, she would find that Sophie had sent it directly to Mr. Larnard's room by Cowpers—who would stalk past Ethel in the hallway as if she had nothing to do with the preparation. Working on a suspicion that Sophie resented being given such orders, Ethel made several attempts to concoct the necessary brews and boilings herself, but she was received with such silent resentment in the kitchen that she quickly made up her mind never again to intrude, and limited herself to making such requests as seldom and tactfully as possible.

But her most tangible objection was to Hodges, the chauffeur, originally a mechanic from a village about ten miles inland from the lake. His contact with the city, made possible by his position with the Larnards, had given Hodges a hale and patronizing superiority to his birthplace, but he had never quite lost the rural belief that city people, particularly rich city people, are fools. With Cowpers in the household, Hodges never condescended to work at anything but driving cars and motor boats and, when they required his special skill, tinkering with the engines. He strutted about with an air of knowing things about you that gave him constant chuckles. Once, when Ethel had first arrived, Hodges had been given occasion to drive her alone to the village. He had started by presuming that between Ethel and himself there would be a winking, almost rib-nudging, camaraderie. When Ethel's laconic responses had finally convinced the man that he was off on the wrong foot—his quick withdrawal into a shell-like formality was very much overdone. His attitude since then had been a series of servile smirks, undershot with continual insinuations.

Everything had fulminated to a household crisis earlier on this same evening. Neville had given his father the only half hour of genuine hilarity he had enjoyed in six weeks by smuggling several pints of Bourbon into the sick room and persuading Henry to die, if he *had* to die, with a few substantial hookers beneath the string belt of his pajamas. Even Hodges, who had stolen upstairs to ask Mr. Larnard how his health went, was taken into confidence, given a drink then and there, and given an unbroken pint for his own disposal as reward for procuring the liquor from a reliable friend of his who bootlegged. Ethel had been the first to discover the jamboree, and the unprofessional nine-tenths of her thought it was not a half-bad idea. But Alfred had discovered the affair and denounced everybody, declared Henry on the point of death, and told Janet and Courtney that something would have to be done about Neville. Courtney had advised Frieda to speak to Neville, but by the time she got to Neville he was quite drunk and on the defensive. The scene ended when Neville was nagged to the pitch of calling his mother a "fancy little slattern." Courtney quietly relayed this remark to Henry, who was by that time losing the jocosity of the whiskey and sinking back to an irritable fatigue. He immediately summoned Neville to give an explanation of the insult to Frieda. Neville's acrid answer was that *Frieda* could explain what he meant if she chose. Frieda looked deeply injured. Courtney said Neville should be given a good horsewhipping. Neville admitted it might be a splendid thing *if* anyone were capable of giving it. Henry told Neville it was the last straw, and promised positively to disinherit him. Courtney was instructed to draw up another will, which Henry swore to sign in the morning.

Ethel had found Neville in the living room shortly before midnight warming his raccoon coat before the enormous, glowing hearth that sent a massive stone chimney to the dark beams of the roof two and a half stories above and filled one-half of the house with warmth. As she came down a branch of the stairways flanking the chimney, Neville looked over the upheld collar of the coat at her and smiled in a sort of embarrassment which was unusual for him.

"Ridiculous, wasn't it?" he said.

"Well, . . . ." she began.

He glared darkly at the gigantic gargoyles on the andirons, and spoke quickly: "Yes, I know. You don't need to say it."

"But you see," she said quietly, "if you hadn't taken quite so much tonight . . . ."

"Of course," he murmured. "I didn't mean to say that to mother. I *meant* it, you understand; but I didn't mean to *say* it. No point in getting father all worked up—unless I tell him the whole thing."

"And you won't do that, will you?"

"Certainly not. I think it's rotten of her, and I think Courtney's a greasy old skunk, but there's no reason why father should be hurt. And he would be—if he knew."

"You're not drunk now, are you?"

"No. I don't get really drunk; that's the trouble. I just lose my temper."

"You don't mind my asking this, do you?" She came down the last three stairs.

"What?"

"Why do you drink?"

"Oh . . . ."

"I mean—so much,"

"But I don't," he looked at her squarely, "ordinarily. But when I'm up here—these people— Oh, I don't know. I just can't stand them. I don't know why I bother—except for father. They'd soon squeeze the life out of him if I left. It's disgusting—day after day—waiting around like leeches." He swung into the coat.

"You're not going out."

"Yes," he answered vaguely, "I—I'm going ashore to—er—meet someone."

"At *this* hour! But who . . . ?"

"I'm sorry," he said, looking amusedly into the fire, "I'd *like* to tell you. But it might place some strain on your professional integrity."

"Oh, I see." She laughed. Sometimes he seemed exceedingly boyish and freshly attractive.

"I'd take Hansel for company," he said, "but I can't find him." His brow was puzzled in annoyed creases. He went over to pull back the huge front door and whistled sharply three times into the eddying wall of snow. There was no answer but a blare of snowy wind about him in the doorway—and the tumultuous haste of wind tearing at the pines outside. He left the door open and disappeared toward the front of the porch. "Hansel!" the shout came harshly. The flames in the hearth shrank and guttered in the cold blast of air. Again, from the storm's depths: "Hansel, Hansel!"—and three, shrill, long-drawn whistles. Then a voice answered.

"Is that you, Mr. Neville?"

"Yes," Neville said, coming back to the door. "Come in, come in this way!"

Hodges appeared behind Neville stamping the caked snow from heavy boots and dusting layers of frosty white from a hunting jacket. "I've been all over the island, Mr. Neville," he said in a worried voice as Neville closed the door against the wind, "and I can't *locate* 'im. Of course, I only had a hand flashlight—and you can't do much in the brush tonight, but I've been along the paths—and he's nowhere!"

"You're sure he isn't shut up in the boathouse?"

"No, I've looked—even up in the loft."

"That's the strangest thing!" Neville muttered. "I could have sworn he was in the launch when Cowpers and I came back from shore to-day—jumped out and ran 'round to the kitchen door to get some meat the second we landed. I can see him doing it now. . . . Maybe I'm mistaken, but I don't think. . . . Still, he *might* have been left ashore."

"He wasn't," Hodges said definitely. "I saw him myself runnin' around outside about an hour before dinner."

"I don't think he could have frozen to death . . . ." Neville brooded.

"Not 'im!" Hodges reassured. "Too active! And there's nowhere on the island he could get to without bein' able to run back in three minutes. Those police dogs don't go under in the cold anyhow. *But*—if you *want* my opinion, although it aint a very *pleasant* one, and I don't like to say it. *I* think he got skippin' around' near the shore—where a lot of snow was held up by thin ice along the edges of the water—skipped out a little too far, went through the thin ice—and got chilled so fast he couldn't swim, or couldn't hoist himself ashore because of the ice."

"Perhaps that's it," Neville said glumly, and then in a brisker voice: "Well, I'll have a look when I'm ashore, anyway."

"D' you want me, Mr. Neville?"

"Never mind, Hodges; I won't be back till late."

"All right, sir; thank you. Good night, sir."

"Good night," Neville murmured, staring dully at the carpet.

Ethel stood by the fire watching Neville as Hodges passed through the room toward the passage under the stairway. She realized that Hodges was pausing, expecting that she would not speak. Simply to baffle him, she said quietly, and as if she meant it: "Good night, Hodges."

Hodges spoke quickly to cover his surprise. "Good night, Miss!"

In actual fact, she *did* mean it. Hodges seemed too ignorant to be genuinely disliked. When she heard the door closing beyond the dining room she spoke to Neville.

"Be careful in the launch," she said. "It must be blowing terribly hard. You won't be able to see with the snow."

"It'll be all right," he said. "Fun. I'll be back in about two hours. So good ni . . . ." He was looking straight into her eyes and he stopped speaking. His mouth closed quickly, twisted a trifle. He came the few steps between them. "God!" he whispered abruptly. "You're the sweetest thing I've ever known."

Before she could answer she was held against him and he was kissing her. He had kissed her many times before, lightly and pleasantly, and even lingeringly, but never like this—this quickening, harsh tenderness. And as he turned away without a word and went to the wide, ponderous outside door, waded into the snow and slammed the door after him, she realized in a numbing warmth how little it would take to make her care more for Neville than anything else in the world.

Alfred was coming brusquely down the stairs and called to her, "Who was that?"

"Neville."

Alfred looked aggravatedly at her as he paused on the stairs, and then, as she looked frankly back at him, he gave a stubborn shrug, passed his fingers lightly and affectedly over the slight grey at his temples, and came on down the stairs. He tried to speak bandyingly. "Going—going ashore, I suppose."

"I suppose so."

Alfred sank his short, thick body onto the lounge before the red and orange warmth of the fire, said "Ha!" and tucked his thumbs into the armholes of his waistcoat. "Mad! Drunk and Mad! Scapegrace!" He settled himself even more comfortably. "Worthless! Worthless waster!"

Janet called from the library, "Did Neville go out?"

"Yes," said Alfred.

"I should think he might," Janet muttered, "although I think Frieda certainly . . . ."

"Did someone call me?" Frieda inquired brittly from the upper bannisters.

"Neville's gone ashore," said Alfred.

These reflections juggled their familiar way through Ethel's mind as she tried to massage a suggestion of warmth from the stingy radiator—reflections all too familiar and all irritating—except the ones about Neville. The more she tried to think clearly of Neville—the more unfamiliar, unreal, and inexplicable he became, and yet when she tried not to think of him—he seemed to be insistently beside her laughing his way into her notice. She paused in front of her bureau mirror to tuck a few strands of pale, fine hair beneath the knot at the back of her head. Her hair resembled coppery tinsel in the lamp's shaded glow, and she wished Neville might always see it by lamplight. She knew that her mouth was firm but uninteresting, and that her nose seemed younger than it should have. She thought the half-blue gray of her eyes was flat and almost deadly, and decided that Neville must have been quite drunk when he spoke to her before the fire. As she went to open the door onto the corridor she felt herself to be a very tired, healthy, sensible, dull person.

Janet's gauntness loomed vaguely in a priestly kimono from her own doorway on the other side of the corridor as Ethel went out.

"I wondered," Janet said stonily, "if you were ever going to get around to answering that buzzer!"

"Oh," Ethel answered quickly, and then paused. "I—I didn't know it woke you up."

"There's no reason why you should. But *everything* wakes me up," Janet said fatally, drew back into her room, and closed the door firmly in Ethel's face.

At this end of the corridor, close by the two doors, the panes of a tall window were being beaten with irregular whips of snow, and the dark oaken sash rattled against the deep sill. At the far end of the hallway the stairway railings and bannisters stood out in even black slashes against a glowing aura that rose from the firelight below. Near the flight of stairs that went down on the right and twisted directly into the living room was Mr. Larnard's door. Halfway up the corridor, on the same side, a door opened to Neville's room, and next this, Janet's. On the other side, next the flight of stairs that branched up again to the guest chambers and Courtney's room on another. corridor, Frieda's door stood opposite Mr. Larnard's. And on this same side, between Frieda's room and Ethel's, and opposite Neville's, was Alfred's doorway.

Neville's door was slightly ajar and as she passed it a frightening blast of cold air blew against her. She thought she could hear someone turning the knob of the door from inside.

"Neville!" she said quietly. There was no answer. The door closed, without a sound, not even a clicking of the latch. She could hear the wind puffing against the great throat of the chimney's shaft. Firelight shadows reached liquidly along the bannisters. A strand of smoke rose languidly and vanished against the gloomy beams above her. The blizzard took the whole house into its impulsive hand, and all the doors along the corridor shook in their frames. A tiny parrot-knocker on Frieda's door rattled and scratched uneasily on its hinges.

Ethel tapped lightly on Mr. Larnard's door and went in. If he had fallen back to sleep she didn't want to waken him, and she had to hold the door firmly to keep it from banging to in a draft of wind.

"Mr. Larnard," but there was no answer. "Are you all right?" She listened for the regular, labored breathing of his sleep, but the buffetings of the gale outside made it impossible to hear. She turned on a heavily shaded lamp by the foot of the bed. Her patient apparently lay on his right side, with the coverlets drawn up over his head, his sallow right hand reaching out across the white sheet toward the push button of the buzzer. Perhaps he had only been too cold. She quietly closed the window to within an inch of the sill. As she turned back to the bed she noticed little pats of snow across the heavy green rug leading from a small door that gave access to Neville's room to the side of Mr. Larnard's bed. Stooping down she saw that they had the fine, criss-cross print of rubber boots or slips, and as she stood up again saw immediately that there was something strange about Mr. Larnard's posture—an angular bulge under one side of the coverlets, as if his left shoulder were far out of joint.

Very gently she drew back the sheet and blankets—and dropped them with a weak gasp as her entire body froze with fright. Sticking out of Mr. Larnard's chest, surrounded with a large, dark patch of blood, was the gleaming hilt of a small dagger, planted directly over his heart. As the paralysis withdrew from her hands she tried to feel his ivory-cold wrist for a pulse, but there was none. He was appallingly dead.

# CHAPTER II

She heard what sounded like the muffled banging of a door in Neville's room and then something falling woodenly on the floor. Softly, and with an hysterical swiftness, she went to the adjoining door and pushed it open against a rush of cold air. Neville's room was completely dark except for the dim light which came from the lamp by the foot of Henry Larnard's bed, just enough to illumine the outside wall and show her that the French door, giving onto the balcony roof of the piazza, was swinging wide open, letting in blinding flurries of snow. The small imprints of snow along the floor from Mr. Larnard's bed led to this open doorway. The glass-paned door swung alarmingly back against heavy, dark window drapes. She tried to look out over the snow-banked roof of the piazza, but the blizzard transformed the outer darkness into a seething, impenetrable vortex of shadow and whiteness.

She closed the door against the storm. Not knowing where the light switch was, she went cautiously to Neville's bed, and reached her hand slowly across the spread. He was not there. The bed had not been slept in. A faint grating sound from Larnard's room brought her stealthily back. Just as she went in she saw the corridor door moving. It closed. She went to turn the handle and heard a precise click. The door was locked. She shrank back from the door, unable for a few seconds to move. As she wheeled to start for the door into Neville's room she saw that close against her, and as her hand snatched at the knob she heard the metallic twist of the lock. She heard again the French door in Neville's room bang open, and raised the window to look out, but the wind-driven snow blinded and choked her. She dropped the sash and ran to the corridor door to beat upon it with her fists and call out as loudly as she could.

Her throat was dry and her voice cracked into shrill harshness as she screamed, "Janet! Janet! Alfred! Frieda! Help, *help!*" She seemed nearly to break the heels of her hands pounding on the heavy panels of the door.

And then Janet's voice from down the corridor, "What is it? What's the matter?"

"Open this door!" She heard Janet fumbling with the knob. "Mr. Larnard's been killed!"

"What!"

"Open the door, *please*," she gasped. "He's been stabbed!"

"Oh!" she heard Janet say in a hoarse, nighttime voice, and then, "I'll open the door to Neville's room. The key isn't here."

"Well, it's not likely to be there, either. Get somebody to break it in—Alfred." But Janet had gone 'round to the other door.

"No, it isn't," she said gruffly. "I'll get Frieda. She may have an extra key."

Janet's calmness wilted Ethel completely. She could only clutch her hands fidgetingly and futilely together, try not to stare with hypnotized fascination at Henry Larnard's angular corpse, and pace nervously back and forth across the thick green carpet, where the little prints of snow were beginning to melt into dark stains around the edges. She could hear Janet calling, "Frieda! *Frieda!*" and switched on the bracket lamps to examine the small imprint cameos of snow. The one nearest the bed had apparently been made by the instep of the shoe or rubber sole. It showed a diamond-shaped trademark—but with one edge notched out as if the mark had been made with an improper die or the sole of the shoe had been cut away at that particular spot. The image was rapidly melting down to a little grayish lump of slush, and Ethel tried to remember vividly what it had looked like. She could hear Janet opening Frieda's door and calling, and then come back to the corridor.

"Frieda's not in her room," Janet croaked suspiciously.

"What's the matter?" she heard Frieda say distantly from the direction of the stairways and the corridor to the guest chambers.

"Henry's been murdered," Janet said quickly, "while you were out of your room apparently."

"What do you mean?"

"Neville's not in his room either, and that nurse says she's locked in there with Henry's body—and there's no key."

"You're mad!" Frieda told her in a shivering voice.

"I'm not mad. I'm noticing that you were not in your room when this happened. Get me a key!"

"But there isn't any."

"Well, then, wake up Alfred or Courtney or Cowpers or somebody and get this door open We can't stand here . . . ."

Alfred's voice sounded sleepily down the corridor. "What's going on?"

"Put on a bathrobe." Janet ordered, "and break in this door. Henry's been stabbed."

"But, my God!" said Alfred as he came nearer. "This is . . . ."

"Never mind what it is. Heave against the door."

Alfred's shoulder, apparently, came bumping against the door. "Much too stout," he said, "to break in. If we had a jimmy or even a chisel, a strong one."

"I'll get Courtney," announced Frieda. "He's much stronger than you are." This spurred Alfred to redouble his efforts against the door, which remained firmly in its frame.

"No use," he said. "There might be a chisel in the cellarway."

"By all means," Janet said, "get it—and hurry."

Ethel began to hate all of them more than ever, and suddenly decided to crawl out the window, drag herself the few yards across the piazza roof through the teeth of the wind, and get into Neville's room through the French door which Janet had closed when she went in, but not bothered to lock. As she opened the door from Neville's room onto the corridor she was glad to see Janet lose enough of her poise to emit a quick "Oh!"

"I thought you were locked in there," Janet finally said, eyeing her gimlet-wise across the accusing finger of the nose.

"I had to crawl out across the roof," Ethel answered, shaking with cold, and flipping the snow from her kimono.

Janet went swiftly by her into Neville's room and tried the door to Henry's. When it did not give she came back staring at Ethel like a vulture that has been done out of its offal.

Ethel tried to laugh through a throbbing rush of anger. "I see! You think *I* did it."

"You might have," Janet said, "just as easily as anyone else. More so! I saw you go to his room. Two minutes later you shout for help. You say you're locked in there, and then appear. Why didn't you come out that way in the first place?"

Ethel stared despisingly at her. "I didn't think."

Janet gave a quick, hard laugh. "That may be so, but you're just as open to suspicion . . . ."

"Yes," Ethel said quickly. "You and I *were* the only ones who were awake when this happened, weren't we?"

"Frieda was not in her room," Janet said evenly.

Courtney came out of the guest corridor bundled into a huge corduroy bathrobe the color of old rose and crossed the stairs rather sleepily.

"She's out now," Janet told him.

"Oh, she is," Courtney said thickly, rubbing his eyes, and then through a yawn, "Who d' you think did it?"

"Stop pretending to be asleep," Janet bit out, "because we all know you weren't."

Courtney's apologetic hand dropped from his wide yawn, and his grey-speckled eyebrows rose indignantly.

"Why, my *dear* girl . . . ." he began in syrupy surprise, "you're certainly not implying that I . . . ."

"Where *was* Frieda then," Janet challenged, leaning at him so that her nose seemed about to pinion the suave attorney against the wall, "if she wasn't . . . ."

"Is the door open yet?" Frieda called, flurrying out of the guest corridor, down over the treads of the stairs, across the landing, and up again, like a shrill, worried sparrow that had temporarily put on cerise lounging pajamas instead of wings. Then, as she glimpsed Ethel, "Oh, they got you out!"

"No. I had to crawl through the window and get in the French door of Neville's room."

Frieda looked at her strangely. "But that door is never unlocked. The roof is very weak in front of it."

"The door was wide open," Janet said, "when I found her locked in there."

"Miss Baines, I take it," said Courtney, "was discovered locked in this room when you . . . ."

"Good, Courtney," Janet snapped, "I'm glad you're keeping up with us."

Courtney merely looked at her, and then back at Ethel. "Now, tell us what happened."

But Janet was speaking. "Henry rang for her about quarter past one."

"Twelve past," Ethel said.

"Whatever it was," Janet went on, "I heard the buzzer ring in her room. I listened, but didn't hear her come out. I thought it might not have wakened her, and I was just going to knock on her door when she came out."

"How long," Courtney asked, "after the buzzer sounded?"

"At least two or three minutes," Ethel said. "I was very cold and terribly sleepy."

Courtney turned quickly on Janet. "What did you do after you saw her come out of her room?"

"I spoke to her and then went back to bed," Janet answered huffily. "I was just falling asleep when I heard a door slam and a window open. Then she began to shout my name and everyone else's and pound on Henry's door, and I got up and came down here and found her incarcerated—at least, so she said. Frieda wasn't in her room and Neville wasn't in his room . . . ."

Alfred was coming up the stairs with a chisel, a small hammer, and a screwdriver. "By the way," he said, "where *is* Neville?"

"Why, he said he was going ashore, didn't he?" exclaimed Frieda.

"But it's half-past one. Isn't he back?"

"He told me," Ethel said, "that he wouldn't be back for two hours."

Courtney spoke quietly. "Did he tell you where he was going, Miss Baines?"

"No," said Ethel, "he—no, he didn't—except that he was going ashore."

"Oh," Courtney murmured, "so that's the way the wind blows!"

Alfred turned from prying the chisel into the door jam opposite the lock. "You certainly don't think Neville did it."

"I only think," Courtney answered quietly, "that Neville will need a pretty good alibi when he returns—*from shore*, if you insist."

"That's pretty vicious of you, I think," said Alfred, and began to pry the chisel against the bolt of the lock. "As a matter of fact, Neville was at the boathouse on shore at ten minutes of one. He couldn't possibly have gotten back in less than half an hour—driving the launch at top speed, and in this storm . . . ."

"How do you know he was at the shore boathouse?" inquired Janet.

"Didn't you hear the telephone ring about that time?" Alfred asked.

"I did," Frieda said, "but it was the shore ring, so I didn't answer it."

"Well, *I* answered it," Alfred said. "I thought Neville was too drunk to answer over there, even if he had gotten ashore. But, apparently, he had, and had gone to meet someone, because when I took up the receiver I heard a voice a long way off say, 'I'm snowed in on the far side of Ticonderoga. I can't get there before two-thirty anyway,' and then Neville's voice saying, 'Alright, I'll be waiting for you ashore. Wake me up in the boathouse if I'm asleep.' So that takes care of Neville, and . . . ." The lock snapped back beneath the pressure of the chisel, and the door into Henry Larnard's chamber swung ajar. ". . . . and this takes care of the door."

"Excuse me," Ethel said, "but—I should think this storm might be very heavy out on the lake. Do you mind if I telephone the boathouse ashore—just to see if Neville's all right, I mean—and tell him what's happened."

"Yes," said Courtney, "in just a minute." He went into Alfred's room—and stopped suddenly. Janet followed him. They stood there without speaking. Ethel could see Janet's under lip, which was thin and chapped, quivering a trifle, and then Janet's teeth bit firmly against it. Alfred went in, paused to glance at Henry; then turned slowly and closed the window. Ethel stood in the hallway as Frieda went hesitantly in.

"I don't know why I'm going in here," Frieda's voice quavered on the verge of sobs, "but I just . . . ." She covered her face with her two slender hands and began to cry hysterically.

Janet turned her head in rigid contempt and fixed her small, stonily-gleaming eyes on Frieda. Frieda drew a deep bravening breath, took her hands away, and for a moment the wide, uncomprehending little ovals of her eyes stared at Henry as if she were staring at a ghastly nothing. The lids closed abruptly, and she shook her head as if trying not to swoon.

"Don't!" Janet ordered. *"Don't faint!"* She led Frieda from the room as she would have led a dirty urchin. "We have too many other things to think about. He didn't mean anything to *you* anyway. We all know that." She opened Frieda's door and switched up the lights, as Frieda began sobbing afresh. "Lie down, Frieda; in heaven's name, lie down. You shouldn't have gone in there anyway. It was a sacrilege." She closed the window in Frieda's room, and said venomously, "It was very clever of you to open your window in here and ruffle up the bedclothes—so we'd think you'd been asleep and just stepped out to the bath. Oh, yes! But it's all coming out now, Frieda, so you can cry yourself sick and see how much difference it makes." Frieda wilted onto the bed. Janet came out and closed the door as if it were one of the small and special compartments of purgatory, and she, one of the trusties. Then she noticed Ethel standing in the hallway. Ethel could see that Janet was shaking with awful anger or excitement. Janet took a step toward her, and reached out her hand vaguely, as if for support. "This is getting quite beyond me, Miss Baines," she said, and then more weakly, almost whispering, "quite beyond me; I'm—I'm terrified." She looked at Ethel from insanely quizzical eyes. "What can we do?" She came closer, and in a very fine whisper, her breath hot against Ethel's cheek, "I'm not afraid of Frieda—but I don't think Frieda did it alone. She couldn't have." She shook her finger menacingly. "I wouldn't trust Courtney—not for two seconds. He's clever, too. Slippery. A snake, Baines, a veritable snake!"

Until now Janet had scraped unbearably on Ethel's sensibilities, but Janet's baleful eyes suddenly seemed like a scared child's beneath their pinched-up lids. Her mouth twisted sickly beneath the angular distortion of her face. Ethel took Janet's hands in her own. They were big-knuckled and crisply dry, almost scratching Ethel with their nervous grasp.

"Well, Miss Larnard," Ethel began hesitantly, "I confess I've always felt out of place in this house, and I don't feel any easier now. I know you don't like me, and I've resented you, too, but—things like this—alter everything."

"Yes," Janet said eagerly.

"And," Ethel went on, "if everybody keeps on suspecting everybody else we'll get nowhere. I know it looks very strange—my being locked in there, but you know very well I didn't do it. I don't think anybody in this house had anything to do with it, and I'm sure Neville could never do a thing like this—drunk or otherwise. It must have been someone who got in from outside—an enemy of Mr. Larnard's, or an insane person—and what worries me now is whether or not he's still on the island, because when Neville comes back . . . ."

Courtney appeared from the doorway. "You seem surprisingly sure of Neville's coming back, Miss Baines. Have you telephoned the shore boathouse?"

Ethel smothered a retort, went to the small table between the upcoming flights of stairs and took up the 'phone.

"At least," Janet said, grasping at some straw to pull herself together, "we can wake up the servants, find out if they heard or saw anything unusual. I'll have Cowpers go over the house and see that doors and windows are all secure," and then, more confidently to Ethel, "I want to see what sort of reaction Hodges makes to this business. There's been something about that chap—for the past year or so—that's aggravated me. Change in his attitude—familiar, presuming—as if he *belonged* here—scraping in front of Neville and Henry and so surly, even fresh, with everyone else." She loped down a short flight of stairs to the landing and up another short flight that went to the door of the servants' corridor on the left wing of the house. Turning, she whispered hoarsely, "Come with me, please! Miss Baines," and pushed the door wide into the dark corridor as Ethel put down the unresponsive 'phone and followed. Janet was reaching vaguely along the wall, a switch clicked, and a shaded bulb of low candlepower began to glow at the far end of the corridor near the back stairway.

Janet stopped before the second door on the right of the hall and hammered on the panel with her bony knuckles. "Hodges!" she called, and then in a coarser, louder voice, "Hodges, *Hodges!*"

From within the answer sounded as if muffled in several blankets, "Yes'm?"

"Come to the door, please."

"Yes, Miss Janet—just a minute, if y' don't mind. I'm dressin'."

"Don't bother about that, Hodges. Please hurry." She turned to Ethel and pointed to the next door, "Wake them and tell them what's happened. Tell Cowpers to look at the windows and doors downstairs, and have Sophie make coffee or something for us . . . ." The door in front of Janet opened about a foot and Hodges squinted at her from his yokelish red face—puffy-eyed in the light. He was shivering and held a sallow yellow bathrobe closely about himself with one hand.

"Hodges, Mr. Larnard's been stabbed to death."

"Mr. Larnard," Hodges repeated, "y' mean he's *dead?*"

"Yes. Come out here where it's warmer, Hodges." Hodges came out of the door and closed it firmly behind him, cutting off the keen draft of air. "Did you hear anything—outside the house?"

"Not me! No, Miss Janet. Didn' hear a blessed thing. Bin asleep, 's matter of fac'."

"You didn't hear anyone—in the hallways—or anywhere?"

"Nope, not a thing. I bin asleep."

"Cowpers," Janet said to the dark face that had appeared in answer to Ethel's knock, "Mr. Larnard's been murdered. Have you heard any commotion?"

"Yes'm, Miss Janet. Ah heered you callin' out a little while back. So'd Sophie. But then the callin' let up, an we jes heered people talkin'—so we thought's all right."

"Did it wake you up?"

"Yes'm, Ma'am! Both of us."

"But," Janet turned back to Hodges, who was scowling at the dusty glass shade over the dim bulb, "it didn't wake you up. Is that right, Hodges?"

"Yes'm, I've bin asleep fer over an hour."

"Fo' an hour?" Cowpers asked blandly.

"An hour," Hodges said tartly, "what's that to you?"

"Why, Ah thought Ah heard you comin' up back stairs about twenty minutes ago. But Ah mus' be wrong. Maybe—someone else."

"It certainly was someone else, because I've bin asleep!" Hodges said with plenty of emphasis.

"Hodges," Janet said in a warning voice, "have you been drinking?"

"Certainly, Miss Janet—that is, I had a drink."

"What do you mean?"

"Mr. Larnard gave me a drink—earlier this evenin'."

"I understand that but I mean—since then."

"No'm. Not a drop."

"But you're intoxicated . . . ." His eyes lifted stubbornly to her gaze, then fell uneasily away. ". . . . aren't you?"

"Well'm, what of it?"

"We won't discuss it," Janet told him crisply, "until you feel better. Meanwhile, get into your clothes, go downstairs, and Sophie'll give you black coffee." And then, as she looked his resentfully stooped hunchy figure up and down, "I thought you said you'd been in bed!"

Hodges' look of injured surprise, although a trifle tardy and hazy, seemed to imply that he certainly had been in bed, but Janet persisted, "You're fully dressed!"

"What'm?" Hodges ventured.

"I say, you're fully dressed."

"I told you," he cut in breezily, "that I was gettin' dressed."

"I'll speak to you downstairs," she concluded curtly, and strode away down the corridor. Ethel followed Janet's lank figure down and up the short runs of stairs, and took up the telephone again. Janet stood beside her for a moment. Ethel shook her head as there was no operator's voice. "Try a bit longer," Janet advised, "the night operators are slow in the village." The long thin hand pressed against the meagre mouth in confused thought. Then she mumbled, "Can't wait for Cowpers. Lock those windows myself," and went stiffly, cautiously down the stairs, her face younger and Indian-colored in the firelight.

"Footprints," Courtney was saying to Alfred, "leading directly to the bed," as he followed them into Neville's room, "through this room to the outside doorway, then out here into the hall."

"I made those into the hallway," Ethel told him, "when I went along the roof and came through Neville's room."

"Then the footprints you discovered went only from the bedside to the French doorway?"

"Yes." She clicked the 'phone hook several times, but could hear only a distant humming.

"Frieda says that door is always locked from the inside," Alfred was telling Courtney.

"But remember," Courtney insinuated, "that Neville might have unlocked this door in his own room before going out."

Janet called up from the living room, "Alfred, I wish you or Courtney would put some more wood on this fire. It's like a barn down here."

"I don't see," Alfred was saying, "why anyone should come in through that doorway when the window was open right here in Henry's room."

"What's the matter, Miss Baines?" Courtney was leering pleasantly. "No answer from the boathouse?"

Ethel put the receiver back on the telephone with a sick feeling of helplessness, and said, "I can't even get the operator."

Courtney's face straightened in serious surprise. Alfred came into the corridor beside him. "Are you— sure, Miss Baines?" She nodded. Alfred came to take the telephone and listen. Janet's haggard face appeared around the mass of the chimney as she leaned up the stairs.

"What's wrong now?" she wanted to know.

"The wires," said Courtney, "have apparently been cut."

"Perhaps the storm only," Ethel suggested.

"That's hardly possible," Courtney told her. "The lines run through a pipe along the ground here on the island to the island boathouse, then through a carefully protected cable about six miles to the boathouse on shore. There are no aerial suspensions more than fifteen feet in length."

"But along the road lines to the town . . . ." Alfred said, as he put down the 'phone definitely.

"That means, I suppose," Janet murmured, "that we can't notify the police."

"Couldn't someone go ashore?" Ethel asked.

"Not very well," Courtney told her. "If Neville's taken the big launch—that is, unless one of us wants to risk his life with the outboard motor. I wouldn't even ask Hodges to try that in this storm."

"What," Janet said suddenly, "if the lake freezes over?"

Courtney went into Henry's room and peered through the window glass, and then turned with a wry smile on his face.

"The thermometer now says six above zero. Fallen twenty degrees since last evening. If the gale keeps the water moving we're all right. But if the wind dies I'm doubly sure Neville won't come back from shore."

"And the ice won't be strong enough for anyone to walk across," Alfred muttered, "for twenty-four hours at the inside."

Janet's breath drew in sharply and her face looked suddenly pale in the firelight. "At least," she said softly, "we might have some more wood in this fireplace. Tell Frieda to come downstairs and get warm."

"What fools we are!" Courtney broke out. "Neville may have cut those wires himself—right here on the island. There's a place in the boathouse or in the cellar. He put in the wiring himself; he knows all about it. I wouldn't be surprised if he'd tapped the wires and made a fake 'phone call—the one *you* overheard, Alfred. He's always fooling around with things like that. He's probably hiding in the island boathouse now. I'm going down there and see, right away." He went over the intervening stairs to his own corridor.

"You oughn't to go alone," Janet called. "Would anybody like some hot tea?"

"I'd like some coffee," Alfred told her. "I'll go along with Courtney."

"Hurry and dress," Courtney called, quite carried away with the thrill of the business. "There's a revolver in Henry's desk down in the library. Get it, will you, Janet."

"All right," Janet answered with deep resignation. "But it certainly is comforting to have you and Alfred sweep out and leave us like this. Whoever did it'll knife you and Alfred from behind a bush and then come in here and finish off the women."

"Neville will be so pleased with himself," Courtney assured her, "that he won't even think of our coming after him,"

"He may have a gun, too," Janet suggested, going to the recesses of the library.

"Not Neville," Courtney called. "He'd think it was frightfully clever *not* to have anything incriminating about him—and then appear back here at the house in about an hour—don't you see?—relying absolutely on the 'phone call."

"But, Alfred," Ethel said, as Alfred was dressing in his room, "what if it isn't Neville? What if it's the only person who could have logically done this—a madman or a criminal?—what happens when you run across *him*?"

"I don't exactly know," Alfred remarked with a hint of humor, "but I can't let Courtney go looking around alone, can I?"

"Here you are," Janet said, as she came up the stairs with a thirty-eight caliber revolver. "I'll leave it here on the telephone table. And please, Miss Baines, lock all the windows on this floor—make sure. I'm going to speak to the servants, and make them stay about with us. Cowpers has a shotgun, and I think a shotgun would be a great comfort at the moment." She went to Frieda's room. "You better come downstairs and have something hot to drink, Frieda." Then she crossed over to Courtney's corridor. "Now, Courtney," she warned, "don't go shooting at people wildly. You may find Neville, but Neville may not have done it. So be careful."

"Don't worry," Courtney laughed, "we won't have to shoot him."

# CHAPTER III

"You see, Miss Baines," Janet was saying to Ethel, as they sat stiffly and apprehensively opposite each other in capacious wing chairs beside the living room hearth ten minutes later, "this household has not been for some time the pleasant circle we tried to affect. That's why all this suspicion, which naturally seems very strange to an outsider like you, comes immediately into the foreground. You may not have gathered . . . ."

"I'd sensed it," Ethel admitted, "but I'd put it down to the irritation of people who were tired of seeing each other day after day under the—well, *trying* circumstances of sickness, and the natural expectations. . . ."

"It goes further back than that," Janet interrupted. "Henry and I were actual brother and sister. Our mother died about two years after I was born. Father married again almost before Henry and I were old enough to resent it. His second wife was a very clever woman, about three years older than father. She already had one child; that was Courtney. And for a while it seemed as if the household would be divided along very definite lines. Then my stepmother made what seemed like a very brilliant move at the time. She allowed herself to have another child by father. This child was supposed to be the little angel of peace, related to us all and holding things lovingly together. Of course, we all spoiled her. Elizabeth was *her* name—you may have heard us mention . . ."

"Yes," Ethel said carefully. "That's her portrait in the library, isn't it?" Ethel was beginning to realize the ambiguity of her own position in the household, and was trying not to tell any flat falsehoods, at the same time recognizing the fact that she must not appear to know too much.

"In some precocious way," Janet mused on, "Elizabeth seemed to know, almost from the time she was born, that she had a great advantage over all of us. Of course, she was in an unassailable position, and as we all babied her she came to take it for granted, and tyrannized everybody accordingly. Even at the age of eight she used to play the two sides against each other, and got herself out of a lot of scrapes that way. Whenever one parent wanted to punish her she scurried off to the other for sympathy and protection, and she was never really punished for anything. She hated me particularly; jealousy I suppose, because I was not bad looking—then, and, being older, I was a great deal stronger. I started intense family quarrels once or twice by deliberately punishing her myself. This was very unwise, because she was extremely treacherous, and subsequently broke my nose—as you see—beyond all repair. She meant to; not necessarily to break my nose; she would have preferred breaking my neck—but she meant to hurt me as much as she could, and when she got a chance one day pushed me off a roof. You can easily see," and Janet grinned with homespun grimness at Ethel, "that I've not been the same since. But that wasn't the end of it . . . ."

Cowpers Freedly came through the door beneath the stairs with a large tray of coffee.

"The doctah and Mist Larnand had theirs in th' kitchen, Miss Janet," he explained, as he rested the tray on a small table by Janet's chair. He was tall and the muscles that tightened beneath his white coat as he stooped over to lower the tray carried through every gesture with an easy suppleness. The rich, coffee-colored skin of his face and the backs of his hands glistened in the firelight while he raised a five-foot log over the andirons as easily as he would have lifted a walking stick. His African composure and the languid, soft tone of his voice brought a sudden, relaxing harmony into the room. The only hint he betrayed of knowing that anything out of the ordinary had broken the stolidity of that midnight house in the storm was in the occasional, swift flashing of his large eyes, and a solemn carefulness that covered his customary, youthful nonchalance.

"Cowpers," Janet said, "you have a gun."

"Yes'm, Miss Janet—that is, jest a—jest a little two-barrel shotgun. Comes in right handy though. Picks off those big rats 'round the woodshed. Almost got one 'o those skunks las' month, too, but Ah couldn't see very well."

"Well, Cowpers, you get down that gun and you stay just inside the dining room, and we'll call you if we need you. Make sure everything's locked up out back and put some coal on the furnace."

"Yes'm, Miss Janet—Ah have."

"Cowpers," Janet called, "did Mr. Larnard and the Doctor go out the back door?"

"Yes'm. They were goin' down to th' boathouse. They think Mist Neville killed him—but Ah don't think so. Mist Neville didn't even like me to kill skunks. He never did that. Sophie says she think Mist Larnand commit suicide. But Ah don't see why he should; tole me he was gonna die anyhow. Guess he *did* alright," and Cowpers' voice drifted through the dining room pantry to the kitchen.

"There's something very comforting about savagery," Janet announced, as she began sipping her coffee, with her second finger crooked into the handle of the cup instead of her forefinger. She hunched her gaunt frame comfortably down in the chair, and planted her vast, sheep-lined pink slippers on the cross-stitched cover of a squat footstool. Her elbows rested heavily on the arms of the chair and her hands crooked awkwardly around cup and saucer. She held them a few inches beneath her nose, which stood out sharply in the ruddy glare from the newly-burning logs. The lids of her eyes wrinkled into narrow concentration as she brooded into the depths of the cup. "Something of a pagan kindliness," she murmured on, "which might very easily kill a man, just as I would destroy a fly, but would never do it with the clandestine venom of Henry's murderer—involving a whole family in a mania of suspicion." Ethel could see that Janet's usual clarity was returning, and that Henry's death had already become a mere puzzle for Janet, in which she might find vent for years of solitary spleen in digging out some factor that would point toward the miscreant. The person who had spoken to Ethel in nerve-agued whispers upstairs in the corridor might have been the Janet as she was half a second after Elizabeth had pushed her off the roof. But the person who spoke now was the Janet whose nose, heart, and self had been broken for many years and who had tenaciously knit herself together into a sinewy, vengeful stubbornness.

"I don't know why I should talk to you like this, Miss Baines, except that you're in an incriminating position along with the rest of us—and you may as well know the family snarl you're up against. I thought for a few minutes that you might be mixed up in the killing, but I realize that's impossible. You have no reason to be—and besides I know enough about people to realize that anyone like you could never do such a thing. I haven't liked you up to now, I admit. Jealousy on my part, I suppose. I'm always subconsciously jealous of attractive, carefree people—particularly women. Resentment—that's all. They always make me feel ugly—and I know I am. But, as you said, we can't go off in separate corners and glare at one another. Must turn to somebody. Neville's the one I'd naturally turn to, but he's not in a position to be of much use. You're completely out of it—the family entanglement, I mean—and if you keep your head as you have so far you may be of some use.

"I was telling you about Elizabeth. The thing didn't finish with the broken nose. About seven years after that, she was about to marry a man who suddenly broke the engagement and bolted. Nobody blamed him. No man who really knew Elizabeth would have thought of marrying her. She was a thorough vixen, but could be very nice when she chose. She took it all very quietly and went to France for about a year. Meanwhile, I met Alfred, and in our unpretentious way we fell in love. There was never anything dashing about Alfred, but he worked hard, gave promise of being a brilliant doctor, and was devoted to me in his own, easy way. Of course, there was nothing exciting about me, but I was fairly staunch, and willing to live on what Alfred could earn. Everything seemed—quite perfect . . . ." Janet drained her cup and turned toward the ornate silver pot to refill it.

"My stepmother," she went on briskly, "had been considerate enough to die. Courtney plumped himself into a law school and became so pleased with his ability that he was charming to Henry and to me. Father was delighted with prospects of a peaceable old age, but he went driving one afternoon—it was Sunday—with a mettlesome horse. My father was an expert with the reins, but the horse shied very suddenly —I think it was a piece of paper blowing in the street—and wheeled around a sharp corner. My father was thrown on his head, when the carriage overturned, and died instantly with a fractured skull.

"This brought Elizabeth back from Europe. My father left a few thousand dollars to Courtney and to me, but the bulk of the fortune was divided between Henry and Elizabeth. Even so—I didn't mind. I was quite happy; but from the minute Elizabeth laid eyes on Alfred I could see what was happening at the back of her mind. She succeeded in getting him away from me, too. It wasn't her money; I'm perfectly sure of that. But she caught Alfred at an angle where he'd never been attacked before. I'd always thought of him as a physician, fairly skeptical about such glamour. But I just hadn't known. Even if I had, there wasn't much I could do. You see me now. Well, I was just a little fresher then, that's all. Otherwise—the same. Elizabeth was devastating, and she devastated Alfred. And until she died—he lived on her fortune and danced on her every whim. He practically gave up his profession for fifteen years—until the money was about gone. Now everything's gone—even Elizabeth. And Alfred!—Alfred, my dear girl, is still naive enough to think that I secretly want him to marry me!

"Alfred is quite afraid of me. He thinks I resent him, and the little money Elizabeth left him. But I pity Alfred; that's all. I might never have made him blissfully happy, but I wouldn't have warped his life the way Elizabeth did, and left him derelict at the end. Of course—and this is a great secret—Alfred *has married again!*"

Ethel's hand froze against her cup, but she continued to stare fascinatedly at Janet.

"Oh, yes," Janet chuckled, "I don't know who the woman is—or where she is—but I've heard—through some friends that see him occasionally in the winter. But you mustn't tell anyone here. It would turn the house into a Bedlam. Elizabeth's sacred memory! And how these people hated her when she was alive! They all despised her, except Henry. Of course, he and Elizabeth broke even on the money, and he was old enough to be above it. But Courtney loathed the very sight of her; wouldn't visit here at the same time with her. And, of course, Courtney's been terribly jealous of Henry for getting the big portion from father. Henry never realized all this. He read books and made more money, and was silly enough to entrust Courtney with most of his legal affairs. You probably have insight enough to know what's going on between Courtney and Frieda. That brings out another aspect . . . ."
She hastily left her saucer and cup on the tray and sprang up the stairs

beside the chimney, peering through the bannisters at the upper hall. When she had regained her chair she no longer sat in ruminative ease, but leaned forward to Ethel—with one big-knuckled hand propping up her square-boned chin. Her eyes were kindling with an excited malice.

"I know you won't breathe this to anyone, because you like Neville, and you're discreet anyway, *but* . . ." the hand stretched away from the chin, and a curved forefinger pointed impressively at Ethel, "Neville, my dear girl, Neville is no more *Henry's* child than you are!" She sat back in smiling, nodding triumph. "Nobody suspects this but me, and even Frieda has never thought that I knew . . . ."

"He's—you don't think he's—Courtney's son, do you?" Ethel wanted to know, quite revolted by the idea that Courtney might ever have had anything to do with Neville.

"Oh, no," Janet assured her, "it goes further back than Courtney. Frieda and Courtney never paid any attention to each other until a few summers ago. Frieda may have told Courtney about Neville, but I don't think so. I don't think she'd trust even Courtney with that tid-bit of confession. It's too strong a card.

"You see, after Elizabeth carried Alfred off, Courtney was at law school, and for several years Henry and I shared a house in New York. Henry, by the way, was always very generous with me. He started giving me an annuity right after father died. But I was telling you . . . ." She paused and twisted her brow and her mouth with the effort to re-member. ". . . . yes! I have it all now. Henry, in his Victorian fashion, was paying court to Frieda. Her family was more than respectable and Henry was eminently qualified. But Henry was always one to let a de-cent interval elapse before he did anything. So the marriage was still in the future. Now then, an intimate friend of mine, the only one I ever had I guess, who had been married about two years, suddenly came to me—completely grief-stricken. Her husband, it seemed, was having an affair with some woman. I wasn't one to give much advice about such things, but this girl apparently trusted me. She loved her husband so much that pride was out of it altogether. She said she'd do anything to get him back. When she found out who the other woman was—it turned out to be Frieda, the little minx! who was hiding the affair under the respectable pretense of Henry's courtship. You can see that I was be-tween two fires. If I told Henry—he'd renounce Frieda, and my friend would probably lose her husband completely to Frieda. I made a point of being quite courageous and broadminded in those days, and went directly to Frieda. I told her that if she didn't give up the other man I *would* tell Henry, but that if she cared enough for Henry to marry him and leave the other man entirely I wouldn't interfere. She was very blushing and sweet—said that Henry had never really proposed to her, and that she was so glad I'd come to her, and that, of course, Henry would mean more than anyone else ever could. So it was settled that way. I spurred Henry to hustle into the marriage, and my friend's home remained intact. Happiness, as you see, prevailed; yes! for exactly two years.

"Frieda always made a great fuss about not being strong enough to have children. She was always rather fragile, and Henry used to send her away to the country while he had to stay in New York, or South in the wintertime. Well, my friend committed suicide; her husband disappeared, and inside of half a year Neville was born. Of course, I have no proof, but Neville has grown to be the image of my friend's husband. Now that may all be conjecture, and so I've never even intimated to a soul what I've grown to believe is the truth. But you can see that there may be a number of uneasy ghosts lurking about this family, and I don't want you to be victimized simply because you don't know what's behind it. There are people in this house who would not scruple at incriminating you or anybody else—even—" She leaned forward more excitedly, "Even *I* have something to explain."

"What do you mean?"

"The dagger," said Janet, trying to squeeze the nervousness from her voice, "which was used to stab him, belongs to me. Yes," she hurried to say, as Ethel felt her mouth gasp open, "I brought it from Tunis three years ago. I've kept it on the desk in my room to open letters. It's been missing for four or five days."

They heard Frieda's measured, soft, slippered tread padding down the stairs. Frieda's eyes, bloodshot from her fit of weeping, stared in dumb hatred at Janet. She had given her face an extraordinary pallor in trying to powder away the irritated redness from crying. As she paused and clutched the bannister viciously with her white-knuckled hand, to keep herself, it seemed, from flying at Janet's throat, Ethel thought she must have overheard the whole story. But Frieda's face cracked into a slight smile, and she spoke in a husky, low voice:

"I wouldn't tell too many people that about the dagger, Janet—if I were you."

"No, Frieda, I won't," Janet grimaced. "I can safely leave that to you. Have some coffee?"

Frieda gave a perfunctory and disgusted "thank you" and came down the rest of the stairs with what appeared to be deliberate slowness, and seated herself tautly on the edge of the upholstered lounge facing the fire, as if weary of waiting for some apprehended hostility to spring at her from ambush. Without a word she took the cup and saucer Janet passed her and stirred her coffee as if it mattered very little, after all, whatever Janet or anyone else might say about her—now that Henry was out of the way, and no one could scamper to him with gossip. She had seen fit to dress herself in a black silk evening gown, tightly bodiced and falling almost to the floor when she walked. Ethel remembered the gown and noticed that Frieda had ripped a large and languorous silver rose from the left waistline. She saw, as well, the carefully chosen gun-metal stockings above the high-heeled black slippers, and marveled at Frieda's timely eye for the details of death decorum, which seemed at the moment, however, blatant and ridiculous. The dress made Frieda's scared and tired face, stripped by the shock of its daily pretences, stand out in simple, drawn lines like that of an undernourished child. With Frieda for a moment quiescent and dumb, Ethel wondered whatever could have made Frieda seem alluring when she was talking and animated. She decided it had been no more than a frequent wrinkling of the small, rather flat nose, insinuating nuances with the eyes, and an inexhaustible repertoire of moues, plus a soothing, babbling, persuasive voice and a habit of leaping from topic to topic, like a drunken gnat, so that you thought you were being dazzled when you were only being confused.

Her hair curved darkly back with the half curl of the grain in wood, almost cultivated in its irregularity, and finished in a small, queenly knot atop the head. The brow was lividly pale with the hair line really beginning not far above the eyes, although the coiffure gave it the appearance of starting much higher, and Ethel always suspected the head must be belittlingly flat on top and that the knot was fixed there with a deceptive purpose.

"This business has had a surprising effect on Courtney," Janet finally threw into the silence. "He's behaving like a boy sleuth of ten—talk of tapping the wires and all that nonsense! If anyone wanted to make a false telephone call in this house all he'd have to do would be to go to one of the extensions—the servants' 'phone in the kitchen, for example—ask the operator to give the boathouse ring, hang up during the ring, then lift up the receiver and begin to talk. But that call Alfred overheard was perfectly genuine. I heard the ring myself and took up the receiver on the upstairs extension. Alfred must have answered from the library."

"What makes you certain the call was genuine?" Frieda demanded. "I was in the bath, right beside the upstairs 'phone, and I didn't hear you answer."

"I didn't speak," Janet told her sharply, "because I heard someone talking. It was not Neville. Neville spoke in a second or two—but it was definitely someone else's voice at first."

"Neville isn't a ventriloquist, to be sure," Frieda. conceded, "but it's be easy enough for him to disguise his voice over the telephone."

"Not quite so easy, Frieda, because *I recognized the other voice.*"

Frieda's face stiffened with astonishment. "But who," she faltered weakly, "who was it?"

"You'll see," Janet smiled. "Henry knew him. I think Alfred's acquainted with him. He's a very good friend to Neville, and has been for years."

Frieda scowled away her chagrin at Janet's omniscience, and went consciously cat-like over to the deeply draped windows near the outside door. She drew the curtains carefully aside and tried to peer into the flurried gloom.

"I wish Alfred and Courtney'd come back," she said. "I think it was extremely foolish of them to go out like this."

"I can well understand," Janet answered, with a grating edge on the words, "how Courtney would feel perfectly safe in going out like this."

Frieda was taking a cigarette from the long, narrow, rug-topped table behind the lounge, but her languor convulsed into a wiry tension as she whipped herself about, her eyes flaring at Janet. "Stop," she said. "Stop talking like thi . . . ."

"I only hope," Janet rasped more loudly, "that Alfred keeps his eyes open—while he's near the water's edge with Courtney." Frieda remained facing her for several seconds, rigid with hatred, and then, as if aware of the futility of working herself into a frenzy and dashing her head against Janet's jewel-hard cynicism, she breathed slowly and deeply in to control herself, let her body wilt into an unnatural ease, and aloofly struck a match to light her cigarette. A log on the fire rolled its glowing length slowly over and whined steadily as it burned in a more settled position.

Frieda reached beneath the thick silken fringe of a red-shaded lamp on the table and pressed on the light, which brought the far end of the living room into dim shape and sent a shadow-bordered circle against the roughly-plastered whiteness of the ceiling. She stood with her back toward the two by the fire and let herself rest indifferently against one corner of the lounge's arm. The brass on the bracket fixtures high on the paneling between the dull maroon window drapes caught an occasional flicker from the fire and turned it to the tiny glare of a sapphire up and down the room. To her left the stressing wind jammed the heavy, nail-studded door against its finger-like hinges of wrought iron, and in one great panel of the long right-hand wall an oil mural done by Neville was a reminiscence of the pale blue lake in late September with its vigilant, mist-crowned mountains and its shoreline of water oaks in flashing scarlet and chrome against the unchanging green of pine and hemlock. Beyond this, at the far extreme of the right-hand wall, a passageway opened to the complete darkness of the library. Between this passage and the corner of the room the bulk of an upright piano stood with its back toward them, completely covered with a wine-hued, oriental rug. At the room's far end—an expanse of windows with their tall, sentinel drapes. Toward these Frieda began a leisured pacing; reached them, turned and paced back again with an aggravating half-swagger. She paused at the table to flick an ash onto a cigarette tray and began pacing again. This was apparently going to continue.

"And why, Miss Baines," Janet inquired with polite detachment, "did you take up nursing as a vocation?"

But Ethel was saved the trouble of an answer by the appearance of Hodges, who came half-sheepish, half-sullen from the dining room, stood hesitantly just behind Janet's chair, and spoke in a throaty but restrained voice:

"Miss Larnard—you wanted to see me."

"Yes, Hodges. D'you feel better?"

"Yes'm," he admitted, "thank you."

"Are you willing to admit now that you'd been drinking?"

"Yes'm."

"You *hadn't* been asleep then?"

"No'm. I was just getting to bed when you knocked."

"*Were* you the one Cowpers heard coming up the back stairs?"

"He didn't say it was me, Miss. He just said . . . ."

"I'm asking *you*, Hodges! Were you?"

"Yes'm," he said quietly.

"Where had you been?"

"Down cellar, Miss Janet—fixing the furnace."

"But, Hodges, you never attend to the furnace. Cowpers is the one . . . ."

"I smelt coal gas in my room, Miss, an' I didn't like to wake Cowpers, Miss . . . ."

"You were *drinking* in the cellar, weren't you?" After a stupified pause he nodded.

"But why . . . ."

"It was like an ice box in my room, Miss Janet. I just wanted a few quiet nips to see me asleep. So I went below to get warmed up. Comin' over the stairs I must 'ave stumbled or somethin'—an' Cowpers thought . . . . He didn't *say* it was me, Miss. No one," his voice became more assertive, "has anything on me, Miss. I was comin' up the back stairs, an' I'd put 'a couple' under my belt—but I'm tellin' you myself, an' I don't want you or anyone to think infumation has to be got from others—about me!"

"I'll get Cowper's story from Cowpers," Janet promised grimly. "How long had you been in the cellar?"

Hodges made much of thinking back. "Well, it was about midnight, Miss, as near as I can figger it when I came back from lookin' fer the dog. Spoke to Mr. Neville here in the livin' room. . . ." He glanced toward Ethel for confirmation, and spoke more deferentially, "Miss Baines can tell you *that*, Miss. She was here. Wished me good night."

"Yes," was all Ethel could say.

"You went to your room," Janet prompted.

"Yes'm. It was so col . . . ." But at a sharp glance from Janet he plunged on. "In about quarter of an hour—went to my tool room in the cellar—an' came upstairs when Cowpers said he heard me. Just a minute or so before one o'clock. I heard the clock strike myself from downstairs."

"And you didn't hear or see anything out of the way—at any time?"

"No, no, Miss. Not a thing. Just—what I've told you."

"Did you hear the telephone ring when you were in the tool room—about ten minutes of one?"

"Yes'm—in the distance." Then he added, "I remember that particular Miss Janet, because I heard someone walking overhead to answer it. An' I popped out the light. Thought whoever it were was comin' down cellar."

"But no one came down cellar?"

"No," he said solemnly, looking Janet straight in the eye. "No one, Miss."

"All right, Hodges. You wait up in the kitchen. Don't drink any more this evening."

"Yes'm. I won't."

# CHAPTER IV

Several minutes later Janet responded to a knock at the outside door to admit three snow-encrusted, bitterly silent men.

Alfred's nose was a short, sharp triangle of venomous red, the rest of his strong-boned face blanched with chill, as he led Neville in quite tentatively by the arm. Alfred seemed to have forgotten that anything existed save his own discomfort, let alone the fact that anyone had been slain in the house. But Courtney came vigorously in, prodding Neville's indifferent back with the barrel of the revolver, never for a second letting the elements overcome his energetic self-importance, but allowing excitement to overcome his sense of the smaller niceties. He wiped his nose freely with his gloved left hand as he slammed the great door and spoke officiously to Neville:

"Take off your coat!"

Neville turned slowly and levelled a look at Courtney, a look such as can only be given by a man soured with too much whiskey who has been sobering himself in a blizzard for two hours.

"I shall take off my coat," he told Courtney with numbing scorn, "*when I choose*. At present I'm too inert with cold to do anything, even to laugh at you." He walked to the hearth and shook the snow from the raccoon garment onto the wide stone, where it hissed and steamed.

Courtney shoved the revolver into Alfred's helpless hands and swung briskly out of his own coat, took back the revolver and crossed to the lounge to warm himself carefully near Neville. Cowpers brought in a shining urn of hot coffee that scented the hearthside with its aroma. With a chattering 'thank God' Neville pounced on the first cup. The coffee brought Alfred stiffly out of his coat and shrinkingly near the fire.

"You're nearly dead, Alfred," Frieda exclaimed with a spurt of the former dancing solicitude. "Don't you want something else—brandy, whiskey . . . ?"

"No," his parched lips emitted, "just don't talk to me please. I'm cold."

"Well, Neville," Janet challenged from her throne by the coffee, "what do *you* think of all this?"

"I'll begin thinking," he gasped, between gulps of coffee, "when these lunatics stop playing charades and tell me what's afoot. Up to now, however, the joke has not been broken to me. I admit we couldn't talk very much when I was *captured* on the launch. Imagine!" He waved his empty cup at Janet, already thawing into his usual voluble buoyancy, "After fighting my way in a shaky craft through miles of gathering ice floes, I'm received by two unreasonable asses with a revolver, who march me up here like a pickpocket . . . . I'd like to know what's happened. I really would." He turned to Ethel. "I ask *you*, my dear, as an impartial outsider, *what* has ever possessed the family that I should . . . ." But the look in her eyes halted him. He stared quizzically at her, his left eyebrow twisting up curiously. Then he turned uncertainly to Frieda, who was watching him from behind the lounge, to the triumphant accusal of Courtney's face, the puzzled intentness of Alfred's, and then to Janet's quiet, inexorable scrutiny. "What's the trouble?" he asked seriously. "*What's happened?*" His face altered to a sudden graveness. "Has—is father worse?"

"That depends on how you look at it," growled Courtney. "He's been murdered."

Neville seemed almost unable to say, "He's been *murdered!* What— how do you mean? I don't . . . ."

"Oh, yes, you do," snapped Courtney, pushing his face out aggressively and shaking the revolver at Neville for emphasis. "Murdered! Stabbed through the heart, Neville, with a dagger—by someone who came in over the piazza roof, leaving footprints of snow across the room someone who came in, Neville, through the veranda door in *your* room. Someone who was malicious enough to lock the nurse in the room with your father's mangled body when she answered a ring for help. Don't pretend you don't know what happened—because *we* know, and we've got you."

"Good God!" Neville breathed. "You—you think *I* did it!"

"Who else," Courtney inquired, "was out of the house?"

"I was on shore—at the boathouse."

"*When* were you at the boathouse?"

"Ever since I left here—discounting the trip over and back."

"Maybe," Courtney ground out, "but you can't *prove* it."

Neville's face tightened, and then he broke out, "Oh, yes, I can—and I will in about an hour."

Courtney allowed an aggravating smile to spread upward from his full, sharply-cut lips and wrinkle into the shadows about his protruding grey-blue eyes. "You mean—the telephone call?" Neville's lips sprang apart in surprise. "Because if you do—we're on to that, too."

"In God's name—on to *what?*"

"How easy it would be," Courtney explained, "and how easy it was—for you to tap the wires right here on the island—maybe here in the house somewhere—and trump up a 'phone call."

"But why should I . . . ."

"To make us *think* you were on shore."

"But, Courtney, it *wasn't* trumped up. I talked with someone—on the other side of Ticonderoga. *He'll tell* you . . . ."

"How will he know," Courtney asked quickly, "where you were when you answered?"

"But he rang the boathouse. He knew I was going to be there."

"It seems very strange that anyone should know you were going to be at the boathouse at this hour of the night. And, anyway, no matter whether he rang the boathouse or not it would ring over here, and it did. It would ring any instrument you might have tapped onto the wires at any point."

Neville merely looked at him again, and then turned with nervous disgust to Janet. "More coffee, please!" Then he turned to Courtney, "Now wait a minute. When you and Alfred came down to the dock you found me coming in the launch from shore, didn't you?"

Courtney smiled agreeably. "You might have been coming from only a few hundred feet off the island. No one could see in the storm until you were right by the dock. We couldn't even hear the engine until you were close at hand. Why did you go ashore?"

"To meet someone."

"Who?"

"The man who spoke with me on the telephone."

"But who was it?" Courtney insisted.

Neville's lips started to speak, and then halted. Then he smiled at Courtney, and said. "I'll tell you later, when the police arrive."

"The police have not been notified, Neville. You made that impossible when you cut the wires."

"Cut the wi . . . ." Neville dropped his cup and saucer smartly onto the mantle and wheeled about to face closer to Courtney. "That's enough. It's a very clever idea, Courtney, to try and trap me—but you've found out now I didn't do it. You should have known anyway. But now we'll stop this tommy-rot." He went quickly to get his coat hanging on the newel post of the stairs.

"Stay where you are," Courtney warned him, and stood up, threatening Neville with the revolver. Neville turned angrily. "Where do you think you're going?"

"Ashore, if the wires are cut here, and notify the police from the boathouse. Incidentally, I'll meet the man who spoke with me over the 'phone."

"You'd better tell us right now who this man is, Neville, because you're *not* going ashore, and we . . . ." Neville visibly tautened to leap at Courtney, but Courtney jumped back warily, and raised a cautioning voice: "Be careful now, or I'll use this thing without any hesitation. I mean business."

"Oh, so *that's* it," Neville laughed, and then his voice hammered out, "well, *I* think you mean a good deal more than that."

"Who is this man?" Courtney demanded again, "you spoke to on the 'phone?"

"Wait, Neville," Janet warned, and then more slowly, "you'd better keep that card up your sleeve. *I* know who it was." Everyone turned quickly toward her. "I heard the call too—from upstairs."

"I'm glad," Neville murmured wearily, as he walked back to the fire, "there's someone who doesn't think I did it."

But Courtney was at him again: "Where's that key?"

"What key?"

"To the engine of the launch."

"In my pocket. Why?"

"Hand it over," Courtney ordered. Neville exercised all his self-control and gave Courtney the key with a shaking hand. "Now," Courtney went on, "the other one!"

"What other one?"

"Or the other two," Courtney said, "that you took out of the doors to your father's room when you locked Miss Baines in there."

Neville broke abruptly into peals of sardonic, almost demented laughter that sounded hideously through the house. Then he smothered it as he drew in a hissing breath and almost spat in Courtney's face. "Christ! What a piece of rotten dirt you are!" His eyes narrowed and his face drew into ferocity, as one hand pointed slowly toward Courtney. "My father's dead, is he? Stabbed! And you think you can wash the blood off your own hands onto mine!" He turned his face to the quiet statue of Janet, and pointed out Courtney for her benefit, as he quoted harshly, "'a man may smile and smile, and be a villain.'" Then back to Courtney, sneering, "'Claudius! to *kill* my father and *marry* with my mother.'" He looked wildly toward Frieda, who watched him pale and afraid from the protection of the lounge. "And you, *Gertrude*, 'to post with such dexterity to incestuous sheets!'" He let himself shriek out with fierce laughter again, and then faced the mantle, burying his head in his arms as the laughter changed to uneven, heaving, half-sobs.

"He's insane," Courtney said shakily.

Neville switched back to him in swift possession of himself, and spoke with significant softness: "'I am but mad north-northwest, but *when* the wind is southerly . . .!'"

"Very effective," Courtney managed to scoff.

"Very! But you'll need more than a melodramatic memory . . . ."

"Yes," Janet said firmly, "this is all quite diverting, but what are we going to do?"

"Less hysteria," Alfred suggested, looking from Neville to Courtney, his eyes searchingly dark under stiff, evenly marked black brows, "on all sides. If I remember correctly, Miss Baines suggested before we went out that everything pointed to someone's coming in from outside, and, as she also told us, the chances of anyone in the household doing this thing were very small. Someone may very easily have approached the island in a boat of some sort and performed the atrocity with some motive we've no reason to suspect—some business enemy of Henry's, a paid killer perhaps, or even one of the criminals he sent to prison while he was a judge . . . ."

"I've changed my mind," Ethel said, "since finding that the dagger . . . ."

"Please," Janet interrupted.

"No, no!" Courtney waved Janet to silence. "Tell us, Miss Baines— what about the dagger?" "Not unless Miss Larnard wishes . . . ."

"Nonsense," Frieda broke in, "the dagger was Janet's. I overheard her telling the nurse. And it's been missing for several days  No point in hiding that, Janet—or *is* there?"

"You don't find out much, Frieda," was Janet's nauseated reply, "if you begin by telling all you know."

"Well," Alfred conceded, "that throws a different light on it. *Must* have been someone who had access to the house."

"What I would like to have explained," Frieda announced, "is Miss Baines' behavior. Why were you so slow in answering the ring?"

Ethel felt herself grow hot under Frieda's glance of cool suspicion. "I was wakened out of a sound sleep, Mrs. Larnard. I was terribly cold and stiff. Tried to warm myself at the radiator . . . ."

"You were sound asleep," Frieda repeated. "Then how does it happen you had your uniform on under your bathrobe?"

Ethel's face was stinging with humiliation. "Because I hadn't—permanently gone to bed."

"That seems a trifle strange. You weren't *expecting* trouble, I hope." Ethel remained in angry silence. "May I ask *why* you hadn't *permanently* gone to bed?"

"Why, I . . . ." Ethel faltered, feeling acutely embarrassed, and then spoke defiantly to Frieda. "I knew Neville had gone out. I—I wanted to speak to him when he came in."

"Oh, I see," said Frieda with glistening innuendo. "*Do* excuse me."

This deflected Courtney's persecution of Neville for an instant. "In that case, Miss Baines, you may be able to help us. Please remember that *you* were the one who discovered the crime, and in—how shall I put it?—very unusual circumstances. Did Neville, by any chance, tell you why he was going ashore?"

"No," said Ethel.

"Didn't you ask him?" Ethel blushed furiously. "Well?"

"Tell him," Neville said. "It's perfectly all right."

"Yes," she said, "I asked him and he said he'd like to tell me, but it might strain my professional integrity."

"Did you know what he meant by that?"

"No. I hadn't any idea."

"It might mean quite a lot," Courtney gloated, turning to Alfred. But Alfred was watching Ethel, and her eyes hurt as they faced his jealous accusal. She knew now that her replies would turn *him* against Neville, but she was afraid of complicating Neville if she invented any hasty falsehoods.

"Yes," Neville said triumphantly, "it does mean quite a lot—as you'll soon see."

"That piazza roof," Frieda remarked casually, staring into the red depths of the fire, "runs all around the house. And every room on that corridor has a door or a window opening on to the roof. It might be very easy to go 'round from one of the rooms by way of the roof, commit the murder, ring the buzzer, and then go back over the roof and *appear* from your room to answer it two minutes later."

"Just whom do you aim that at?" Janet wanted to know.

"Why, I couldn't help thinking again of Miss Baines. She seemed so adroit in hopping about the roof."

This almost convinced Ethel that Frieda had done the thing herself, but she tried to remember that Frieda *did* have every reason to suspect *her*.

"I'm quite sure Miss Baines had nothing to do with it," Alfred said, as he smiled reassuringly at Ethel.

"But, of course, Alfred," Frieda said, "we've had to take *your* word for Miss Baines all along. You're the only one who's ever seen her before."

"I'm perfectly willing," Ethel flared, "to tell everything I know of this, immediately, to the police, which is more than some of the people here seem to want."

"That's my idea, too," Neville said, and then, slyly, "but there must be some *reason* why we're not anxious to have the police know, some reason why it's more comfortable to have Courtney's legal subtlety playing on the thing."

"I shall go ashore," Courtney said, "when the storm clears. Just at present I don't care to risk . . . ."

"By the time the storm clears—you won't be able to get the launch ashore," Neville laughed. "There was ice forming when I came in."

Courtney spoke imperviously: "Neville, a few more questions, if you don't mind."

"Certainly."

"Will you, or will you not, admit that you have the technical knowledge necessary to tap these telephone wires."

"Why, of course!" Neville answered easily. "I put in the wiring, didn't I?"

"Then," Courtney probed on, "will you tell us whether or not there might be the necessary equipment, 'phone receivers, mouthpieces, et cetera, among your collections of mechanical junk here in the house?"

"There's enough equipment to set up a whole switchboard."

"Well," Courtney smiled, spreading his large hands apart as he turned to the others for applause, "Quod erat demonstrandum." Then, to Neville, "One more thing—you went ashore, you say, to meet someone. He 'phones you he is delayed. You promise to wait for him at the shore boathouse. Then—you appear here on the island without him. What motivates that?"

"Why," Neville answered quickly, "I had to come back to keep a channel of water open through the ice that was beginning to form. Otherwise, I'd have been stranded ashore—and you'd be stranded out here, as you will be inside an hour."

"If Elizabeth were only here," Janet yawned, "there'd be no question about who'd killed Henry." Alfred seemed acutely hurt at this, and looked reproachfully at her.

"That," Courtney admonished, "was quite unnecessary."

"The truth," Janet smiled, "is seldom necessary, but often very pertinent."

"Cowpers!" Neville called with startling loudness. "Cowpers! Come here please." Cowpers brought his athletic frame sleepily from the dining room, a shotgun dangling from one hand. Courtney clutched the revolver beside him on the upholstery of the lounge. "Cowpers," Neville said, "when did you last go ashore?"

"Why— Ah was shore this mawnin, to pick up groceries, 'fore the storm set in."

Neville turned to them. "As you all know, nobody went ashore this afternoon or this evening—except me, and I went after midnight."

"Granted," Courtney said, "except for the fact that you *did* go ashore after midnight."

"Cowpers," Neville said, "when you came back this morning—you remember you told me something was wrong with something in the boathouse. Tell them what it was."

"Why," Cowpers mused, "Alls Ah remembah is tellin' Mist Neville that th' clock upstairs in th' boathouse was run down an' stopped, and Ah couldn't find key t' wind it."

"Thank you, Cowpers. That's all." Cowpers lounged back to the dining room. "Now then," Neville said smartly, "anyone who's interested may go ashore and see that the clock is running. I found the key. It had fallen into a crack between the floorboards. This establishes the fact that I *did* go ashore. I left here about one minute before twelve. It takes thirty-five minutes each way, and more in this storm. But granting me thirty-five minutes each way, with about two minutes ashore to fix my alibi, when would I have returned to the island ?"

"About two minutes before the crime was discovered," Courtney said quickly.

"Then, in order to have been here to do the stabbing, I must have been on my way back—almost midway between here and shore—at ten minutes of one."

"What of it?" Courtney inquired blankly.

"That happens to be the time when I received the 'phone call, the time when you accuse me of tapping a cable several fathoms below the keel of the boat in freezing water."

"But I don't say you tapped the *cable*," Courtney flustered. "You may have stayed on the island, tapped the wires here at ten of one, committed the crime at quarter past, and *then* gone ashore."

"But you brought me into this room at quarter past two—just a little early for my return if I followed your second theory."

"That clock business sounds a little funny," Janet observed. "I believe it. I believe you and Cowpers, but most people who didn't know either of you would say that story had been cooked up. It's too neat."

Ethel was glancing unobstrusively at Neville as he stood, back to the fire with his profile to her, on the hearthstone. Every time he shifted from one foot to the other, placing the heel of one boot up against the andiron to dry the sole, she tried to see if there was any trade marking under the instep. Of course, they would have to take her word for the presence of the trade marking on the snow footprint in Mr. Larnard's room. It had probably melted away before Alfred and Courtney had examined the traces. But her word was as good as anyone's. This might prove . . . . As he lifted the sole of his left boot . . . . she thought it was worn clean away, with no marking of any sort. Yet it might have been on the other shoe. The boots were laced to the calf of his legs. They didn't seem new—the dark, mahogany leather of the tops scratched, and stained with machine oil, mud, and wet patches where snow must have melted. But she did not dare to raise the question of the footprint openly, for fear it *might* have been Neville. Although sure of his innocence, she had a maddening desire to protect him whatever he had done. She would wait and see for herself—without telling anyone. If she found that the right boot had that peculiar, broken-rimmed diamond marking she would . . . . *what* exactly? And then she knew, in a tense wave of apprehension, that she would be terribly afraid of Neville, but would care for him perhaps even more, with a gnawing wish to allay the agonized repentance she knew would surge impulsively through him when he had thought the horror through. And she would never whisper what she knew to anyone—except, well, perhaps to Neville himself. But he *couldn't* have done it. He *mustn't*, he simply mustn't have. She realized that Courtney was speaking—speaking again with the dogged, untiring, and hypnotizing persistence of a butcher slicing an endless sausage.

"You realize, of course, Neville, the sharp suspicion that will fall on Miss Baines if you go on claiming you had nothing to do with this. Now I know you well enough to be sure that you'd be quite willing to stab your . . . ." he paused, and Ethel saw Frieda's restless hands tense together " . . . . father, if the mood struck you, or anyone else for that matter, but I didn't think you'd deliberately incriminate an innocent . . . ."

"If there weren't several innocent people here, liable to be shot in the scuffle, that revolver wouldn't keep me from wringing your neck."

"It might," Courtney smiled, clutching the revolver firmly in his right hand, "but to avoid any such contingency, I was just going to ask you to let us lock you in your room, temporarily, at least. What do you say to that?"

Neville shrugged. "Not much I *can* say, is there?"

"He could very easily get out," Frieda laughed, "through the door or windows onto the roof."

"Naturally," Courtney said, and spoke to Alfred. "I think if you get Cowpers to help you nail those windows up on the outside . . . ."

"All right," Alfred hesitated as he got stiffly up from the lounge, "but it seems pretty high-handed to me. And it'll look very bad for all of us if we lock Neville up while someone else may have done it and is making a clean getaway."

"It's all very well," Frieda said, "to be polite to guests—but I still don't feel quite easy about Miss Baines."

Courtney looked at them all in turn. "Has anyone else a plan of action?"

"Neville's already offered to go ashore," Janet reminded them, "and 'phone the police. You or Alfred can go along with him if you think he's trying to make an escape."

"I feel apprehensive enough," Courtney said, "with Neville at large in the house. In the launch, off shore in a storm like this why, he's *already* threatened to wring my neck."

Alfred came in from the dining room with Cowpers, who had temporarily taken up hammer and nails in place of the shotgun. He glanced guiltily at Neville and ambled up the stairs behind the chimney. "Ah dunno," he was saying, "whether Ah oughta do this. Seem to me Mist Neville the las' person . . . ."

"You do as you're told, Cowpers," Courtney called, "and stop thinking about it."

"Yes, *suh!*" and then he could be heard saying with a religious certainty to Alfred: "But Ah won't go into *that* room, suh—not while *it's* there!"

Courtney was explaining to Janet. "I wouldn't be so sure about Neville—if he hadn't left the house under the threat of being disinherited by Henry immediately. In fact, I was already drawing up another will."

"Were there any other changes in it?"

"None." Neville merely clenched his fingers viciously into the palms of his hands so that the knuckles stood out in little red and white bulges. It required, apparently, every fiber of control to keep him from leaping wolf-like at Courtney and tearing his throat open. Ethel began to understand what Courtney had meant a few minutes before when he had accused Neville of being capable of stabbing his father or anyone else if the mood struck him. His mouth became a compressed, brutal curve. His nostrils twitched with quirks of hatred as his breathing became uneven, almost hoarse. His eyes narrowed to small, dark triangles of glowing venom. Courtney let his urbane gaze meet Neville's for several seconds before speaking.

"Neville, this is going to go hard with you, but not as hard as it might—if you behave, now, with some consideration for us. I'll forget that you locked Miss Baines in that room and that you let suspicion fall on Janet by taking that knife. I'll forget your insidious cleverness in fixing up your alibis, and try to make things as easy as I can for you. If you confess this thing and clear the rest of us—I'll defend you in the courts on grounds of insanity. I think Alfred can be persuaded to testify that your mind is *not* what it might be. You can plead guilty, and you'll probably be shut up for some time but you won't necessarily have to be electrocuted or even be in prison . . . ." Neville's mouth jerked, as if to speak, but Courtney made a quieting motion with the revolver. "Now, wait a minute. Think this over before you make any absurd move. We've got you, Neville, and nobody in the family is over-fond of you. You *were* pretty vicious, I admit, but it's done now. Your father might have died anyway—of his illness, so you can comfort your conscience with that. But you *have* made a mess of things, for yourself and the rest of us. My idea is to fix it up as easily as possible for all involved."

"Damned decent of you," Neville murmured between his teeth, "but it still strikes me as mighty strange that you don't want the police here."

"The police will be here soon enough," Courtney assured him. "Right now I'd like to have you hand over those keys to your father's room."

Neville raised his arms and rested them along the mantle. "Search me," he said agreeably, "do!"

"Thrown them away, of course," Frieda said, "if he had them."

Courtney drew his senatorial figure up and, holding the revolver against Neville's chest, went through his pockets, while Neville drummed nonchalantly on the mantle with his fingers. Courtney kept his eyes constantly on Neville's eyes, and Neville continued to smile insultingly back at him.

"Now turn 'round."

Courtney's substantial, well-manicured fingers searched the pockets of the corduroy riding breeches, and plunged again into the side pockets of the formless tweed coat, while Neville's lean fingers went on thrumming against the mantle.

Alfred called from the upper bannisters: "Everything's ready."

"Now, Neville," Courtney said encouragingly, "if you don't mind." Neville walked casually upstairs, turned on the landing by the chimney, waved elaborately.

"Good night, everybody. Now that the felon is safely in hand, I hope you all have delightful dreams."

Courtney followed him, still somewhat self-conscious about the revolver, and spoke to Alfred:

"Now the door from his room to Henry's is already locked, and I guess he's thrown the key away. So we'll just lock the corridor door. He'll have to break the window frames to get out to the roof, and we'd hear that."

"If you think I'm going to stay awake!" came distantly from Neville, and then a laugh, "I'll be the only one in the house who'll dare to sleep because I shall be securely locked in. There are bolts on the *inside*, too, you know."

Cowpers came vaguely downstairs, looking back mildly aghast at Neville.

"Do Mist Neville say he did it?"

"No, Cowpers," said Janet.

"Good night, Cowpers," Frieda said quickly.

"Good night, Ma'am," Cowpers answered, and quickened his step into the dining room.

"You'll stay in the dining room, Cowpers, with that shotgun," Janet called.

"Yes'm, Ma'am."

# CHAPTER V

"I don't see," Alfred protested to Courtney, as they came down the stairs, "why we shouldn't give him a little whiskey if he wants it. Been out in the cold. Like a little myself for that matter. Probably much easier to keep him safe and quiet if you give him a drink, but," he shrugged himself close to the radiant fantasies of the fire, "you seem to know."

"Well," Courtney told him severely, "considering the fact that a certain dipsomania is probably at the root of this whole ghastly business, I hardly see . . . ."

"Cowpers," Frieda called, "bring some whiskey for Dr. Trevor." She spoke cuttingly to Courtney, "Of course, if you think for one instant you can keep Neville boxed up . . . ."

"How about that man on the telephone?" Janet demanded. "Are we supposed to let him wait at the shore boathouse all night? Courtney, stop nursing that gun like a sick kitten!"

Courtney placed the revolver carefully on the side of the mantle and rubbed his hands administerially together.

"I should never have been so forward in securing Neville in this high-handed fashion," he explained, "if it weren't for the fact that this is probably going to be very skittish for us all. We realize, I presume," he said with grave unction, "that Neville is the only one so far who has attempted anything in the nature of a definite alibi, at least—an alibi backed up by someone else, namely, Cowpers."

"Wait," said Frieda. "Is Neville securely locked up—are you sure?"

"The door to Henry's room," Courtney told her, "was locked anyway, and I searched Neville, as you know—to make sure about the key. He must have thrown it away as you said. The shutters outside the windows have been nailed to the frames. He could batter those down,

71

but they're storm shutters, made of solid hard pine, and we'd be sure to hear him."

"But the door onto the roof?"

"Locked. With a few nails at the sides, just in case. I have the key to it, also the key to the corridor door."

"Now we've got him there," Alfred said, "what the devil are we going to do with him?" Cowpers came in with an air of offended dignity and placed a tray of whiskey and small glasses silently on the long table behind the lounge. "Thanks," Alfred said as Cowpers began to fuss over the bottle, "I'll fix it." Cowpers nodded tacitly and withdrew. "There's this man who is supposed to be waiting at the shore boathouse to be reckoned with. I take it he's a friend of Neville's, and I suppose he was coming out here to the island. If one of *us* goes to meet him and sends him away—he'll begin to think things, and if we tell him the whole story or bring him out here—he's going to make trouble."

"We can't have any stranger coming out here," Courtney agreed, "with things as they are—particularly a friend of Neville's."

"This man," Frieda suggested, "may have been mixed up in it from the start—unless the whole telephone conversation was a trick."

"Trick or not," said Janet, "I recognized the voice."

Courtney glowered at her. "Why won't you tell us who it was?"

Janet's lips hinted at a smile. "I'd rather see what your plans are first."

Courtney's jaw muscles tightened under his razor-reddened skin. He shook a threatening finger at her. "All these little—side-steppings will be remembered, Janet, when the showdown comes. It isn't at all likely Neville was alone in this thing. We won't forget whose property the dagger is either."

Alfred handed Janet a small glass of whiskey that gleamed like a large, misshapen, dark sapphire in the ember-light. The shiny skin of her fingers crooked about it affectionately. Her eyes peered searingly at Courtney from beneath her scraggly, grey-threaded eyebrows. "If you've nothing to hide, Courtney, why are you afraid to go ashore and bring this man out here—no matter who he is?"

"You're not *afraid* to, are you?" Alfred asked lightly, but paused in pouring the whiskey to watch Courtney for an answer.

"I think," Courtney hurried to say, "that it would be a pity to complicate the situation—now that we have it clearly defined—by getting another person mixed up with it before we tell the police. As a matter of fact I doubt if there *is* such a man waiting at the boathouse. We have to take Janet's word that the conversation was not bogus." Alfred lowered the bottle slowly to the tray, but Courtney went on: "That in itself is very strange—that and the dagger. I call you all to witness that Janet is the only person in the house Neville has even been civil to since his father was taken sick . . . ."

"Just a minute," Janet broke in. "You have Alfred's word as well as mine on that 'phone call." She waved an empty glass irritatedly at Alfred. "Think, now Alfred. Didn't you recognize that voice?"

"Not at the time," Alfred assured her.

"But as you think it over . . . ." Courtney began.

"I know," Alfred said with a puzzled quirk about his eyebrows, "I know—I've heard it before. In fact—as I think it over the sound of it was very familiar, but I can't place it with a name—or even a face. It was a man; I'm sure of that, and I should say—a middle-aged man."

"That's right!" Janet said snappingly.

"We can soon find out," Alfred said, "by going ashore in the launch."

"Telephone the police from the boathouse," Janet added.

"Yes," said Alfred, "or one of us can drive to the town if the storm has been responsible for the 'phone here being out of commission. I mean, if the main lines are out of order, too."

"And while you're gone," Janet nodded, "we'll see if . . . ." But she levelled her eyes at Courtney and stopped.

"If what?" Courtney wanted to know.

"Never mind," she told him, "we'll see anyway."

"There you are!" Courtney expostulated. "Don't you understand what she's trying to do?" He turned to Alfred. "She thinks with us out of the way she can get Neville out of this. Hand in glove with him! I'm not going to leave the house—at least, not unless you promise, Alfred, to keep things just as they are till I get back."

"I'm sure Alfred will risk going ashore," Janet smiled at Courtney, "if *you* think the boat would be too treacherous in this . . . ."

Courtney almost shouted: "That's not the point, dammit! You know perfectly well why I want to stay here, and *I* know perfectly well why you want me to go."

"The thing is," Frieda said languidly, "can you *get* ashore. Neville said the lake . . . ."

"The wind has certainly gone down," Alfred remarked, and poured himself another glass of whiskey.

From her chair at the left of the fire Ethel could see the upper stairway leading to the hall overhead. Several stairs from the top she thought she glimpsed something moving slowly in the shadows. Her quick instinct was to gasp and point toward it, but almost instantly another thought occurred to her—of course—Neville! She leaned her head casually back against the chair and glanced up again. The figure had moved silently two steps further down, and she recognized the knee boots as their leather picked up the flare of the fire in two dull lines of reflection. They remained stationary. She tried to look into the white-edged embers with perfect unconcern.

"Another thing," Courtney was saying, "about this business of informing the police. If we could wait and get a confession from Neville it would save the rest of us a lot of—well, embarrassment."

"It certainly would save *you* a lot of embarrassment," Janet assured him.

"We're all Henry's heirs," Courtney continued, "and if Neville wants to he can probably have us all subjected to a lot of inconvenience before the police get it through their heads that he was the one who did it, and while I've nothing of any real importance to hide—I still don't like the idea of having this become current gossip."

"Well," Alfred admitted, "it would be quite easy to keep the whole thing from the police, provided we can dispense with the friend on the telephone."

"How do you mean?"

Alfred shrugged. "Largely depends on Neville's attitude. I still don't feel sure he did it, but the facts *are* pretty incriminating. Perhaps when he thinks it over and realizes what a case there is against him—he'll see reason, provided, of course, that he *was* the one. In that event, we can bargain with him. If he'll admit doing it . . . ."

"He won't," Courtney replied. "You know he'll never admit it, even if it's true; but go on."

"Well, the only people outside the family who know about this are Cowpers, Sophie and Hodges.

"*And* Miss Baines," was Frieda's reminder.

"Yes, of course," Alfred laughed, "but somehow we've come to consider Miss Baines as practically a part of the family, and I know she'd be willing to abide by our judgment in this. My idea is to keep this crime a secret, taking Miss Baines and the servants into our confidence, and executing the necessary punishment ourselves.

"Here we are," he went on to explain, "icebound on the island. We are naturally unable to secure undertakers and such. Necessity compels us to perform an impromptu embalming, which I think can be managed quite easily, and temporarily inter the body, with the assistance of Cowpers, in a board casket of our own manufacture. The next step depends on how long we are ice-bound here. If we're unable to get ashore for four or five days the most feasible scheme is to cremate the remains ourselves here on the island, and subsequently explain the necessity to the authorities. In any case I will submit a physician's report, pronouncing the death to be from the natural cause—pneumonia."

"And what," Courtney inquired with fascinated but apprehensive enthusiasm, "if the ice breaks up within the next two days?"

"Then—we transport the body ashore in our own casket and make arrangements to have it cremated in the usual fashion. Our own casket will probably be quite satisfactory for the purpose and will doubtless not even be opened by the crematory workmen. However, if they *do* have cause to put the remains in a different receptacle—the body will be laid out in the usual clothing and will betray no evidence of violence. You see, the transportation to New York will require another day, or even two—and I think the chances of our own casket being opened are comparatively small. It was commonly understood that Henry was seriously stricken with pneumonia, and everything will appear quite natural."

"But," Courtney half-objected, "don't we thereby become Neville's accomplices—in attempting to conceal the crime."

"Technically," Alfred admitted, "we may. But morally we relieve ourselves of all responsibility by dealing with Neville according to our own lights."

"How?" Janet barked at him.

"By committing him to an asylum for the insane."

This turn in the conversation had chastened Frieda's venom to a quiet, scared curiosity, implying that she sanctioned the idea inwardly without quite having the courage to admit it. "Do you think," she wanted to know, "that Neville will ever consent to such a thing?"

"I'm recommending it," Alfred assured her, "as much out of regard for Neville as for the rest of us. I think the customary treatment of criminals is not only inhumane but illogical. A murderer is not possessed of the devil, nor is he a vicious agent by his own volition. He is mentally sick, dangerously sick."

Alfred was drawing a short-stemmed, large-bowled pipe from his pocket. The dark wood shone dully in the firelight, much like Neville's boots on the upper stairway. Ethel let her eyes look upward slowly to get another glimpse of the figure on the upper stairs, but there was nothing beyond the bannisters now but the flickering of shadows and firelight on the woodwork. Alfred went 'round to the table behind the lounge to open an oriental canister covered with hair-fine, golden scroll work and scoop the bowl of the pipe into the quantities of Henry's own blend of smoking tobacco.

"Even," he continued, "if Neville were not executed by the authorities, even if a plea of insanity succeeded in removing the death penalty—he would still be faced with a life term in some asylum and be treated as a criminal instead of being cured as a patient should be. Whereas, if *I* commit him to an asylum, as a curable victim of temporary nervous derangement—I will someday be able to have him removed."

"But," Courtney reminded him quietly, "do we ever want him removed?"

Alfred smiled with wry pathos. "I can't help looking at it from Neville's point of view," he said. "Neville isn't thirty years old yet. It might mean fifty horrible years of confinement—think of that! Half a century. No crime warrants that—at least, not a crime like this." He paused to pass a lighted match back and forth across the bowl of the pipe. "I admit it *looks* brutal, but even from Henry's angle it's not really such an atrocious piece of work. Henry was far from being a young man. And his physical condition made him much older than his years even when he was well. Although I tried to be optimistic about his illness, I have been quite sure from the start that he would not recover. Neville only hastened something that was bound to come very soon anyway."

"And you think that makes it less brutal," Janet said harshly, "for someone to stab him!"

"But if Neville did this," Frieda said quickly, "I see no point in trying to consider his feelings. He's never had the slightest consideration for the rest of us. And if he's dangerous enough to . . . ."

"At the same time," Alfred told her with calming assurance, in an even, direct tone that practically amounted to accusal, "there are circumstances which *some of us* would prefer to keep out of court gossip." He looked from Frieda to Courtney, who was fumbling in the pocket of his jacket for a cigarette.

"To be sure," Courtney stammered, "yes—er—decidedly!"

"For one thing," Alfred went on, turning back to Frieda, who sat rather shrinkingly on the arm of the lounge, "the causes of the quarrel between Neville and Henry earlier this evening, which brought on Henry's threat to disinherit him. Neville was considerate enough of you, Frieda, not to try to explain to Henry *why* he'd insulted you and why it might be justified. And you were cowardly enough to let it pass."

"Yes!" Janet hissed.

Frieda changed to quick, very obvious indignation. "What do you mean?"

Alfred's level gaze continued to drill into her eyes until she shook her head and looked away injuredly. "You were not in your own room, Frieda, when this happened." Frieda's eyes widened back at him. "I mean, when Henry was stabbed. I'm not saying you had anything to do with the crime itself. But I *do* think it may be a little embarrassing to explain—if you insist on bringing this to an open fight in the courts. I'm sure you and Courtney . . . ."

"This is all quite unnecessary," Courtney exploded.

"Wait," Alfred said firmly, "this is no time to mince matters. *We* all know what's been going on, and we may pretend to understand—because we knew how unreasonable Henry could be at times, and because we know you and Frieda. But," his voice became harder and more resonant, "outsiders won't understand; the courts won't understand. And, believe me, Neville won't hesitate to tell them, and the rest of us will have to admit that whatever he says about you and Frieda is probably true."

"Are you trying to threaten me?" Courtney asked.

Alfred looked for confirmation at Janet. "I'm just showing you how things line up. Janet, am I right?"

"Perfectly!"

"In that case." Alfred said more quietly, "you may understand how I'm going to have my way about dealing humanely with Neville, even to the extent of bargaining with him."

Courtney's solid, flushed neck twisted 'round like a wind-warped tree, so that he was looking closely into Alfred's face. "Why," he inquired thickly, "are you so anxious to protect Neville? Why should you want to keep this thing a secret?"

Alfred's eyes, in jumping away from this unexpected thrust, met Ethel's, and looked away hastily. Ethel felt a sudden rush of blood in her cheeks, and in trying to avoid Alfred's furtive gaze as casually as possible glanced up across the mantle at the higher stairway. The figure was there again, motionless, the boots betraying two dull, vertical reflections from the fire light.

"Because," Alfred answered, "this thing incriminates us all. Our rooms are all on that corridor, except yours, and Frieda was in your room. Neville's extremely clever, and we can't take any chances. If we have to bargain with him to keep this quiet—I think it's worth it."

"Perhaps you're right," Courtney admitted quickly.

"And now," Alfred said, as he went 'round to the table to pour himself another thimbleful of whiskey, "I suggest that one of us goes ashore in the launch to stave off this friend of Neville's, or take him into our confidence, whatever may seem best, depending on what sort of a person he appears to be. Maybe if he sees it's for Neville's interests he'll be willing to help us."

The figure on the stairs moved silently down two steps. Ethel could see Neville's face above the bannisters pale in the shadows, his eyes gleaming like steel in momentary flarings of firelight.

"Very well," Courtney acquiesced, as he drew himself wearily up from the lounge and stooped down to lift another log onto the fire, "I suppose Hodges and I can handle the launch."

"The storm must be nearly over," said Frieda.

Ethel could see Neville watching Courtney with the intensity of a leopard about to spring. But he realized in a second that Ethel had seen him. He remained rigid, staring at her, apparently certain that she had seen him, but not knowing whether she was going to cry out or remain silent. Ethel let her head nod the slightest fraction, and then focused her eyes on Courtney's profile. Courtney was taking the small, flat key to the engine of the launch from his pocket, as he stood back to the fire. She could see Neville's hand moving upward in the shadows, and saw that he was pointing one finger at Courtney, apparently for her benefit. She watched closely, and saw the hand move a trifle to the right. She understood—get Courtney away from the fire—but how?

"You'll have a hard time with the launch," Alfred said, "if the wind's gone down. Ice must be forming."

Ethel felt her body convulse tensely as a thought flashed through her.

"What," she said, trying to keep her voice from trembling with excitement, "what's the temperature now? Has it gone down . . . ?" But before she finished asking, Courtney went casually to the window near the outside door; and was drawing the drape aside to peer out at a thermometer.

Neville's body shot down to the landing. As his boots thudded on the carpet, one hand caught the bannister and swung him 'round the bend. Courtney wheeled at the window and shouted, "Alfred!" Alfred dropped his whiskey glass and darted around the lounge, but Neville practically slid down three more steps and reached across the mantle to grab the revolver. His hand clenched shakingly on it as he waved the shining steel from Alfred to Courtney.

"Stop right where you are," he said in a quick, hoarse whisper.

Courtney's quick rush faltered to a crouching halt, and Alfred stopped between the lounge and the stairway. Ethel was halfway out of her chair, ready to trip Courtney in his bee-line for the mantle, but sank back with a weak feeling of relief. Frieda had apparently seen Neville before the men did and her mouth was open for a scream which did not issue forth. Janet calmly turned her head to look at the revolver pointing a few feet above the back of her chair.

"Good work, Neville!" she said.

"Mother," Neville ordered, "sit down on the lounge—in the middle of it." And when she had done so, he pointed to Courtney and Alfred in turn. "You sit on that side—and you over here. And if you make any false moves somebody's going to be hurt. I don't care *who* it is."

"How did you get out, Neville?" Janet wanted to know.

"Whoever," Neville answered, "locked Miss Baines in father's room was nice enough to toss the keys into a drawer with my neckties, doubtless to further incriminate me. But we'll see!" He came slowly down the last few stairs, still covering them all alertly with the revolver.

"Neville," Janet suggested, "the first thing I think you'd better do is question Hodges again."

"What about Hodges?" Courtney asked quickly.

"He knows something," Janet said. "He lied to me at first. Said he'd been asleep in his room for an hour. When Cowpers said he'd heard someone on the backstairs—Hodges finally backed down and said he'd been drinking in the tool room off the cellar."

"Why didn't you tell us that before?" Alfred demanded.

"There wasn't a chance," was the hard reply. "You and Courtney were baying so hard on Neville's trail."

"Cowpers," Neville was calling through the dining room, "ask Hodges to come in here, please." Then he turned and said easily, with a motion toward the large dining table, "We may as well question him in here—where we can all sit down." The dining table was rectangular and had three chairs on each of the long sides, and one more massive chair at either end. Neville stood aside as the others passed silently through the corridor under the stairs and came last into the dining room as Cowpers hovered in from the kitchen.

"Mist' Neville—he's just went down cellar."

Neville started through the pantry and came upon Hodges just rounding the corner from the kitchen.

"I'm here," Hodges said groggily.

Neville led him by the arm into the white glow from the glass-decked chandelier. "What is all this, Hodges? Cowpers says you just went into the cellar again."

"I did," was the stolid answer.

"I told you," Janet reminded him from her solitary chair at the far end of the table, "to wait in the kitchen."

Hodges smoldered. "Kitchen's not my place to wait," he said shortly.

"You do as you're told, my man," Courtney advised judicially, "or you'll find yourself in a lot of trouble."

"We'll never get anywhere," Alfred muttered, "if we all start badgering the poor devil at once."

This encouraged Hodges to whine something about just dropping down for another nip of a drink, "which I certainly need if I'm to be questioned and bullied by those I can't answer back to."

"Now take it easy, Hodges," Neville said. "Sit down and tell us what we want to know." This suggestion seemed to cover Hodges with embarrassment, as everyone but Janet was standing up. Neville waved them all into chairs and pocketed the revolver. Hodges was still muddled, appearing not to be able to decide whether it would be better to be militant and show them he could tell as little or as much as he pleased—or cringe his way into their sympathies. Frieda, Courtney, and Ethel were sitting on one side of the table—with Frieda nearest Janet at the head. Neville pulled back the middle chair on the opposite side for Hodges, and sat next him. Alfred sat on the other side of Hodges, near Janet.

"When I went upstairs tonight," Neville began, "to take my father some whiskey—it was a little after nine o'clock—*you* were in the room talking with him."

"Yes, Mr. Neville, I was," Hodges admitted in a very civil tone.

"You seemed embarrassed and wanted to leave at once, but father made you sit down and have a drink. We all had a drink and talked for about five minutes."

"Yes, sir. We talked about—where Hansel was. And I said I'd go out and look for him around the island, which I did—once just after I left you and Mr. Larnard, and again, on the other side of the island, just before midnight—when I met you at the front door."

"While I was at the bureau," Neville said with explicit recollection, "pouring a second drink, I could see you out of the corner of my eye picking up a piece of paper from the little table beside father's bed. He must have seen you himself, because he was looking right at you. When I turned 'round—you were putting something in your pocket. You refused a second drink. Father gave you a pint of whiskey, and you said goodnight. After you'd gone I asked father about the paper. He said it was a little message he'd given you to take to someone, so I forgot about it. But I'd like to know now—exactly what the paper was."

Hodges was staring at his heavy red hands on the table. He turned to Neville and spoke with more genuine spirit, and yet more reservedly, than he had shown before. "I wish, Mr. Neville, you wouldn't ask me about that. It's just a matter between—your father an' me . . . . I swear to Almighty God it's got nothin' to do with your father's death."

The skeptical silence was broken by Courtney. "Wait a minute, Neville!" He leaned across the table from his place directly opposite Hodges, planted the palms of his hands flat, fingers outspread, on the polished wood. "You've told Miss Janet you were out of your room. For how long, Hodges—and when?"

"From about quarter past twelve, sir, until just a mite before one o'clock."

"And you were in the cellar?"

"Yes, sir. In the tool room."

"The telephone call," Courtney reminded them all, "came at *ten to one.*"

"I heard a telephone ring, sir, upstairs. I heard someone walking overhead—to answer it, I suppose—but I thought they were comin' down cellar so I turned out the light in the tool room."

"I was the one he heard," Alfred said. "I overheard the call from the downstairs instrument in the library."

"But," Courtney said eagerly, "you and I, Alfred, have been over the wiring in the boat-house here on the island, and there's no evidence of the lines being tampered with. The only possible place now is the cellar."

"Cowpers," Neville said quickly, "go down cellar, look over the telephone wiring, see if there's a bottle of whiskey in the tool room—and bring it up here."

Hodges fists were clenching and unclenching until Cowpers could be heard plodding down the cellar stairs. Then Hodges broke out, as if unable to restrain himself.

"I didn't do that to the wires. I was in the tool roo . . . ."

"Do *what* to the wires?" Neville demanded.

"Whatever meddlin' *was* done to 'em. I didn't do it. Someone scraped the insulation off—I could see 'em workin' at it from the tool room. That's why I just went down again now to make sure."

Janet bent toward him across the table: "Who was it, Hodges?" But Hodges' mouth closed stubbornly and he stared immovably at the table's surface.

"Come on, Hodges," Neville prodded.

"Couldn't you see who it was?" Alfred demanded quietly.

"No, sir. I couldn't. When I put out my light—there was no light but the flashlight the person had—and it wa'n't pointed toward the face at any time."

"No one had any right fussing with those wires," Courtney observed. "Why didn't you speak out and put a stop to it?"

"I had no right there either," Hodges weakened, "drinking in the tool room."

"How did this person get into the cellar?" Alfred wanted to know.

"Heard 'em on the steps."

"Which steps?" Alfred continued, "the ones from the bulkhead outside, or those from the kitchen."

"I dunno. I was just plannin' to go upstairs myself. I hadn't put the light on again after once puttin' it out. I'd left the tool room and was just by the furnace when I heard a noise—of someone's footsteps—very soft. I ducked back to the tool room. Saw a flashlight, and got behind a door out of sight. When I looked out again I could hear this small scrapin' sound. Saw a figure—back to me—one arm holdin' the light—other arm workin' away at the wires. In about two minutes—light went out. I heard a few little noises—further away. Nothin' more. Then I sneaked upstairs to my own room."

"Did the person," Courtney inquired, "have any instruments?"

"Not that I got sight of. No, sir."

"When was this?" Neville asked.

"Just a couple of minutes after I heard the telephone ringin'."

Cowpers appeared with a half empty pint of whiskey, a small glass, and a few tarry-looking shreds of black rubber in the palm of one hand.

"Foun' these, suh, jes' unerneath wires—where wires show through th' insulation—insulation pared off. Wires aint cut though."

Neville placed the black shreds on the table and poked at them pensively with one fingernail. He took the bottle and glass from Cowpers, and looked thoughtfully at the bottle before placing it on the table.

"Never mind that, Neville," Courtney said edgily, "you've had enough."

"Cowpers," Neville said immediately, "bring some small glasses." He turned to Hodges, "You'll have another, Hodges?"

Hodges seemed uncertain.

"I will," said Alfred.

As Neville poured an inch or so of whiskey into small glasses for himself and Hodges and passed the bottle to Alfred, he said in a low, metallic voice, "This, Hodges, may refresh your powers of recollection."

Alfred was pouring himself a tiny glassful.

"Yes, sir," Hodges said more brightly, and raised the glass. "Here's the best, sir."

"Wait!" Neville took the glass from him and placed it on the table. "If you can't tell us who it was you saw in the cellar—you'll have to give us a little more light on that business in my father's room this evening."

"Yes," Courtney agreed, "—about that message. Have you still got it?"

"N—No, sir."

"You delivered it?" Hodges nodded. "To whom?"

Hodges sighed, laboriously drew a worn wallet from the inside pocket of his coat, took from it a rectangular slip of paper which he handed to Courtney.

"A cheque," Courtney observed, "for two hundred dollars, made out to Hodges by your father." He tossed the cheque to Neville. "What was this, Hodges?"

"A gift, sir."

"A gift?—for two hundred dollars?" Hodges said nothing. "But Mr. Larnard was not in the habit of making gifts. He was a most economical man. Cowpers," Courtney continued, "has Mr. Larnard ever made you a gift of money?"

"No, suh—jes' at Chris-mas—ten dollars, an' a day off fo' ma' birthday."

"You receive your regular salary," Courtney stated, "from *Mrs.* Larnard."

"Yes, sir. This was another thing. I was hard up."

"Hard up?" Courtney repeated. "What do you mean? You have your regular salary. There's nothing to spend it on up here. You're given board and lodging."

"Yes, sir; but I got relations to take care of."

"Who and where?"

"My sister."

"But your sister," Frieda reminded him, "left our employ to get married two years ago."

"I know," Hodges said glumly. "The man left her with a year-old kid to take care of—and no money."

"Well," Neville said, "that's nothing to be ashamed of. Why didn't you tell us in the first place?"

"Why should I, sir? Your father didn't tell you, did he? Now you've forced me to make him out a . . . ."

"That'll do!" Neville glared at him.

"I wonder," Courtney said to Neville, "exactly *why* your father didn't tell you what he'd given Hodges."

"Because," Hodges said excitedly, "he wasn't one—like you—to bully a man about his private business and make him ashamed of takin' charity! If I wa'n't in the position I am in this house, and under the circumstances there are, don't think I'd stay here and be talked to like this. Not for one minute!" He was on his feet, facing Neville. "And if you get me up to answer questions like this before the police—there'll be a pile o' trouble, and it won't be only for me!"

"If you're innocent," Neville said, "you won't get into trouble—provided you tell us what you know—who the person was in the cellar—and all the rest of it."

"I couldn't tell," Hodges wavered, "who it was—there was only a flash . . . ."

"Come on," Neville said more calmly, "sit down, take your drink like a man, and speak out . . . ."

"Please!" Courtney interjected, and started into the living room. "Before you go any further! I've an idea." He could be heard hurrying up the stairs.

Neville was gulping his whiskey. Hodges, a bit dubiously, was following suit. Alfred was just lifting a glass to his own lips. His face turned to a horrified grimace in the midst of a deep breath. He dashed the untouched glass on to the table and turned to stare transfixed for half a second at Hodges. With an electric gesture, as if unable to speak, he grabbed Hodges by the shoulder with his right hand, snatched the almost empty little glass from Hodges' lips with his left. "That's poison," he was whispering hoarsely, but he was too late. Hodges had drawn in one swift, rasping breath, his hands clutching stiffly at the coat over his chest. Hodges' face was a convulsed mask, his eyes bulging and terrified, his mouth gasping jerkily. "Sharp pain . . . ." he managed to say and wilted forward onto the table.

Alfred's hand fell limply from the hunched, dead shoulders. His eyes glowered accusingly at Neville. "You poisoned him, Neville, and you tried to poison me."

"That's a lie," Neville said calmly, and held up his own glass—empty. "I drank it and I'm not dead."

"You poured your own glass," Alfred told him, "and then put something in the bottle."

"What makes you think," Janet asked, "Hodges didn't do it himself."

"After Neville's drink was poured," Alfred told her, "Neville and I were the only ones who touched that bottle."

Courtney was speaking excitedly as he came over the stairs into the living room. "During the past years Henry has made at least eight payments of two hundred dollars to Hodges . . . ." But as he reached the doorway the sight of the figure on the table stopped him. He held a large cheque ledger under one arm. Neville was taking the cheque from the table to fold it and place in his pocket with the fragments of rubber insulation. The pint bottle, about one-quarter full, he locked in the sideboard, dropping the key into the pocket of his trousers. Without a word he started to pass Courtney on his way to the living room.

"Hold on a minute, Neville," Alfred called, and Courtney edged over as if to block Neville's path. Neville took the revolver from his pocket, and Courtney stood aside.

"I'd like those keys, Courtney—to the launch and the corridor door of my room." Courtney handed him the keys with resentful submission, and Neville went into the living room. In several seconds the front door was pulled to with a heavy slam.

# CHAPTER VI

When the swift collapse of Hodges had been outlined for Courtney's benefit he assumed a most saturnine expression and pronounced that everything—fallen glasses, angles of chairs, and particularly Hodge's' corpse—should be left exactly as it had been.

"Although Neville," he said regretfully, "has removed the most essential item by locking up the bottle."

With the most recent murder conveniently sidetracked and everyone assembled in the less harrowing atmosphere of the living room, Courtney again brought forward his discovery—the cheque book. He handled it with a reverence which might have been justified if he had made the bulky folder and made the monies recorded in it with his own two hands. Individually he compelled them to examine the stub of each cheque, and when Janet finally showed the general lack of interest by saying flatly, "What of it, Courtney? The important thing about Hodges is what he saw, or did, in the cellar about those wires. He may have been killed to keep him from telling on someone else, or he may have poisoned himself—because he was caught. You've got to have more than cheques . . . ."

"I have," Courtney exclaimed, "if you'll give me a chance to explain . . . . As you know, I have been entrusted with Henry's will and the drawing up of it. In the past five years he has probably instructed me to compose fifty-odd differing dispositions of his fortunes. Now—with minor variations they have always been essentially the same—with this exception: dating from two years ago—all wills made have included a *secret* bequest."

He glanced about for gathering curiosity, and Janet nursed his feelings to the extent of saying, "Secret bequest?"

"A specified amount of money—fifty thousand dollars to be exact—to be handed over to a certain bank, the interest therefrom to be paid by the bank according to instructions given in some other way by Henry to the bank. I wouldn't be one bit surprised," he said complacently, "if Hodges turned out to be the beneficiary of this bequest. Of course, we'll never have any way of finding out."

When a clock sounding from the library interposed a chime in the conversation half an hour later, Frieda said drearily, "If Neville doesn't come back soon—we'll be convinced he was responsible for the whole thing."

"Yes," Courtney agreed, "and if he doesn't come back—and force a path through that gathering ice—the lake will be definitely frozen up—and we'll be ice-bound out here while he makes his getaway. He can probably leave the country during the several days we'll be tied up here with no way of notifying anybody. Of course," he triumphed, "the minute he came downstairs I was certain of his guilt. The fact that he had the key from his door to Henry's just about clinched the thing as far as I was concerned. And then, naturally, the business with Hodges was too absurd."

"But," Ethel objected, "if Neville had locked up that room—he certainly wouldn't have been fool enough to leave the key in his own bureau. He would, as Mrs. Larnard has already suggested, have thrown it away. And as for the whiskey . . . ."

"Yes," Courtney insisted, "as for the whiskey . . . ?"

"Several people handled the bottle before it got into the glass at the table. Hodges was the one who brought the liquor to Neville in the first place. Neville gave it to Mr. Larnard—and Mr. Larnard handed it over to Hodges. No one knows what happened to it when Hodges left it in the cellar. Cowpers brought it upstairs. Neville poured himself a glass which seemed to be alright . . . ."

"*Seemed* to be . . . ?" Frieda echoed.

Then Ethel felt herself blanching—in the sudden fear that she had given Neville away.

"At least," she said quickly, "we saw him drink it."

"But did you?" Courtney cut in quickly.

"The glass was empty."

"Certainly," Courtney reasoned, "but he might easily have tossed the contents under the table."

"You remember," Ethel went on, "how long it took Hodges to get down to taking his drink."

"But," Alfred objected, "if Neville knew there was something wrong with it don't forget that he was letting *me* drink the stuff."

"But he didn't," Ethel exclaimed. "You didn't drink yours."

Janet raised one conclusive finger. "If Neville knew there was something in that whiskey—and let Hodges take it . . . ."

"But," Ethel hurried to say, "he may not have known. He may have pretended to drink it—I mean, he may have tossed it onto the floor—to clear himself—when he found he'd invited Hodges to take what turned out to be poison. My theory is," she went on, "that, aside from what Neville did, *Hodges died altogether too suddenly.* Why, he scarcely had time to swallow before he was overcome."

"You mean," Alfred suggested, "that he had been poisoned before he came into the room by a slow poison in the whiskey which he drank down cellar."

"That's exactly what I mean."

"Which," Courtney smiled, "only throws it back onto Neville."

"*Or* onto Hodges, himself," Ethel corrected, "or Mr. Larnard, who gave Hodges the whiskey."

"How dare you!" Frieda bristled up. "A perfect stranger in this house, insinuating that my husband . . . . It's unthinkable!"

"We're all on an equal footing," Ethel reminded her quickly, "as far as suspicion is concerned—strangers or not. You sit by quite passively when your son is accused right and left . . . . And yet the minute I try to show it might be someone other than Neville . . . ."

"Why," Courtney demanded, "should you undertake to defend Neville, Miss Baines? It must be quite obvious that you'll have trouble enough defending yourself. We know much more about the servants in this house than we know about you."

"Please!" Alfred interrupted. "Miss Baines is a professional nurse with excellent credentials. I'll testify . . . ."

"Which," Courtney interrupted, "only serves to place you under suspicion, Alfred. As a matter of fact—you handled that bottle along with the rest of them."

Alfred's precision was withering. "I poured a drink for myself, Courtney, the last one to touch the bottle. Hodges was given his whiskey by Neville. Everyone saw what happened. I'd be dead myself if I hadn't smelled something wrong in the glass, and if I'd been a quarter of a minute sooner—Hodges would be alive. Don't let your enthusiasm make a fool of you, particularly when you weren't even in the room. Why, by the way, did you leave the room?"

"To get the cheque book!" Courtney sputtered.

"Oh—of course!"

"Of course," Frieda told them, "no one's thought of Cowpers as being mixed up in this, but at the same time . . . ."

"Everyone's thought of Cowpers," Janet assured her, "and everyone with any sense has promptly forgotten about Cowpers. It's absurd."

"I don't know," Frieda said, half scowling in trying to affect a customary pretense of using her intelligence. "It seems to me I read of a valet once in the newspapers who . . . ."

Janet pounded her fist impatiently on the arm of her chair. "What are we going to do, Courtney?"

"It seems unsafe," Courtney brooded, "to leave things entirely unguarded, since, of course, Neville might . . . . But it's ridiculous for us all to sit here falling asleep in our chairs." He turned to Alfred. "So I think if Janet, Frieda, and Miss Baines go upstairs to bed, you and I can stay down here, and one of us can keep our eyes open—in case Neville . . . ."

"But if he comes back and looks in," Frieda said, glancing nervously about her, "he can easily see what's happened and sneak away—or get in a window, or perhaps shoot both of you."

"There's no way he can see through those curtains," Janet said with chilly brevity, "and everything's locked up—except the front door."

"On second thought," Courtney decided, "I think I'd prefer to have you stay down here with us, Janet." Janet smiled, relaxing in her chair.

"Give me a cigarette," she said, and Alfred passed her a box from the lounge table.

"You two better get some sleep," Courtney said.

"I don't want to go up there," Frieda quavered.

"I'm sorry," Courtney said, "but if Neville does come bursting in that door, I don't think it will be best for many people to be in this room. In fact, Alfred, I think you'd better sit in the library with Janet. If he doesn't come back in the next hour I don't think we have anything to worry about—except the problem of getting ashore and notifying the police, so they can watch for Neville on outgoing liners and so forth. Of course, if we can't get ashore, we can't, and that's all there is to it."

Ethel started up the stairs, with Frieda timidly behind her, as Alfred followed Janet into the library. Janet was accepting the situation more and more in an attitude of quiet, derisive amusement, punctuated by frequent chuckling snorts at each fresh twist of Courtney's plans. When Ethel rounded the landing and climbed the upper portion of the stairs, she could see Courtney seating himself ironly in the chair by the hearth which Janet had just left, with the shotgun resting on the arms in front of him—and then twisting the chair a fraction to the right so that he had a direct view of the front door.

Ethel was trying to conceal an impulse to get to her own room as hastily as she could to find out if there were any way in which she could climb down from the roof outside her window in order to meet Neville, whom she felt sure was coming back as he had promised, and warn him. Light came from all the doors along the corridor, except Neville's, which was closed.

"Good night," she said impersonally to Frieda, as she went along the hall.

"Good night," Frieda said quietly. As Ethel turned to enter her own room, she noticed that Frieda was standing motionless in front of Henry Larnard's doorway. Frieda turned, apparently saw Ethel watching her, and then began to sob as she went into the room where the murder had been committed. The sobbing stopped with a dull cry, and Frieda rushed out the doorway to the head of the stairs.

"Courtney," she called, "he's gone."

"What?" came from Courtney, already half way up the stairs. Ethel started toward her.

"Henry," Frieda was saying, "the body—it isn't in there."

Courtney crossed from the head of the stairs to Henry's room, the shotgun still in one hand, saying, "What do you mean?" Frieda followed him in, and Ethel stood in the doorway. The bedding had been flung back, and there was a great blotch of dark redness on the under sheet. Courtney confronted this alteration completely dumbfounded.

"I simply had to come in here," Frieda was explaining. "Morbid. I don't know why. Wanted to—see him, again. Miss Baines saw me come in. And this was what I found. Gone."

Courtney stooped down to look under the bed. Janet and Alfred were coming up the stairs. "What is it now?" Janet called.

"Everyone stay out of here," Courtney said quickly, and pushed Frieda and Ethel firmly into the hallway. "And don't disturb anything in any of the rooms. Alfred, stay near Janet." Courtney was examining the rug. He breathed a faint exclamation and moved over to the door into Neville's room. The door was shut, and between the rug and the threshold was a dark stain, still moist. He ran his finger over it and stood up.

"Of course," he said, and tried the door. "Locked."

"Hamlet," said Alfred, "must have lugged the guts into the neighbor room."

"Don't," said Frieda, "please!"

Alfred was trying the corridor door to Neville's room. It would not give. "And the room is nailed up from the outside," he said.

"Listen," Frieda whispered harshly, "what's that?"

"Where?" Courtney wanted to know, coming attentively into the hallway. They all heard an insistent thumping sound, barely audible above the moans of the abating wind.

"You don't suppose Neville's got back into that room through the windows," Frieda said, "from outside."

"No," Courtney whispered, already down to the landing beside the chimney. "It's the front door. Someone . . . ." A definite, heavy, knocking interrupted him.

"Can't be Neville," Alfred said, "or he'd come right in."

"No," Courtney answered, "because I bolted the door from the inside before I came upstairs." Alfred started down to the landing, but Courtney made a quick gesture with his hand. "Listen!"

A man's voice came in a muffled cry out of the echoes of the storm. "Hello-o-oh, hello-o-oh! Let us in." And the pounding was renewed more vigorously.

"That's not Neville," Janet said, as she leaned over the bannisters.

"Everybody else stay up here out of the way," Alfred told them, and then to Courtney, "I'll open the door and stand aside, while you cover the entrance with that gun."

"Alright," Courtney said, as they both crept hurriedly down the stairs, and Courtney took a position by the lounge with the shotgun half raised, his hand over the trigger. Alfred circled the lounge, walking softly, and approached the door from one side. "Pull it wide open," Courtney suggested, "and get back out of the way quickly."

Alfred slid the bolt aside with a sharp snap and swung the door swiftly back, standing behind it. A flurry of snow whirled through the doorway; the fire gasped in the draft. A man walked in carrying Neville's limp figure in his arms.

"This boy's nearly dead," he said, between exhausted breaths, and carried Neville quickly over to the lounge, where he put him down slowly and with labored difficulty, "and I don't feel very smart myself." Alfred had closed the door and came a few steps toward the fire, but the man was talking to Courtney, who seemed thoroughly puzzled and unwilling to put aside the gun. "You'd better get some whiskey," the man went on in a low voice, "and something hot. Forget about murder for a few minutes, or you'll have something else . . ." He was unbuttoning Neville's coat and unlacing the heavy boots, which were thickly encrusted with ice. The lower part of the coat was covered in the same way and held itself rigid as the man pulled it away from Neville's figure.

"Hello, Doctor," Alfred said, coming 'round to the lounge and stooping to unfasten Neville's necktie and shirt, "what happened?"

"Oh! Hello, Doctor," the man returned, after a second's surprise. "We got stopped by thick ice coming across . . ."

"Dr. Harvey," Janet called calmly, coming down the stairs. Ethel followed her and hurried to pour out some whiskey from the quart bottle on the table.

"How d' y' do," the man said, with a half-glance up at Janet, and then, as he noticed Ethel with the glass of whiskey, "Why, Mrs. Trevor . . . ! Thanks." He tasted the whiskey and poured it between Neville's inert, blanched lips. Ethel knew that she was visibly startled, but thought everyone was too absorbed to notice what he had called her. She recognized him now, and the name . . . Harvey. Of course! He had been consulting physician at the hospital where she and Alfred had worked during one winter. Even though he was too worried about Neville to remove his own hat and muffler, she could discern the full, strong nose, the weather-varnished face, the heavy grey eyes, encased with deep seams.

But she realized that Frieda had come almost to the foot of the stairs and was watching her. In a swift look at Frieda she saw intense suspicion in Frieda's eyes. Frieda's parted lips moved.

"Mrs.—*Trevor*," Frieda murmured, but nobody else heard her, except Courtney. Ethel saw him watching her narrowly when he rested the shotgun against the arm of a chair, and took up Neville's boots, as Harvey removed them, to place them absent-mindedly and methodically to dry out on the hearth.

"Some warm blankets," Harvey was saying, "and hot coffee . . . ."

"Yes," Janet responded, "Miss Baines—blankets—the linen closet upstairs. Warm them in front of the fire. I'll get Sophie to start some more coffee."

Neville's eyes were opening weakly, and Harvey poured more whiskey between his lips. Neville tried to smile and winced as the whiskey stung his mouth. Alfred was massaging his bare, white, muscular arms and chest, while Harvey tried to slap circulation into action through the thighs and knees. Ethel went upstairs for the blankets.

When she came down the Doctor was explaining: "Ran into ice, which stopped the boat completely. Neville crawled up along the bow to break it away with a boathook, but the decking was covered with a slippery coating, and he tumbled in. Went in up to the waist I guess. Held a rope until I climbed forward and hauled him out. Then we had to wait while I broke the ice away in that spot, and we were held up in another place, too. And I'm not much of a hand with a boat. Guess ten or fifteen minutes more would have been pretty serious for him. That's right," he smiled as Ethel tucked the hot blankets about the motionless figure on the lounge. Frieda began chafing Neville's wrists in a pathetic attempt to help without getting in the way.

"Sophie'll have the coffee going again in a minute," Janet announced, as she came in carrying a tray with two tall glasses filled with steaming hot water and cut lemon. "Meanwhile, perhaps, a strong whiskey sour."

"You, too, Doctor," Alfred said, satisfied that Neville's life forces had begun to function again. "Let me help you off with your things— must be soaked yourself."

Harvey laughed and took off his snow-stained slouch hat, revealing a high, tanned forehead topped with steely-grey hair that was closely trimmed and combed compactly to his large, squarish head. "No," he said, "I didn't fall in, but I could stand warming up a little; I'll admit that." He began to unstrap a waterproof coat which he wore over his heavy ulster. The two combined to give his solid, tall figure a massive appearance, but when Alfred had helped him strip them off, Dr. Harvey seemed merely a ruggedly built man, inclined to heaviness about the waist and the slightly-stooped shoulders. When he turned to watch Janet, who was adding whiskey to the glasses and giving one to Neville, his head moved quickly and thrust itself slightly forward. His eyelids creased up close about his eyes when he stared at anyone, doubtless from a certain near-sightedness, because he proceeded to draw a pair of steel-rimmed spectacles from the pocket of his vest and adjust them above the little indentation on his nose just between the eyes. He paused before taking his glass, looked at Courtney and the shotgun resting against the chair, then at Frieda, who sat on the edge of the lounge staring mutely at Neville's exhausted face, and he smiled guardedly at Janet as she handed him the tumbler.

"I thought I recognized your voice," Janet said to him, "over the 'phone. I overhead that . . . ."

Harvey nodded. "So Neville told me, and . . . ." he turned to Alfred, "and you overheard, too, Doctor . . . ."

"Yes," Alfred smiled, with an unobstrusive but needlelike glance at Janet, "and I believe I was the first to let on about the conversation, the only leg Neville has to stand on, as it were. I knew I'd heard that voice before, but for the life of me I couldn't place it."

"You can vouch that the conversation was authentic then," Harvey urged.

Alfred was beginning an emphatic affirmative, but Courtney stepped forward. "No one," he said, "questioned the validity of the *conversation*. But there *was* some doubt about where Neville was when he spoke to you."

"Yes, he told me," Harvey agreed. "You apparently, think he was in the middle of the lake. But to anyone who's been out on the lake this evening, that would seem to involve a few technical difficulties."

"Well," Courtney said, "if you're determined to be belligerent about it perhaps you can tell us exactly what you're supposed to be doing here this evening." He turned to meet Neville's calm, fatigued gaze. "Perhaps Neville can explain why he chose to abduct the corpse . . . ."

"And lock it in his own room?" Harvey said quickly. "Well, I'm sure he can, because he explained it to me quite satisfactorily." Harvey ignored their surprise by taking a long drink from the steaming tumbler.

"It looks as if we'd better sit down comfortably," Janet suggested, drawing up a chair from under the stairway, "and talk this over. Sit there, Doctor, by the fire." At this point Sophie bundled in a large tray of coffee with frightened efficiency.

Courtney reached languidly over to take the shotgun from the arm chair in which Harvey was seating himself, but Harvey placed it in a corner of the framing about the fireplace.

"If you don't mind," he said easily, "I don't think any more of that will be necessary." He tucked his right hand reassuringly into the angularly bulging pocket of his jacket.

Frieda remained in puzzled silence on the edge of the lounge beside Neville. Ethel sat in her former chair, opposite Harvey. Alfred and Courtney drew up chairs beside her. As she leaned over, ostensibly to place Neville's boots in a position to dry more quickly, Ethel turned them over and saw that the soles of both were cleanly worn away with no suggestion of any trade marking.

# CHAPTER VII

"You may wonder," Harvey began, "why we didn't bring the police. When Neville met me just now over at the shore boathouse—he tried to 'phone them immediately. It so happens that since I telephoned Neville at ten to one the whole telephone system has been put out of commission along the lake shore by the storm. Well," he rambled on, "you'd think one of us would have driven to the village to get authorities. But when I drove along the lake shore coming out the road was just barely passable, and we figured it would be at least an hour before we could get a machine through those drifts to the village and back to the boathouse with policemen. By that time, according to our calculations and the temperature, the lake would have been impassable, so we decided to come right on out. All of us here are the people implicated. We might as well figure it out for ourselves.

"It's some time since I've visited the house," he went on, "and I've lost track of the arrangement of rooms as well as external layout—in relation to the surrounding shore, size of the island, and so forth. So if someone would be willing to sketch me a little map . . ." He let this demand fall toward Courtney.

"Certainly!" Courtney replied, assuming that the request was a mark of extreme confidence. He went back of the table, took a plain sheet of paper from the drawer, planted a straight chair near the table and sat down to draw the oval-shaped shore of the lake, the Larnard Island equidistant from three shore points at one end of the oval, the road over which Harvey had just driven—tangenting close to the shore from the village, following the shore halfway 'round, then veering away again. Neville hoisted himself up to lean on the back of the couch to watch this diagraming. Harvey and Alfred stood on either side of Courtney as the sketching was explained.

"The lake, Doctor," Courtney began, "is about eight miles long and three miles wide. Here on the island we are not more than a mile and a half distant from the shore on three sides, but this is the undeveloped end of the lake and the shore is one solid wilderness until you get halfway to the other end. The road you followed coming out hits the lake shore at this point, follows 'round the egg-shaped tip of the lake here—and passes our shore boathouse right here. So, in order to reach a civilized part of the shore, we have to travel by launch a good six and a half miles.

"The island itself has approximately the shape of a triangle a quarter of a mile on each side, with its base facing the near shore—and its point in the direction of the far shore at the other end of the lake. There is a boathouse on this tip of the island—and the house itself is here—in just about the center, facing the boathouse.

"The house itself is composed of three large wings—put together, roughly speaking, like the top pieces of a cross." He drew the accompanying map and identified the rooms for Harvey's benefit.

"You see," Harvey said genially, as he drew out a curved-bowl pipe and Alfred passed him the tobacco canister from the table, "anyone of us might have murdered Henry and the chauffeur—anyone now in this house, including the servants."

"Anyone except you," Courtney said, implying the opposite.

"Oh, no," Harvey laughed, "I flatter myself that I might just as plausibly have done it as anyone else. As you see, I *can* handle a power launch—and for all you know I may have secured one at some point along the lake shore, come out here, accomplished the business, and returned to shore to meet Neville."

"But you," Alfred objected, "couldn't have faked the telephone call—and if Henry was murdered at twelve minutes past one and the call came at ten minutes of . . . ."

"I could have tapped wires just as skillfully as Neville, for that matter," Harvey replied, "right here on the island. I'm fairly familiar with the house; I've visited here often. I'm something of a mechanic . . . . You see, I might have hitched on a piece of apparatus at the island boathouse or even somewhere inside the house."

"But," Courtney objected, seriously this time, "you couldn't have poisoned Hodges."

"Why not?" Harvey exclaimed. "The poison might have been put in the bottle while it was in the cellar."

"But Neville," Alfred reminded him, "said he drank a glassful from the bottle—and Neville's not dead."

"Under the circumstances," Harvey smiled, "that was the natural thing for Neville to say."

"Just what are you driving at?" Courtney wanted to know.

"I'm simply trying to show that any of us could have done this. But I'm positive I didn't do it, and I'm reasonably sure Neville didn't. But since you seem to have cooked up a pretty convincing case against Neville, and since all the circumstances *are* against him—the quarrel with his father and mother this evening—Neville having taken too much to drink, as he admits—the evidence against him might very easily convince the literal-minded authorities, if they were called in, so I've decided to come out here and discover what's been going on."

"That doesn't explain why you were planning to come here to meet Neville in the first place," Courtney objected, "and you must have arranged to do that long before the crime was committed."

"Late in the afternoon, to be exact," Harvey said. "Neville called me on the telephone at the hospital in Syracuse. He thought Henry wasn't doing so well as he might and wanted me to come out and consult on the case."

"It's very peculiar," Frieda said, "that he didn't tell any of the rest of us about getting you out here. I was certainly entitled to know who was being called to attend my husband."

"According to Neville," the Doctor replied, "Henry knew that I was coming and didn't want anybody told for fear of hurting Dr. Trevor's feelings. I wrote to Henry about two weeks ago that I would be visiting the clinic in Syracuse for a month or so and would like to spend a week-end out here with several colleagues—to do a little shooting. I thought, of course, that no one would be here but a caretaker. I didn't know Henry was ill or that you hadn't moved back to town. Apparently when the letter was forwarded to him he decided to have me come out and see him anyway—and not wanting to offend Dr. Trevor—he sent the message by Neville. I was to just 'happen along' as you might say—and spend the night. But when the storm came up—the 'happening along' began to seem more and more phony. And since Dr. Trevor heard me talking over the 'phone there's not much point in trying to hide the fact that I *had* arranged to come here." He returned the canister to the table, and sat back in his chair puffing conclusively on his pipe. "That much for *my* being here."

Frieda sat erect on the lounge watching Harvey closely all through this. "Please," she said pungently, "you wrote to Henry about two weeks ago?"

"I mailed the letter a week ago Sunday. This is—Thursday."

"Where did you mail the letter?"

"In Chicago."

"But if you thought we had moved back to New York how did you happen to send the letter here?"

"I didn't," Harvey said tolerantly, as if talking to a child. "I think I mentioned that the letter was *forwarded* to your husband. I sent it originally to the New York address."

"Thank you," Frieda said shortly, got up quickly, and hurried up-stairs.

"What's the matter?" Courtney called, starting to rise from his chair.

"Never mind," she threw back with airy brevity. "I'll be right down."

"She's going into Henry's room," Janet declared, and started toward the stairs.

"You mustn't disturb anything in there!" Courtney called loudly. "Wait till the Doctor's had a chance to look around."

"Alfred," Janet said, "do stop her. There's no telling what she may . . . ." But Frieda had reappeared at the head of the stairs and came quickly down with a letter in her hand.

"He kept all his mail in the drawer of that little bedside table while he was sick. This must be the one—postmarked Chicago, then another postmark of New York and the forwarding address." She drew the letter from the envelope.

"Yes," Harvey admitted, not startled, but in a more serious tone, "and, if you don't mind . . . ." he reached for the letter, "it will be better, I'm sure, for everyone if you let me have that without reading it."

"Not at all," Courtney snapped out. "If there's anything in that letter—we're all going to know what's there, if you don't mind, Doctor."

Harvey made an indifferent gesture with his pipe. "You speak of my *minding*, as though it made any difference to *me*. All I warn you of is this—if you read that letter you may destroy our chances of discovering who did the murders."

"I'm sorry," Courtney said, as he took the letter from Frieda, "but you can't protect yourself at our expense."

"Would you mind, then," Harvey suggested, "reading it to yourself only, Mr. Larnard?"

"Why, er . . . ?" Courtney's surprise was equaled by his pleased sense of flattery.

"Nothing of the kind," Janet remarked. "We'll all hear it."

Harvey pursed his lips with a fatal amusement as he looked deeply into Janet from under his down-slanting brows. "Very well," he conceded, and settled himself behind the slow swirling of smoke from the rounded bowl of his pipe to watch the gradual twistings of vapor as they lengthened above the small circle of people.

"Miss Baines," Courtney said, "would you mind watching this letter with me as I read—just to assure everyone that I read it correctly?" Ethel leaned to look over Courtney's shoulder, trying not to notice Harvey's quickly parting lips as Courtney called her 'Miss Baines.' She knew that she must be blushing guiltily, and that she must turn and meet his cool, blue, unfathomable eyes or seem even more ill at ease than she really was.

"This is how it reads," Courtney began, "'Dear Henry, trusting that you have recovered by this time, I send this to New York . . . .'" Courtney broke off and looked at Harvey. "Apparently, then, you did know he was ill."

"He wrote me when he was taken with a severe cold or grippe during October. I had no idea it was anything serious."

"Oh, he wrote *you* first."

"You'll see," Harvey told him, "if you persist with the letter."

"Well," Courtney continued, "'I certainly will see you immediately I come East, which I expect to do within a week. I do recall the incident you mention and understand your reticence in committing the matter to writing. I must admit, now you bring up the subject, that there was one point on which I was never quite clear myself—one, and possibly two. My first doubt concerns her reason for doing such a thing, and the second concerns a small but, I think, now you mention the business again, highly significant fact—which I have so far never mentioned to anyone and will not entrust to writing. Originally it caused me only a second's wonder, but now that two of us are inclined to suspicion, my original doubts return to me more forcefully. I was never fully aware of the family tension, as, of course, you were, and I had no reason to look for anything deeper than the apparent event, which seemed tragic enough. I agree with you that if there is anything more sinister behind it, we would find it interesting, if not imperative, to ferret through the mystery. I shall be in Syracuse at the hospital after this week and will get in touch with you from there when I find out what plans have already been made for me. Ever sincerely, Gerald Harvey. Sunday, November Fourth.'" Courtney raised his eyes meditatively, with the beginnings of a smile, to study the Middle-Western Doctor, who sat watching him back as motionless and unperturbed as a figure of Buddha, the firelight gleaming fixedly on his spectacles, the smoke wreathing undisturbed from the dark bowl of his pipe.

"Then," said Alfred, "there must be something behind all this that none of us has suspected."

Harvey nodded inscrutably and took the pipe slowly from his mouth as he stretched the drenched extremes of his trouser legs closer to the fire. "That's probably quite true," he admitted, "although there was no indication in the letter I previously received from him that he foresaw the event that took place tonight. But I haven't any doubt but that the business that *did* take place tonight goes back to the episode which is hinted at in that letter."

"What *is* the episode referred to—if you don't object to telling us," Janet inquired, "and who is the 'she' mentioned in your letter to him?"

"I think it will be better," Harvey said, directly to her, "if we let that rest—for the present. But," he added, "*you* should know, Miss Larnard."

"Have you the letter my husband sent to you?" Frieda asked him.

"Yes," Harvey said briefly, "and I shall keep it."

"Places you in rather a strange position, Doctor," Courtney reminded him.

"Yes," Harvey returned, "a—a position which is shared, however, by everyone here."

"Well, what do you propose to do?"

"I'll just glance through the dining room," Harvey answered, "and ask Neville to let me unlock that pint in the sideboard." Neville handed him the key and Harvey remained noiselessly in the dining room for five minutes. When he came absent-mindedly back he seconded Courtney's suggestion of leaving Hodges' body as it was—at least during the night. "It may be possible," he brooded, "when I have tested this whiskey to ascertain exactly how long it would take to poison a man—and whether he had taken the fatal dose before entering the dining room or not. And now . . . . I should like to look things over upstairs," he said, "and then perhaps have all of you reconstruct the events for me."

"Henry's body, as you know," Courtney told him, getting efficiently to his feet, "has been moved, but we can soon . . . ."

Harvey waved him aside. "If it doesn't make any particular difference to you," he said, "I'll just go up alone first—and look around."

"Just one minute!" Courtney objected.

But Neville had raised his head, propping it up on one arm. "Cowpers," he called.

Cowpers appeared with the quickness of a shadow from the dining room.

"Take your shotgun, Cowpers," Neville demanded, "and see that everyone does as Dr. Harvey wishes."

Harvey had already silenced Courtney by placing his right hand in the angularly-bulging pocket of his coat. "I'm sorry," he explained, as Cowpers took up a station at one side of the room, "to have to seem peremptory about this. But I've taken up quite a responsibility by coming out here, and I don't want anything to happen. I have Neville's revolver, and I'm afraid I'll have to use it if anyone interferes with me." He plodded deliberately upstairs as if he were going to do no more than see a patient. At the landing he turned and came back. "Oh, Neville," he remarked, "could I just have that key to the adjoining door?" Neville handed it to him, and Harvey disappeared silently up the stairs.

Frieda started impulsively after him, but Neville shouted weakly at her as she reached the stairs:

"Stop, mother; for God's sake—d' you want to be shot."

"But those letters," she protested, turning to Courtney. "He knows where they are now. He'll get them."

"What of it?" Janet said harshly. "What letters?"

"Why, I just mentioned where Henry kept his correspondence, and now this man can get at whatever letters are there—and destroy any evidence."

"What of that?" Janet insisted.

"Is there anything in Henry's correspondence you want to conceal, Frieda?" Alfred inquired.

Janet laughed at Frieda's amazed face. "Not now," she said. "If there *was* anything—Frieda's had her chance to get hold of it herself."

"Oh, but I didn't," Frieda insisted. "I simply brought down that one letter. This is getting more horrible every minute! Nobody can breathe here without being accused of something."

"Sit down," Neville suggested. "Let Harvey take care of it."

Frieda went over to Neville and sat beside him. "Do you know," she implored, "*what* he has in mind?"

"Of course," he said quietly. "I wouldn't have brought him out here if I hadn't thought he could help."

"And you refuse to tell us, Neville," Courtney said, "what it is he has up his sleeve?"

"Why should I tell you?" Neville demanded angrily. "I didn't notice that you trusted me very completely."

"But to protect all of us," Courtney said. "Why, this man may have . . . ."

"Go to hell," Neville sighed.

"It's all perfectly simple," Janet sneered. "There are only two women in this family who've ever done anything with any element of 'mystery' in it." She was looking at Frieda with a tired animosity.

Frieda's eyes widened until she managed to say, "What—what do you mean?"

"Elizabeth was one," Janet told her, "and you're the other."

"I—I don't understand," Frieda faltered. "You mean about—Elizabeth's suicide?"

"That—for Elizabeth," Janet conceded, "and, of course, you realize what I mean about—you."

"But I don't."

"Suicide!" Ethel murmured, remembering that Alfred had told her about Elizabeth's ending her own life, but thinking this a good chance to prove that she knew as little as she was supposed to know about the family, in case Dr. Harvey's slip in calling her 'Mrs. Trevor' had been taken seriously by Frieda and anyone else who might have pretended not to hear.

"Yes," Janet explained, "I didn't tell you about that, Miss Baines. But Elizabeth deliberately took poison while she was ill here two summers ago. And I always think there's a certain element of mystery when anyone as proud, conceited, and well off as Elizabeth was, commits suicide. And I presume that's what Dr. Harvey has in mind. He was here at the time. Everyone but Courtney was here." She turned back to Frieda. "Those letters couldn't have referred to you, Frieda, because, so far as I know, Henry and Dr. Harvey had no way of realizing there was any mystery in your life. I'm the only one. You'll remember—it was many years ago."

"And you—" Frieda tried to recover, "you think the Doctor has come here because of . . . ."

"Because of—Elizabeth, Frieda—and not because of you. So don't worry." Alfred and Courtney were hanging on Janet's words with a baffled interest. "Did it ever occur to you," Janet asked them all, "that Elizabeth left very little money for a woman who should have been nearly as well off as Henry at one time?"

"Squandered it all," Courtney remarked. He turned to Alfred. "You two lived fairly high, didn't you?" Alfred nodded, and Courtney went on matter-of-factly, "Europe—Florida estate—innumerable costly gowns, a new car of the most expensive make whenever she wanted one. And she left you very comfortable, Alfred, as I remember it."

"Well," Alfred said dubiously, "I had to start practicing medicine again to stay alive. The income I get from Elizabeth's estate amounts to about twelve hundred dollars a year."

"Look here!" Courtney said to Janet. "You brought this up. How do you know why Harvey's here?"

"It may not be the reason," Janet admitted. "We'll see."

"Yes, but why should you . . . . Let's see, you said something awhile back about—what was it? Oh, yes! We'd all know perfectly well who'd done this if Elizabeth were only here. What did you mean?"

"At the time," Janet answered, "I meant nothing. Neville, why did you take Henry's body into your room, when you went out, and lock it up?"

"Because I heard what you were all planning down here—about getting me into an asylum and disguising it from the police. I simply locked up the material evidence of the crime. I couldn't lock it up in his own room because you'd smashed in the door."

"You were here, Neville," Courtney observed, "when Elizabeth died."

"Everyone was here," Neville replied, "except you, Courtney. You, as I remember, always seemed very reluctant about seeing Elizabeth under any circumstances."

"I'd a perfect right to be," Courtney snapped at him. "She duped my father out of leaving me a descent portion of the . . . ."

"Your *step*-father," Janet corrected.

"Well," Courtney parried, "she did the same thing to you, and he was your own father."

"I always thought," Janet said, "that it was *your* mother who threw everything Elizabeth's way."

"We all know you two hate each other," Neville yawned, "and that you both hated Elizabeth. Where does that get us?"

Harvey's footsteps came down the stairs to the landing.

"Well—?" Courtney said expectantly.

"Just one thing," Harvey said, "that nobody seems to have noticed so far. At least no one told me about it."

"What's that?" Neville asked.

"The stab wounds on the body."

"Right through the heart," Courtney said.

"Yes," Harvey mused, "but also—a wound across the left arm, as if—yes, that must have been it as if whoever it was tried to stab him in the dark, and missed the first blow, catching Henry a side glance across the arm. And before he made the second thrust, which went to the heart, Henry had just time enough to press the buzzer."

"But why didn't he cry out," Alfred wanted to know, "if he was stabbed in the arm, surely . . . ."

"Perhaps he did cry out," Harvey said, and looked at Janet. "You were awake, weren't you?"

"Yes."

"And you didn't hear any cry?"

"No. I heard the buzzer ring in Miss Baines' room."

"Who is Miss Baines?" and then as his eyes met a glance which Ethel meant to be communicative. "Oh, er— Oh, yes; of course—the room opposite yours, Janet."

"I heard the buzzer," Janet went on, "and started to go across and wake Miss Baines. Met her coming out of her own door. When she went down to Henry's room I went back to bed. The first time I heard any cry was when she called for help and began pounding on the door."

"There might have been a cry, of course," Harvey decided, "and you might not have heard it."

"I suppose not," Janet said, "with the wind outside."

"But you heard Miss Baines when she called you."

"Well, she shouted, and she kept on shouting, and hammering on the door."

"It strikes me," Harvey suggested, "that a man who's been stabbed once, and has every reason to suppose he's going to be stabbed again, would shout, too; and shout pretty loudly."

"Perhaps," Janet said, "but there may have been a way of keeping him from shouting."

"Quite true. Strangled or smothered, but there's no evidence of that. And anyone who'd have a man sufficiently overpowered to keep him from calling out would probably see to it that the victim didn't ring the buzzer, too." They seemed to recognize that Harvey knew what he was about, and no one spoke. He lounged down the rest of the stairs and stood with his back to the fire to stare pensively down at the hearthstone. There were two deep wrinkles across his swarthy, shining forehead and his mouth puckered itself up into a slender, ruminative line. He murmured something to his shoes, and his eyebrows arched up sharply as he looked at Frieda.

"You—er—were not in your room, Mrs. Larnard, when this happened?"

"No." She shot a defensive glance at him. "How do you know where we all were?"

"I don't. Nobody does. But Neville told me where all of you said you were." He scratched a match on the stone of the fireplace and it flared close to the long-drawn mouth of his ruddy face as he relit the pipe. "You were in the bath, possibly?"

"Yes—I—" and then, as she saw Janet's mouth harden, "that is, Sophie—had been cleaning upstairs today."

"Oh, Sophie had been cleaning upstairs." He turned to Janet. "How long has the dagger been missing from your room?"

"Since—Monday, I think it was. Yes, it must have gone sometime Monday, because I noticed it wasn't there Tuesday morning when I went up to answer my correspondence."

"You're apt to be pretty careful about your correspondence, Miss Larnard?"

"What do you mean—careful?"

"You—er—*always* keep your letters?"

"Why, why, no! Why should I? I destroy them."

"Why?"

Janet's mouth twitched in perplexity. "Well, the way everyone does—of course."

"Always?" Harvey persisted.

Janet's face tightened perceptibly. She spoke with accusing anger. "You—you've been at my desk—meddling with my letters."

"But I thought you just told me you always destroyed them." Janet merely looked at him with a sickened horror. "Didn't you?"

She held out her long hand which was trembling. "Give me those," she said. "*Give them to me!* You haven't any right . . . . Those letters haven't anything to do with what's happened—*to-night.*"

"Anything in the house," he said, "may have something to do with what's happened to-night, and not just to-night either,"

"Then," Janet concluded, summoning her control, "I was right. It *is* something to do with Elizabeth."

After Harvey had let his glance penetrate hers for several seconds, he spoke again. "I haven't taken your letters, Miss Larnard. Your desk drawer is locked. How could I? I didn't even know you had letters in it, until you told me just now. But it looks as if they were on your mind somehow." He looked again at Frieda. "You were saying—about Sophie cleaning upstairs."

"Oh, yes. I wasn't sure whether she'd left any clean towels for Courtney—in the bath room off the guest room, on the other corridor. And I knocked on his door to make sure."

"Yes. What time was this?"

"Why—just before Janet saw me coming back, when Miss Baines was locked in that room."

"You were coming back then?"

"Yes." Frieda hesitated, and then went on:

"I knocked on Courtney's door. He said to come in. I opened the door and asked him . . . ."

"Was he asleep?"

"No. He—he was reading in bed."

Harvey switched his eyes to Courtney. "What were you reading?"

"Just a magazine."

"Your room is on the other corridor—the last guest room on the left?"

"Yes," Courtney said, slightly puzzled.

"What magazine were you reading?"

Courtney tapped his head, as if trying to recall. "Oh, damn! What the devil is the name of it—that thing with the maroon cover—you know . . . ."

"Where did you put it?"

"What do you mean?"

"I mean that I didn't see any magazine when I went into that room just now. You were called in a hurry. By rights you should have dropped it on the bed covers."

"Probably—slipped under the bed or something. I may have taken it out with me—hurrying like that."

Janet leaned forward. "You didn't have any magazine with you when I saw you, and you were pretending to have been asleep."

"Wanted," said Harvey, "a magazine with a maroon cover. Now then—" He levelled the stem of his pipe at Frieda once more, "you asked him—about the clean linen."

"Yes," Frieda said eagerly. "He didn't have any Turkish towels, and I was just going to the linen closet . . . ."

"Where's that?"

"In a spare room on the same corridor."

"You were just getting the towels when you heard—what?"

"Pounding, and shouting—I guess it was Miss Baines. Then I heard Janet calling me—just as I got there."

"So you didn't have time to get the towels?"

"No. I was just opening the door of the linen closet—when I heard . . . ."

"But there are plenty of towels in that bath room."

"Oh, yes, but I mean the large—Turkish towels." Frieda laughed nervously.

"Yes," Harvey nodded, "that's what I mean, too—large, Turkish towels—two of them—hanging on a rack. Now another thing! How long would you say you'd been out of your room when you heard the call from Miss Baines and Janet?"

"Why, just before. Couldn't have been more than a minute or so."

"Did you see Miss Larnard or Miss Baines when you went through the hall to the other corridor?"

"No—No. Miss Baines must have been in Henry's room then."

"What makes you think so?"

"Why—" Frieda flustered, "the—the time it was."

"Did you notice anyone in the hallway locking Miss Baines into Mr. Larnard's room?"

"Of course not."

"Miss Baines," Harvey asked, "how long after you went into Mr. Larnard's room did you call for help?"

"Why—let's see—I went in, put on the light, closed the window . . . ."

"Why the window?"

"Because—I spoke to him when I went in and put on the light, and he seemed to be asleep. The covers were pulled up around him, sort of over his head, and one arm was reaching toward the buzzer. So I thought he was only cold."

"I see—so you shut the window . . . ."

"Yes—then I noticed snow—on the rug—as if someone had walked across the room from outside. Footprints led from the door to Neville's room over to the bed. Then I noticed something strange about Mr. Larnard's position—it was the dagger holding the bedding up on one side. Just as I threw back the covers to see what it was I heard a noise in Neville's room. When I went in I saw it was the outside door hitting back against the wall. I closed it and went over to see if Neville was in bed. He wasn't, and I heard a noise in Mr. Larnard's room and went back. The hall door was closing just as I got there. When I tried to open it, the door was locked. And just as I ran to the other door—that closed, too, and somebody locked it. Then I heard the outside door in Neville's room open. I opened the window and tried to see if anyone was on the roof, but the wind and snow blinded me. Then I called for help."

Harvey faced Frieda again. "So you see, Mrs. Larnard, what was going on as you were leaving your own room."

"Well, it must have been before then that I left. I can't tell—a few minutes, more or less."

"Excuse me," Janet interrupted, "but where were you, Frieda, at ten minutes of one?"

"Why—in my room."

"You were not. I knocked on your door just after I overheard the 'phone call—and you weren't there."

"I must have been in the bath."

"Strange. Because I went directly into the bath myself and I didn't see you anywhere."

"Oh, how can you expect me to remember," Frieda broke out, "with things like this happening? I stopped and chatted with Courtney for a few minutes possibly."

"For fully twenty minutes," Harvey reminded her, "if you weren't in your room at ten minutes of one."

"No, I remember," Frieda said, "I went downstairs then to get a book."

"Was anyone else downstairs?"

"I was," Alfred said. "I overheard the call from the downstairs end of the wire."

"Did you see Mrs. Larnard?"

"No."

Harvey began, "What book did you . . ."

"*The Rise of Silas Lapham*," Frieda flung promptly at him.

Harvey took a pace to one side of the hearth. "Dr. Trevor," he said, "you were the last one downstairs?"

"Yes. I went up to my room about five minutes of one."

"You went to bed right away?"

"Yes. I was already in bed when I wound my watch, and it was one o'clock then. I fell asleep within two or three minutes. The next thing I knew I heard someone shouting, and recognized Janet's voice."

"You didn't see your patient before retiring?"

"I opened the door as I went by his room, and asked him quietly if he was alright. He didn't speak. I could hear him breathing regularly.

The room seemed a trifle stuffy. The window was only open about two inches. I opened it almost wide. I left without waking Henry, and went to my own room."

"You didn't put on a light?"

"No. I was afraid it would disturb him. I could see my way around from the light in the hall."

"You're sure he was alright when you left him?"

"Positive. He was breathing soundly; noisily, of course, because of his lung condition; but I'm sure he was asleep and comfortable."

"That's the last thing you did before going to your own room?"

"Yes," Alfred said, "I switched off the light in the hall. Apparently everyone else had retired—except Neville, and I knew from the 'phone conversation that he wouldn't be back for sometime.

"Now, Miss Baines," Harvey began again, "you mentioned footprints of snow in Mr. Larnard's room. Was there anything definite about them?"

"Yes," Ethel said quickly. "While I was waiting for them to unlock the door and get me out of the room I had a chance to look at them before they melted. And on one there was a criss-cross marking—and the imprint of a trademark."

"Do you remember the mark?"

"Yes. Very well! A diamond shape—with a tiny piece broken out of one edge."

Harvey's jaw stiffened and he looked at her more acutely. "You—you're sure of that, Miss Baines?"

"Positive."

Harvey picked up Neville's boots from the hearthstone and glanced dubiously at the soles.

"They weren't Neville's boots," Ethel exclaimed. "I've looked at those already."

"Yes, but . . . ." Harvey paused. "Well, I'm sorry, Neville, to have to say this. I went carefully through all the closets upstairs just now—looking for any evidence of wet clothing. And in your closet there's a pair of rubbers—with a trademark like that. The reason I looked at them was on account of their being obviously wet. They were standing in little pools of water on the floor of your closet."

# CHAPTER VIII

"Do you suppose," Neville was asking languidly, as he reached up one arm to take the whiskey bottle from the table, "that I'd be silly enough to leave the footwear in my own closet—if I'd had the presence of mind to remove them after doing a stabbing."

"Well," Courtney told him, "there was that key you said you found in a drawer of your room. It's not unlikely that you're clever enough to make suspicion point to yourself just so you *won't* be suspected."

"'S absurd," Neville said, trying to pour himself a drink from his reclining position.

"Wait a minute," Alfred warned him. "If you're going to have more whiskey—you better take it in something hot."

"Yes," Harvey said.

Alfred took one of the tall glasses and went past Cowpers into the dining room.

"I'm alright now," Neville protested, sitting up, "and I won't lie here any longer with evidence piling up around me."

"Stay there," Harvey ordered. "There's no point in straining yourself now. How far is it from the roof of the piazza to the ground below?"

"Not more than twelve feet," Courtney told him. "A very simple jump—especially with drifts of snow to break the fall. And with the storm in progress—anyone who jumped would leave absolutely no traces."

"I can't understand," Janet observed moodily, "why anyone would go in through the door in Neville's room when the window in Henry's room was wide open."

"Simply this," Harvey said, "that anyone dragging himself through a window would be liable to give Henry some cause for alarm, if he happened to be awake, whereas anyone coming in from Neville's room would seem quite natural."

"But if it *wasn't* Neville . . . ." Janet objected.

"With no light on he'd presume it *was* Neville, until he'd been stabbed. He was probably asleep anyway."

"If we really knew whether or not the wires had been tapped," Courtney said efficiently, "we'd have a very definite case against Neville. I think I'll check the wiring in the cellar."

As he got up, Janet rose with him, and Harvey paused in a gesture of stopping them. "All right," Janet said, "I'll go down with you. Although, as I said before, a call could easily have been made from the servants' 'phone in the kitchen. If we find the wires have not been tampered with it won't prove anything one way or the other."

They passed Alfred as he came back with a tumbler of steaming hot water and lemons.

"Now don't be stingy!" Neville pleaded, when Alfred poured a few fingers of whiskey into the hot glassful.

"It may seem callous of me," Frieda sighed, "but I can't stay here any longer haggling over this thing. I'm quite exhausted. If you want me," she said over her shoulder, as her high heels clumped slowly up the stairs, "I'll be in my room."

"I think we all should give Neville a chance to do a little quiet sleeping," Alfred suggested. "You haven't fully recovered from that cool plunge yet, Neville."

"Oh, I'll go up in a few minutes," Neville replied. "Just let me get this sour down, won't you?"

"You don't need to go upstairs," Harvey smiled. "No sense in that. The—er—that is, your room is still in something of a muddle."

"That's right," said Neville, and buried his nose in the tumbler. "Well, I can sleep here all right. I could sleep anywhere to-night I guess, even if I had to run the danger of being stabbed." His short laugh finished in a gulp of whiskey.

"Of course," Alfred said to Harvey, "if we had any way of figuring out finger prints on that dagger there'd be no trouble at all in identifying the person."

"Well, there isn't any way," Harvey brooded absently, refilling his pipe," until we get hold of the police, and this storm seems to be mustering up again." Bits of melted snow from the cavernous chimney were hissing into the pale embers of the fire, and the great front door tugged staunchly at its hinges. "What's more, whoever did this, seems to have been fairly clever. Not much chance that finger prints have been left behind. By simply rubbing the handle of the knife with one of the bed sheets any prints could have been wiped off. The door handles have been turned by several people since the murder. No traces possible in the drifting snow outside. It was Miss Larnard's dagger. Neville's rubbers correspond with the print in the snow. The family is full of bitterness which goes in several directions, and almost everyone has something to hide—even you and Miss Baines, if I remember rightly . . . ."

Alfred was standing behind the lounge. He pointed at Neville quickly behind Neville's back, and then raised his finger to his lips in a cautioning way. Neville seemed to be asleep.

"If you just come into the library," Alfred whispered, "I can explain that—nothing really," he continued quietly as Harvey followed him into the next room, "except a matter of tact." Alfred turned to smile back at Ethel and switched on the lamps in the library.

Ethel went over to sit on the lounge beside Neville, who opened his eyes, sleepy and darkly blue in a dreamy contentment. Cowpers stirred uneasily in his chair.

"Go into the dining room, Cowpers," Neville said. "Miss Baines is going to massage my headache away."

Cowpers withdrew with a lazy, drooping-eyed indifference, and Ethel pressed her hands on Neville's cheeks where the dull, healthy flush was beginning to come back.

"I'm sorry," she said, and leaned over to kiss him on the forehead, but he pulled her mouth against his own and held her strongly close to him for several seconds. She gave a breathless little laugh and tried to draw away from him. He held her arms with a desperate firmness.

"Why?" he asked. "Why—sorry?"

"About the footprints. I thought I'd get you out of it that way. I'd have mentioned it before—only I didn't get a chance to look at the soles of your boots."

"You don't think I did it, do you?"

"You couldn't have," she said, and kissed him again.

"What," he inquired through a quizzical smile, "makes you so sure?"

"You're so—nice, I guess. That's all."

"You're—more than nice," he told her. For the moment the wish she thought she saw in Neville's eyes was all that mattered, and his willful mouth, and his hands gently smoothing the hair back from her brow. "What did Harvey mean," he said vaguely, "about you and Alfred having something to hide?"

She felt frightened and taut as she looked into his eyes. "You—won't tell anyone?" she said.

"No, of course."

"Well, you see, Alfred's my husband. He thought we shouldn't tell because of . . . ." She felt his hands twitch. His eyebrows drew together as if a little wave of pain had gone through his head. His mouth puckered a trifle down on one side.

"Oh!" he said, as if unable to realize what she meant, and then, "that's—too bad."

"Why?"

"Because—I love you."

"Oh, no you don't," she tried to say. "You're only . . . . It's just—attraction."

"I don't know what it is," he told her after several seconds, and his eyes looked away, "but it's—terribly important." His eyes were searching hers again. "Isn't it?"

"Yes," she nodded, "terribly!"

The indistinct mutter of Alfred's voice came from the library, followed by a barely audible answer from Harvey.

Neville's tired, perplexed eyes flashed.

"I wonder what's going on between those two."

"Alfred's just explaining about my being . . . ."

"No, no," Neville whispered sharply, "it wouldn't take all that time. They're up to something. I think Harvey is beginning to suspect me in spite of himself." He raised himself on one elbow and listened.

"I'm sure," Harvey's voice was insisting, "that it goes way back . . . ." and then his words blurred into a soft, confident muttering.

"God!" Neville murmured, "I wish I knew what they're hatching up."

"Has it got something to do with Elizabeth?" Ethel asked quietly. "I mean, Harvey's coming here?"

"Yes. Father sent for him, or wrote him a letter some time ago, when he was first taken ill, apparently. He hasn't told me the whole story. Something's come up about a trust fund that Elizabeth left secretly to some man no one in the family ever heard of. It was just left to him during his life, and when he died a London banker wrote to father wanting to know if Elizabeth had made any provision in her will for the disposal of the trust, as she hadn't left any provision with him. That throws a new light on her suicide. You see, the banker wrote that Elizabeth had made a temporary arrangement about it, promising to send him word later what should be done with the money in case the man it was made for died. Before doing anything about it she took poison. Father thought that she certainly would have cleared up the thing before killing herself, and it made him wonder if she'd done it deliberately or, if perhaps, she'd been poisoned by someone else . . . ." The voices in the next room had softened to a whispering drone. "If I didn't feel so damned weak . . . ." Neville complained, "I could get to hear some of this." Then he took Ethel's arm. "Please," he said quietly, "go over there by the other door, near the piano, and see if you can't hear what they're saying."

"Alfred would be furious . . . ."

"You don't care whether Alfred's furious or not, do you?"

"I guess not. But you see I *was* discovered locked in that room, and if anything . . . ."

"Oh, never mind then." He started to get up.

"Stay there," she told him hastily. "If they come in through this door—tell them I've gone upstairs."

"Alright," and he sank back weakly on the lounge.

She went cautiously along the room to the opening into the library at the other end. Alfred and Harvey were apparently seated on a sofa backed up to the wall right beside the archway. Heavy portieres were part way drawn and she stayed in the shadow from one of them. Through a half-inch opening between the portiere and the arch she saw the back of Alfred's left shoulder as he leaned over to flick a cigarette ash onto a tray. Harvey was out of sight to the right of him. She heard a crackling of paper and saw Alfred hold up a letter to catch the light from a lamp.

"That's the one from London," Harvey was saying. "I found it with the others in Henry's drawer upstairs. That particular one must have started Henry thinking. Then there are several others with very scanty replies to his attempt to get information about the man for whom the trust was left. Henry, of course, suspected him, and so would I—but for the fact that he definitely died last summer, and I'm sure that all three murders, provided they *were* murders, must have been performed by the same agency. Now, that leaves this mysterious man out of its completely. Oh, by the way, you're sure your wife never mentioned him to you?"

"Never," Alfred assured him. "I didn't even know she had enough money left, to make a trust fund of that size. But I still don't see—about Elizabeth's poisoning—where there can be any doubt."

"Now, think back, Doctor," Harvey said. "I was here at the time, and I remember it exactly. She was confined to bed because of that infection of the foot. Stepped on a sharp pebble on the beach or something of the sort. You remember. You and I had both forbidden her to get out of bed. And she raised such a fuss that we finally had to get her a nurse. Now, if I recall correctly—Elizabeth had the room Henry has been using recently."

"Yes," Alfred said, "Henry and Frieda had the room that Courtney's using now. That was before Frieda definitely . . . . well . . . ."

"Quite," said Harvey, "we'll let that rest. Anyway, Elizabeth was in Henry's room. Her nurse used the room that Miss—er—Baines has been in, and Janet had the same room she has now. It was the middle of the evening. Neville and his father were on the lake trying out a new launch. Frieda was entertaining some friends from shore downstairs at bridge. Janet had gone to her room immediately after supper. You and I were sorting out some trout flies in your room. We heard the buzzer ring in the nurse's room next yours, and thinking Elizabeth just wanted someone to fret at paid no attention to it. The nurse, as it turned out later, was in the kitchen at the time. We heard the buzzer again, and thought we'd better see what the trouble was. When we went into the hall we ran into Janet, who told us the nurse was downstairs, just as she was going in to attend to Elizabeth. Janet went into the room and reappeared in about three seconds to tell us what was the trouble. Elizabeth had apparently died just after ringing the buzzer the second time, and there was an overturned glass on the table beside her bed. From what little was left in the glass we concluded she must have taken an enormous dose of strychnine. But," he spoke more slowly, "nobody *saw* her take it. Nobody knows she took it voluntarily, or at least that she *knew* she was drinking poison. No one had seen Janet since dinner time, and we found Janet in the hallway. She may have been going *to* Elizabeth's room, but she may just as well have been coming *from* it. Everyone in the family knew that Janet hated Elizabeth, and you, Doctor, if I remember correctly, must realize that she had a pretty good reason for hating Elizabeth."

"Yes," Alfred said, "decidedly. Janet's never gotten over having her face deformed by that fall."

"No," Harvey continued, "I wasn't referring to the fall. It was the broken engagement between you and Janet long ago, and Elizabeth's part in it."

"Oh," Alfred said, almost inaudibly. "Yes. Very—difficult situation—but I always thought Janet had thoroughly gotten over that. Best thing—all 'round."

"If I'm right," Harvey said, "she didn't get over it and hasn't yet. By the way, she was to get a pretty substantial portion in Henry's will, wasn't she?"

Ethel heard hasty footsteps coming down the stairs into the living room. She stood close to the arch till she could see Frieda just going into the dining room.

"Cowpers!" Frieda called, "did Miss Baines go upstairs?"

"Do you want me?" Ethel said, quietly walking toward the lounge. Neville was breathing audibly in deep sleep.

Frieda turned in the dining room door and came slowly toward her. "Oh!" she exclaimed, "Neville told me a few minutes ago that you'd gone upstairs."

"I—I had," Ethel said, "but I came down again."

"That's peculiar. My door was open and I didn't hear you go by."

"Didn't you?" was all Ethel could say.

"Where were you when I came through this room just now?"

"I—I was just starting into the library to get a book, and I heard you ask Cowpers . . . ."

"You *didn't* go upstairs, did you?" Frieda insisted.

"*Why*, Mrs. Larnard? Were you looking for me—for any particular reason?"

"Yes," Frieda said slowly, "*Mrs. Trevor*. I wanted to ask you exactly why you came to this house under an assumed name, and why you and Alfred wanted to conceal the fact that you are his wife."

"I don't see," Ethel hesitated, "what makes you think . . . ."

"I heard the slip Dr. Harvey made when he first came in. He caught on very quickly, but it was quite obvious that he didn't know you as 'Miss Baines.'"

"What's all this?" Janet inquired militantly, as she came in from the dining room followed by a more profound and satisfied-looking Courtney "What are you bothering Miss Baines about?"

Frieda gave Janet a thin little smile. "This," she said, very much pleased with her acumen, nodding toward Ethel, "is *Mrs. Trevor*. Alfred's *wife*, it seems!"

Ethel tried to meet Janet's sudden, uncomprehending stare, and saw the eyes widen fiercely above the beak nose and then narrow conclusively. Courtney, who had started to putter with the fire, stood up, the tongs poised indecisively in his hands, his lips parting with astonishment.

"What—what makes you think so?" he managed to ask.

"You can find out from Dr. Harvey," Frieda assured him. "He recognized her right away. The rest of you were so concerned with Neville you didn't notice. But I did, although they tried to cover it up right away."

Janet's chapped, pale lips moved. "Alfred's wife!" came from them in a searing whisper.

"No wonder," Frieda laughed metallically, "she was found locked in the room. Little innocence personified!"

Alfred appeared somewhat apprehensively from the library with Harvey just behind him.

"I thought we were going to let Neville have a chance to sleep quietly," he said.

"Perhaps you can explain," Janet turned on him, "why you brought this woman into the house without telling us she was your wife!"

"Certainly," Alfred said with composure. "I already have—to Dr. Harvey's satisfaction. Perhaps you can explain, Janet, why you . . . ."

"Just a moment, Doctor," Harvey enjoined calmly. "If it's all the same—we won't go into that now." He turned to Janet. "It was a matter of tact, Miss Larnard, nothing else."

"Tact!" Janet exclaimed. "Nothing else! Why it might very conceivably explain the whole thing. Not just this, but . . . ."

"Please," Alfred said firmly. "We can talk about this somewhere else. No need of waking Neville."

"I should think," Courtney suggested, "that it might relieve Neville's mind to hear about this!" "Neville knows who I am," Ethel answered.

"Oh," Courtney said, "he does! Well, that might explain even more."

"He didn't know till just now. I told him while you were all out of the room."

Alfred's eyes were glazing at her. "Why?" he inquired thickly, and then with more precision, "Why did you suddenly find it necessary to tell Neville?"

"Please, Doctor," Harvey urged. "It's a wonder Neville isn't awake now."

"He's had enough whiskey this evening . . . ." Courtney began, but Harvey raised a peremptory hand.

"Let's discuss it in here," he said, leading the way into the library. Neville's exhausted, sonorous breathing continued with convincing regularity. His face was thinner and older when he was asleep, extraordinarily pale, and his impudent lips drooped above the firmly rounded chin. Usually his moodiness and impetuous ardor were made to seem quite natural by his ingratiating ease of doing his will or his forceful charm even when violently petulant. But in sleep the sparkling laughter had left his face completely, giving place to a marble sadness. The discouraged, tired fixity of it was almost terrifying, and bore not the least resemblance to the vivacious self of Neville when awake. The idea of awakening him tempted Ethel in a fleeting, unreasonable impulse to make the real Neville present himself immediately, although whether the self she had been charmed by was real or only a glamourous disguise for the impassive, dejected figure now recumbent on the lounge, she could not tell. She recalled a similar impulse to awaken Alfred once when he had fallen asleep in her arms. It had been almost a passive pain in his relaxed face that she had wanted to massage away quickly. But that had been— yes, more than a year ago, when she had still not

minded his embracing love, when Alfred's love had been—she wondered, as she looked at Neville, how it *could* have been ever—happily
satisfying. His finicking exactness had only been amusing. Since then
it had grown to a continual peevish worry. His mature assurance had
at one time sustained her and provided a balance for the fluctuations of
her own disposition. But recently it seemed to have become a pompous
smugness. When she thought about it, which was seldom, she had what
she thought was an inexcusably ingenue desire to tantalize and explode
it by some piece of perverse impertinence. She knew it was such a desire that had prompted her into the flirtation with Neville. But now
Neville had become so—yes, his own word was the best—"important"
that the beginnings of the affair were reduced to utter silliness. Alfred
was watching her from the nearer of the library doors. She pretended
to be professionally tucking the blankets about Neville and went past
Alfred's scrutiny as aloofly as she could.

"The matter of Mr. and Mrs. Trevor," Harvey was assuring them all,
"will be quite understandable, I think; not altogether sensible, but at
least an excusable deception."

"It's very far from understandable," Janet glowered, "and along
with half a dozen other peculiar circumstances, will have to be looked
into pretty thoroughly before I'm satisfied."

"If you object to my methods," Harvey said easily, "perhaps you'd
prefer to take over the handling of this yourself, Miss Larnard."

"Do as you please," Janet bit out. "I only say these things will all
have to be explained before we're finished."

"The wires," Courtney began, with a fresh delight in his own acumen, "*have* been tapped, just as I presumed from the first."

"Well," Janet admitted, "something's been done to them, covering
or— what was it Cowpers called it? . . . ."

"Insulation," Courtney prompted, "scraped away."

"And what I want to know," Janet blurted at him, "is how and why
you seemed to know from the first that something had been done to
the wires?"

"Why," Courtney flushed, "it's the obvious conclusion. Neville's
supposed to be ashore. He's overheard on the 'phone. Then it looks as
if he committed a crime here on the island. He can't be in two places at

once—so we naturally conclude the 'phone business might have been a hoax."

"Of course," Janet said, "*if* Neville was the one."

"Where was *Miss Baines*," Frieda demanded, "when I came downstairs looking for her just now. Neville said she'd gone to her room. I pass through the living room. She's not there. Just as I come in here to ask Cowpers—she appears behind me."

"Well," Alfred returned with some irritation, "why were you looking for her?"

"I suddenly found it quite imperative," Frieda sneered, "to speak with Mrs. Trevor."

Through this exchange of questions Harvey was inquiring of Courtney, "Exactly what had been done to those telephone wires?"

"Insulation pared off," Courtney replied, "over in that corner of the cellar where they enter a pipe to pass underground."

"Did you find the piece of apparatus that had been hitched on?"

"Well, not specifically," Courtney told him. "But there's plenty of stuff, in that electrical workshop of Neville's down there, that could very easily have been used. Several telephone units could be assembled . . . ."

"I see," Harvey broke in. "Better have a look down there myself later. And now, Mrs. Larnard . . . ." He leaned over the table in Frieda's direction, "in the light of the various complications that seemed to develop from your story—do you still insist that you left your own room just before twelve minutes past one."

"I don't see that it makes any startling difference," Frieda retorted with an affected remoteness, "but if you must pry into the thing, I was in Courtney's room from about twelve thirty until I heard Janet call. I don't see what business it is of anyone else's where I . . . ."

"It wouldn't be," Janet broke in quickly, "if you didn't try to lie about it."

"Miss Larnard," Harvey suddenly challenged Janet, "considering the fact that those letters we spoke of caused you such alarm—don't you think perhaps you'd better let me have a look at them—just to clear up . . . ."

"Certainly not." she said with a grieved sort of anger. "I certainly will not. There's no reason why my personal correspondence . . . ."

Harvey made a little gesture of immediate concession with his hands. "Just as you wish, Miss Larnard, but it means that for the present I have nothing more to contribute to the work of solving this thing. I'm only meddling in this with the confidence that everyone wants me to. When I find someone who puts obstacles in my way I am, I admit, quite powerless to overcome them. But I can't help becoming somewhat suspicious of the person who tries to thwart my inspection. I'll do what I can without your assistance."

"But it's certainly unreasonable," Janet plead, "to expect me to show you letters that have no bearing. Why, I got them *years* ago."

"Oh, I see," was all Harvey said, and glanced at Alfred, whose face was expressionless, except for his eyes, which were sullen little shadows with their centers burning at Janet from beneath his black, stiff eyebrows. Perceptible little spots of red were beginning to show on the skin drawn tightly over his cheek bones. For a second Janet saw and seemed to recognize the shame on Alfred's face. Her mouth contorted and she bit her lips tightly together. Ethel felt very sorry for her and quite ashamed of Alfred, and felt herself partly guilty of Janet's obvious hurt. She suddenly felt the same uprush of tender friendliness toward Janet that she experienced when she saw Janet's unstrung nerves break into helpless, spinstery fear a few hours before in the upstairs hallway.

Janet rose uncertainly from her chair, steadied herself with one hand against the polished arm of it, closed her eyes and then opened them quickly wide as if trying to outstare something that would not be banished. Immediately she seemed to have her customary gnarled control of herself.

"If that's all," she told Harvey, "I'm going upstairs to lie down. Can't keep on sitting up hour after hour—" she went through the door to the living room "—getting more and more wrought up over this thing. Drive us all mad." Her slippers could be heard padding listlessly up the stairs.

"I think she's right about that," Frieda said, in a voice that was thin with fatigue. "If you've asked all the questions you have in mind, Doctor?"

"Certainly," Harvey nodded. "I'm going to have a look at those wires downstairs, and then figure out a few items with Dr. Trevor. But the rest of you might as well go to bed."

Frieda left the room without saying another word. Courtney asked if he could be of any help to anyone, and on being assured that he couldn't—rubbed his eyes irritably and went upstairs after Frieda.

"You might as well go to bed, Cowpers," Harvey said to the somnolent figure propped in a chair in one far corner of the living room. "I'll be around myself. Everything will be alright."

Cowpers nodded vaguely and trailed his shotgun after him on his tired shamble into the kitchen. Ethel had started upstairs when Alfred came in from the library and spoke softly to her.

"I want to talk with you later," he said.

"Well," she told him, "I'll be in my room." She expected he was angry with her, and thought the involuntary curtness of her reply would aggravate him. But she could not bring herself to be more than meagerly civil. Her answer did not, however, seem to dampen the assumption of intimacy he had suddenly taken on. He took her hand, looked furtively back toward the figure of Harvey lighting his imposing pipe at the dining room table, and then tried to draw Ethel confidentially to him.

"What's the matter with you?" she asked him. If he had been undeniably hurt by her interest in Neville, if he had come out in the open and showed her that he was jealous, as she felt sure he was, if he had plead with her or fought with her about Neville—she knew she might have found traces of sympathy for Alfred. But it was his cold tolerance which aggravated her, and the superficial scorn with which he treated Neville maddened her. Acting not as if she were hurting him, but as if she were making a silly mistake, which she would soon discover for herself and which he would manage to overlook, Alfred had apparently decided to treat her like a little girl. In the face of Alfred's maturity, assumed or actual, she did feel incompetently young and, in spite of herself, somewhat silly—never completely, but somewhat—at certain moments. This did anything but make Alfred appear lovable. It made her begin to hate him.

"Harvey," Alfred was whispering excitedly, "thinks Janet did it. He has several items . . . ."

Then, simply to get rid of him, she placed her finger against her lips, and pointed to Neville asleep on the lounge. "Don't you think you'd better wait," she said, "until you talk with me later." He pressed her hand in quick assent and went to speak with Harvey in the dining room. As Ethel reached the landing she realized that Janet was standing by the upper bannisters at the top of the stairs. She stared at Ethel with a look of long-suffering hatred poorly concealed by a transparent mask of patience.

"He thinks I did it, does he?" she said. "Perhaps that's why my desk has been broken open and my letters stolen."

"When?" Ethel asked her.

"When he came upstairs to look around, I suppose. How do I know? Can't trust anybody, it seems. Frieda was upstairs, too. She might have taken them. You might have taken them yourself. I heard Frieda say you disappeared at one time." She emitted a small, snorting laugh and came down past Ethel to assail Harvey in the dining room.

"But *I* didn't take them, Miss Larnard," she heard Harvey say. "I wouldn't have bothered to ask you for them if I'd taken them."

"Well, if you've got them—you'll keep them, I suppose. But you might *show* them to Alfred. He'd be interested in them." Ethel heard her coming back through the living room and hurried along the corridor to her own door. Even after she had closed the door of her own room she could hear Janet muttering along the hallway. The door to Janet's room slammed with a decisive bang that seemed to shake that whole section of the house. The wind sounded fiercer outside and the snow was being driven against the window with the sound of thousands of needle-sized bullets. Annoyed at the idea of having to talk alone with Alfred, she was partially comforted by a sensation of complete weariness that made her almost indifferent to everything that had happened so absurdly, hysterically and horribly during the night—all garish impossibilities—except Neville's eager, persuasive words, "God, you're the dearest . . . ." No, it hadn't been that. It had been—yes, " . . . . you're the *sweetest* thing I've ever known . . . ." She let herself sink onto the bed and drew a spare blanket over her shoulders. She wondered how it was possible for a person you had once cared moderately about to become the pathetic, boor-seeming sort that Alfred had become. She shuddered with thinking that perhaps people could alter like that without knowing it. She grimaced at the fear that she herself might . . . . and there was Neville's ardent, laughing face, and his quiet, sincere answer, "I don't know what it is—but it's terribly important."

# CHAPTER IX

She didn't realize that she had fallen asleep until something woke her. She found herself sitting upright on the bed, knowing that she had heard something—uncertain in a frightened way as to exactly what it had been. Muffled voices possibly, a brief, dull scuffling sound—she couldn't remember, except that she had been finally and definitely wakened by a hard, sharp noise like the quick closing of a door. Or it might only have been a broken tree branch whisked against her window by the wind.

Then she was sure she *did* hear a door close, not loudly, but near at hand. It must have been Janet's door. This was followed by a distinguishable scuffing of footsteps down the corridor, along with other footsteps which were heavier, more like those of a man's shoes. Ethel knew that she must have been asleep about twenty minutes when she looked at her watch and saw that it said four minutes of five. She sensed that the storm had increased to a more deadly intensity as she stole tip-toe across the room to draw her door slowly and noiselessly open. The lamps had been put out in the hallway, but a long sliver of light showed under Janet's closed door. A faint illumination in the stair shaft beyond the bannisters indicated that the fire had fallen to a dull, ash-covered glow. Against this pale remnant of firelight she could see Janet's tall figure just entering Henry's room. She heard Janet's low voice speaking to someone in the room.

"Where did you say they were?" Janet was asking, but whoever was in the room with her made a quick hushing sound, and Janet's voice changed to a whispering murmur. Ethel was intrigued by a violent desire to creep along the corridor and hear what they were saying, but could not help remembering what had happened when she had tried that once before during the evening and was afraid of placing herself in the same position again. Now that everyone knew she was Alfred's wife she realized that everyone had begun to suspect her of having something to do with the stabbing, and that, on top of the fact that she had been locked in Larnard's room, had obviously renewed even Janet's distrust. She was very sure that Harvey was not particularly impressed by Alfred's explanation about the secrecy of her own relationship with Alfred—and in glossing over it so suavely she thought Harvey had revealed a strong, inner suspicion that all was not as clear as it might be. In spite of her growing dislike for Alfred she definitely did not want to do something out of mere curiosity that would compromise him. So she made herself close her door and remain restlessly in her room, wondering why Alfred hadn't come to talk to her as he had promised. The idea of knocking on his door occurred to her, but she thought it would be better to wait until Janet was out of the way. Of course, it might be Alfred who had gone into Henry's room with Janet, or he might still be downstairs talking with Harvey. That was probably it. She didn't think he and Janet would be on sufficient terms to be hatching up such secrecy in Henry's room, and was sure that if Alfred had come upstairs he would have come immediately to her room. It was, she realized suddenly, the first time she had yielded him an opportunity of seeing her alone since she had come to the island. She was certain it was not the first time he had wanted to be with her.

It was five minutes after five when she heard easy footsteps in the hall again. She waited—it seemed interminably—to hear Janet's door close. She observed the second hand of her watch, and when two minutes had gone by decided it was silly to wait there doing nothing. She would knock at Alfred's door. If he hadn't come upstairs, certainly it would be unreasonable for him to expect her to wait any later. If she did not find him in his room, she would scribble a note, come back and go to bed—permanently, homicide or no homicide.

The light that had been showing beneath Janet's door had vanished. She must have returned very stealthily to her room. But there was a glimmer showing beneath Alfred's door, and she knocked gently on the panel. Alfred opened the door in his shirt sleeves.

"Oh, hello, dear," he said, "I thought you'd gone to sleep. Come in." She went over to sit in a low armchair by the tall chest of drawers. "Your light was out when I came up, so I thought I wouldn't bother you." He sat comfortably back against the pillows at the head of the large wooden bedstead and took a cigarette from a small table beside it.

"I dozed off waiting for you," she said indifferently. "When did you come up?"

"About a quarter of an hour ago."

"Did you see Janet?"

"Why, yes. She came downstairs just after you'd gone up. Somebody's taken her letters . . . ."

"I don't mean then. I mean a few minutes ago."

"No. Why?"

"She was in Mr. Larnard's room talking with someone."

"Oh, yes. I thought I heard those unmistakable slippers of hers clopping along the hall with someone. I imagine it was Harvey come up to pacify her for the loss of the letters."

"Was he really the one who took them?"

"Swears he didn't. Told me he found her desk locked when he came upstairs that time. Thought there was a chance there might be something in it—naturally, letters. And he thinks Janet did it anyway. He has a theory that she poisoned Elizabeth, too. Quite far-fetched—but seems to link up. You see, Henry had some correspondence from bankers in London indicating that Elizabeth had left the disposal of a trust fund hanging in the air."

"Oh," Ethel brought herself to exclaim. "Trust fund—for you?"

"No, strangely—for some man I'd never even heard of. Not even a remote relative."

"That is peculiar," Ethel remarked.

"It certainly is. Probably some—affair she had on the sly. She was in France often. Didn't always take me with her. Extraordinary. I never thought of her as carrying on with anybody else. And yet she was just the type that would. I suppose I was so relieved to be away from her at times that I didn't think about it. I should have." He tapped an ash from his cigarette calculatingly onto a small tray, and carefully destroyed the burnt form of the ash. "If I'd known about this man I could have divorced her."

"Did you want to?"

"From about six months after I'd married her. I despised myself for continuing to need her, but I did—and she knew it. It seemed impossible that I could go on needing her when we really meant nothing to each other. She treated me like a small boy half the time and like a servant the other half. Of course, she had the money and that gave her the upper hand."

"I don't quite see why you couldn't be independent."

"Because the only means I had lay in my practice, and that dwindled away soon after we were married. You can't start a substantial practice of medicine while you're bobbing around from one place to another. I often objected to being trailed about like that. She'd say if I preferred to be a drudge I could stay in one place when she went abroad the next time, and she'd leave me here. By the time she came back I'd want her so much that I'd lose all reason—and everything would be patched up for a while until I got sick of her again—and sick of my own weakness. Gradually I got to depend on her so completely—on her money and on what little affection she gave me—that any break was out of the question."

"I don't see why she ever married you in the first place if she didn't care any more than that for you."

"She married me simply to take me away from Janet. I was engaged to Janet. I—I lost my head. After the marriage she kept me just because I was a convenient—man. Nothing more than that."

"And this is all supposed to be the motive for Janet's poisoning Elizabeth?"

"That's what Henry thinks."

"But I don't see what connection that has with killing Mr. Larnard."

"Well, if she got wind of the fact that Henry was beginning to suspect that Elizabeth didn't die of her own accord—she'd put him out of the way before he had a chance to find out things."

"But how would she know that he suspected about Elizabeth's death?"

"I don't know. He may have confided to her, thinking someone else did it."

"And that's how she knew it was Harvey on the telephone?"

"I suppose so." Alfred pressed the glowing end of his cigarette into the tray.

"Do *you* think Janet did it?"

"No, I don't. I know her or I did at one time better than most people, and I'm dead sure she's not capable of a thing like that."

"Who do you think did it?"

"Neville, I'm afraid."

Ethel gave a slight gasp. "But that's impossible."

Alfred leaned toward her tensely. "Why?" She found nothing to say, and he repeated the question, "Why?"

"Because," she dared to look him full in the eyes, knowing that he must realize what she meant, "I think I know Neville better than most people, and I'm sure *he's* not capable . . . ."

Alfred came over and stood in front of her. "Are you," he asked, "in love with Neville?" suppressing the excitement in his voice to a low vibrancy.

She had to look away, and then back at his eyes. "I—I don't know," she said. Alfred was on his knees in front of her. The nearness of his face seemed suddenly gross as he tried to force his arms around her waist. She pushed his arms way, but he was ignoring her disgust. "Please," she said, "please."

"I know," he said firmly, "ever since you came here you've disliked me and you've been liking him more and more. I've seen it. I've tried to be reasonable about it, and not say anything that would make you see how unhappy I was. But I can't keep it up. I can't stand it. I can't even bear to have you pretend to love someone else."

"I haven't been pretending."

His lips were suddenly motionless. The look of slavish worship in his eyes altered to an incredulous, pained stare. It frightened her that fixed look of maddened disappointment, an agonized, hungry look. She realized that every shred of desire she might once have had for him had gone. The expression in his eyes made him seem even more alien than he appeared when ordinarily talking to her. She shrank slightly from his hands pressing against her back. His face was leaning toward her. She knew, almost with a twinge of nausea, that he was going to kiss her. "Please, can't you see . . . ." she was saying, and turned her face quickly away. His lips were shaking and hot against her cheek. The fine stubble of his beard scratched her,. He seemed old, furtive, and disgusting. She pushed him away with a quick shudder and stood up.

"Is that all you wanted to see me about?" she asked him quickly.

He stood there, wearily stooped, his eyes cowed under the heavy dark brows, his hurt mouth sagging weakly. He seemed like a dog that could not understand why he had been kicked. She was frightened and felt cruel at the same time. Red splotches were beginning to burn on his prominent cheeks, and his mouth hardened.

"I'm sorry," he said huskily, and then in a harder voice, "I suppose I should have waited till you were over your," he paused, looked down, and then into her eyes again, "infatuation for Neville. Perhaps it's taking longer than I thought it would for you to find out what he is. He'll never—think of marrying you, you know, if you leave me. It isn't the *first* time he's meddled with other people—and he's never married anyone before." She turned to the door to keep herself from answering, because in the furious uprush of answers that swarmed into her head she recognized nothing coherent that she could say, only words of blind, angry meanness. But Alfred's tone was different when he said, "Don't. Don't go away. Please forgive me—I couldn't help it. I know I'm being unreasonable." She faced him. "But I—love you so. It does—the most horrible things to me. I can't think straight. Please, stay and talk it over anyway. You've hardly said a word so far."

"I don't think there's anything much to say," she told him, but went back to sit in the chair. "This isn't very pleasant for either of us. I don't want to be mean, Alfred; I don't want to hurt you. But I don't love you any more; that's all; and I do love Neville. He didn't even know I was your wife until tonight."

"You led him on, didn't you?"

"Oh, yes. I was just furious at you for bringing me up here without telling anyone who I was. And I thought . . . . Well, it doesn't make any difference *why* it happened. But that's the way it is now. He's never said anything about marrying me. But I'm not going on being your wife if I love him—whether he marries me or not."

"But you—you'll probably get over this," Alfred said, trying to calm himself, and apparently saying anything that came into his head. "I don't . . . . well, of course, it hurts me, but . . . ." he sat on the bed and looked at her bravely, "I love you and want you anyway. There's nothing I can do though. But I'll do anything you say if—if you'll only came back to me. This won't last—with him. He's not your sort. He's a fool, just an attractive, crazy boy. But I won't—mind so much perhaps, if you'll come back to me after you . . . . You will, won't you?"

"What's that?" she said, sitting up suddenly alert in the chair. It seemed to her that the buzzer in her own room . . . . And then again, through the low keening of the storm—three long fierce rings on the buzzer.

"Your room," Alfred said quickly, "the buzzer—from Henry's room." He went across the room and cautiously opened the corridor door to look out. "No light in Henry's room," he said over his shoulder. Then he called down the corridor, "Anything wrong?" There was no answer but the deep-throated moaning of the wind about the house.

He turned in the doorway. "Did you hear that, too—the buzzer ringing in your room?"

"Yes," she said, "I'm certain of it."

"I can't understand it," he muttered. "No light in Henry's room and the door's open. And yet I'm sure . . . ."

"Perhaps it was something outside."

"Maybe." He left the door wide open and came back to light a cigarette. "Damned strange. We must be nervous to be hearing things like that." He sat down again on the bed, still glancing apprehensively down the hallway through the open door.

"There must be a window open somewhere," she said, "the air coming through that door is like ice . . . ."

"Perhaps someone's come in again over the piazza roof," he was saying, when she tightened in every muscle as the buzzer sounded again. Two short rings, but through the open door into the hall, and through the door she had left open into her own room it came penetratingly and raspingly.

"Must be someone . . . ." Alfred began in a low whisper as he hurried to the doorway. She followed him. There was a draft of chilling air in the hallway. Without making a sound they went to Henry's door. She held his arm.

"Don't go in," she said in a barely audible whisper. His hand caught her own in a second's desperate clasp, Then he pushed her gently back against the wall, took two quiet steps forward, and stood looking into the blackness beyond the open door.

"Who's there?" he said hoarsely.

The only reply was a rush of cold wind coming through the door.

"Window *is* open," Alfred said, as he walked into the room and switched on the light. "Somebody must have been prowling around in the dark and . . . ."

Ethel saw a sudden, frozen expression fix itself on his face as he turned from the lamp by the foot of the bed, She went in to see what he was looking at. Janet lay motionless on the bed, one arm reached out toward the button on the wall, her head turned away from it so that her open eyes were gazing at them with a dead, bulging, terrified stare, her shiny nose sharply outlined in the lamplight. She was still wrapped in her loose, heavy bathrobe, and her legs stretched awkwardly over the side of the bed. One of the ungainly woolen slippers had fallen to the floor, leaving one bare foot pointing toward them in angular rigidity.

"Christ!" Alfred gasped, and stepped over to look closely into the eyes. He held one wrist for a few seconds—and one of his eyebrows gave a surprised twist upward as he pulled the heavy collar away from the throat. There were red, bruise-like marks about the neck. His eyes turned aghast to Ethel as he pointed to the marks.

"Strangled," he murmured, and bent his head down to place one ear against the chest. As he was straightening up slowly his eyes quickly widened. "Of course," he exclaimed, "the window!" and leaped across the room. The window was already open. He pushed it wider and dragged himself through it. The driving snow had lightened, and a greyness was pushing its way upward in the eastern distance behind the looming, dark mountains. From the window she could see Alfred standing on the edge of the roof looking downward. He abruptly turned and ran toward her shouting excitedly.

"Somebody down there—in the snow," and then, as he struggled to get his large body through the window, "Get Harvey—quick. There's a man down there in the snow right beside the front door."

She ran from the room and down the stairs, calling to Harvey, but the house was silent. As she reached the foot of the stairs she could see, in the subdued remnants of firelight, that the lounge was empty. Neville had disappeared. She called again, and started into the dining room as Alfred hurried down the stairs behind her and ran to the front door. He flung it open and rushed out into the snow.

"Dr. Harvey!" she called again, and went through the dining room, where the lights were still ablaze on the chandelier. She called Neville's name. Then she noticed with a sharp start that the corpse of Hodges was no longer in the middle chair on the far side of the table. The overturned glasses and stains of whiskey had been carefully wiped away from the table top. She could still see the marks of a damp cloth along the surface. There was no indication anywhere in the room that anything out of the way had occurred there. The kitchen was empty. She could hear Frieda answering from upstairs, and when she ran back to the living room Frieda was just coming down with Courtney.

"What's the matter . . . ." Frieda was asking, but before Ethel could reply the front door banged wide open and Alfred appeared dragging the snow-spattered form of a man. He let the figure flop onto the floor, and turned to slam the door behind him. As Alfred let the arm drop the face fell into full view. It was Neville. He lay there on the floor, apparently unconscious.

Frieda and Courtney came forward in a puzzled way to watch, as Alfred stooped down to examine Neville.

"I don't understand," he was saying. He felt Neville's pulse. "He's alive apparently—must have fallen from the roof." He pulled the lower lids down from Neville's eyes and looked carefully at the red membrane. Then his hands felt their way carefully behind Neville's jaw bone, up under the back of the neck and about the head. His eyes flashed as he turned the head over to pull the hair aside and examine the scalp. "That must be it," he said, "bad bruise. Must have fallen against the piazza railing when he jumped, or landed on a boulder underneath the snow. Bad concussion." He was lifting Neville to carry him over to the lounge, and said to Ethel, "Where's Harvey?"

"I don't know. He's not in the dining room or the kitchen. And Hodges' body has disappeared."

"What started all this?" Courtney was asking. "What's been going on."

"Bathe his head in cold water," Alfred said to Ethel, "and get my medicine case upstairs in my room. May have to take a stitch in that head." Then he turned to Courtney, and began to tell him what had happened. Suddenly, just as Ethel was going upstairs, he turned to Frieda. "Didn't you hear us upstairs? Where were you?"

"I was in Courtney's room, talking."

"Oh."

"What's happened to Harvey?" Courtney wanted to know.

"That's what I'd like to find out," Alfred replied. "And Hodges' body, too. You might hunt around for them."

Ethel went into the room where Janet's strangled body lay on the bed, and closed the window against the blast of freezing air and the slow rising of the winter dawn. Her mind whirled with uncertainties and fears. Her head felt sickeningly giddy. Neville . . . . She could not think it, and yet it seemed undeniable.

# CHAPTER X

Neville was still unconscious when she went downstairs with Alfred's worn leather medicine bag. His boots were on, but she remembered that he had not had his coat on when Alfred brought him in. Frieda was helping to prop his inert head on two cushions and hovered about flutteringly until Alfred sent her to get hot water.

"Superficial cut," Alfred murmured, as Ethel held a mop of curling black hair back from the head while Alfred swabbed into the wound with cotton soaked in iodine, "but a bad blow, I guess. Everything seems to be sound though. Nothing fractured. Good thing if he doesn't come to until we've got this fixed up." He took a straight razor from his kit and shaved away a small circle of hair, and Ethel put lysol in the hot water Frieda brought to wash the cut. "One stitch," Alfred said, and strung a thread-fine piece of catgut through a curved needle. "Can't quite understand why he's still unconscious. Don't like to give him any more whiskey. He wasn't in any condition to lie out there in the snow. Guess he wasn't there long anyway." Ethel held Neville's head again on one side when Alfred bent over with the needle. She saw Frieda turn away and sit near the fire, with her back toward them. Courtney came in quite breathlessly from the dinning room—his shoes covered with snow.

"Door to the cellar stairs is locked," he told them. "No key, either."

"Perhaps it's on the other side," Alfred muttered.

"No. I poked into the lock with an ice pick. No key there at all. I knocked on the door and called to Harvey. No answer."

Alfred straightened up and tucked his instruments back in the bag. "Is there any other way into the cel . . . . yes, of course."

"The outside bulkhead," Courtney said. "I tried that, but it's locked, too; bolted on the inside."

"Something's wrong," Alfred said. "We'd better force that door."

Courtney leaned over to revive the fire, lowered a log onto the embers, and reached over to the stand for the fire-irons. "Whe—where's the poker?" he exclaimed. "It was here a while ago. I remember . . . . Huh! That's strange." He prodded the embers cursorily with the shovel and followed Alfred through the dining room to the kitchen.

"You—discovered Janet—in there," Frieda said, as Ethel placed a gauze dressing over the sewn cut and strapped it in place with adhesive tape.

"Yes. I was talking with Alfred in his room. We heard the buzzer ring in my room . . . ."

"It seems quite extraordinary," Frieda said, "that *you* should be the one to discover these things every time. You found Henry, and now you and Alfred find Janet. You're going to have a hard time explaining why you came here under an assumed name. Harvey may understand it, but *I* don't—in the light of what's happened."

They could hear poundings from the kitchen and finally a splintering crash. Ethel was putting a protecting wad of gauze over the dressing. She took Neville's pulse, which was slow and feeble. Frieda fidgeted helplessly in her chair, and started about the room pulling aside the heavy drapes that covered the windows. The great room was filling with wraith-like half-shadows in the greyish light. Muffled voices sounded from the cellar beneath them. Neville's face stood out gaunt and shining in the new light. Gently Ethel pushed his dark hair back so that it clustered over the dressing, almost hiding it, and marveled at his impersonally handsome features. When Frieda came over to stand by the lounge and look down contemptuously at him, Ethel was diligently taking his pulse again, making some show of looking at the watch on her wrist.

"You thought yourself very clever, I suppose," she said, "in carrying on that flirtation with Neville to throw off all suspici . . . ." Ethel's eyes must have appeared very much the way she felt, because Frieda stopped short, and said, "Don't look at me like that. You look depraved. What's the matter with you?" Ethel could only look away dumbly and watch the tall rectangles of light that broke the dark walls and were turning slowly, imperceptibly from gray to white. Six coldly musical strokes sounded from the bell of the clock in the library.

"I think I'll go upstairs," Frieda began more civilly, "and wake Cowpers and Sophie."

"Why?" was all Ethel could think of murmuring.

Frieda turned on the stairs with a look of the blankest surprise. She appeared to be more uncertain about Ethel than anything else she had ever confronted. Then she gave a half-shrug and went up to open the door into the servants' corridor. A numbing silence closed in on Ethel for several long seconds, a silence which was devastatingly complete except for faint, regular monotony of Neville's breathing. She was startled out of a submissive trance when her gaze suddenly comprehended the snow still caked onto his boots. She realized that he had been lying out in the drifts—and that this second exposure might make him fatally sick. She seized the blankets from the foot of the lounge and held them to warm before the freshly blazing fire.

As Frieda appeared again on the landing, Courtney came in out of breath from a quick rush up the cellar stairs. "Found Harvey," he said to Ethel, "lying—right on the floor—at the foot of the cellar stairway." He brandished the fire poker emphatically at her, "and this right beside him. Bad wallop on the head—knocked him out—just coming to. Get some more stuff—ready to fix his head. And," he continued breathlessly, as if he could scarcely believe what he was saying, "Hodges' body on the floor about ten feet away partially stripped and defaced with an axe." He waved the poker toward the figure on the lounge. "That boy's an absolute devil—insane—criminally insane." He dropped the poker with a clatter back against the stand, and fussed with the chair beside the fire. He started back through the dining room, speaking over his shoulder. "Harvey says he can walk, though—must be alright—Alfred says no fracture or anything. Wicked situation!"

"What was he doing in the cellar?" Frieda called, but Courtney was already in the kitchen bustling solicitously about Harvey, who was pushing both Courtney and Alfred aside to come in slowly through the dining room, saying he could navigate perfectly well by himself.

"Just hit over the head," he said, as he dropped himself easily into the chair by the fire and raised a hand to touch his fingers gently and tentatively over the back of his head. "Just a bump." He scowled. "Seems to be bleeding a little though. Perhaps, if you don't mind, Doctor, a little disinfectant."

"Better get off a little of that hair," Alfred said, as Ethel drew the bottle of iodine from the satchel.

"No, no. No need of that. Just clean it out. I would like a look at it though. Probably feels worse than it is. If I had a little hand mirror . . . ."

"I'll get you one," Frieda volunteered, and skipped up the stairs. "Men think hand mirrors are such affectations."

Harvey winced and screwed his face up distastefully when Alfred applied the iodine. He grunted and shook his head. "Times when you want to swear," he said. And then his eyes changed interestedly as he seemed to notice Neville. "He been asleep all this time? What's he doing with his boots on?"

"We found him lying out in the snow, unconscious, just after we found Janet strangled in Henry's room," Alfred said calmly. "He'd apparently hit his head on the railing when he tried to jump from the roof above just outside Henry's open window."

"Miss Larnard—strangled?" Harvey said incredulously. "Why, but I was dead sure . . . ." He broke off as his eyes widened with a start. "Then her story—Great God! This is becoming inconceivable!—her story about the letters must have been straight. I didn't believe her for a minute. I thought . . . ." Frieda came down and handed him a silver-backed mirror, which he held absently above his head, only to put it aside immediately. He stood up. "In Henry's room, you say?"

"Take it easy now, Doctor," Courtney warned him. "We can fix everything up later. You've had a nasty crack on the head."

"I was just coming out of the cellarway," Harvey explained. "I went down to have a look at those telephone wires that someone's supposed to have tapped. It was about five minutes after you went upstairs, Doctor. You remember we came in here to see if Neville was mulling along alright. You went upstairs. I went back to the dining room and got out that pint of whiskey, planning to analyse it. I slipped it into the left-hand pocket of my coat." He patted the pocket with a discouraged look. "Now it's gone. Then I went into the cellarway, and looked over all the wiring down there. I found the little scraped places that Cowpers, Janet and Courtney had mentioned. When I came up the stairs, I turned out the light and was just stepping through the door. Something hit me hard on the head, and that's all I remember until I came to and found you splashing cold water on my face."

"You were hit with the poker," Courtney told him. "I found it right beside you down cellar. Whoever did it must have been standing behind the door, and when you came through he cracked you a good one, carried you and the poker downstairs, locked the door and threw the key away unless . . . ." He went over to Neville and began searching his pockets. From the left-hand trouser pocket he drew out a key. "He *didn't* throw it away. I'll see if it fits that lock." He dashed into the dining room.

"You were saying something about Janet's letters," Alfred reminded Harvey.

"Oh, yes. I thought her story about having the desk broken into was all nonsense. I thought she must have broken the lock herself, hidden the letters, and then told us that yarn so we wouldn't suspect her for not being willing to show them to us. But apparently—yes, I must have been completely wrong about this whole thing. She . . . ." His eyes were fixed on Neville, and he blinked and shook his head. He seemed unable to accept any more readily than Ethel could. "I—I can't tell you all how this makes me feel. I undertook, in a way, the responsibility—and now Janet." He tried to breathe deeply and bracingly. "We—we'll have to put Neville in some secure place. But, tell me—is he—hasn't he come to yet?"

"Concussion, I presume," Alfred told him. "I wasn't any too anxious to waken him while we were putting in the stitches. And he's had so much stimulant in the course of the night . . . ."

"Yes," Harvey agreed vaguely. "But we—better get him locked up somewhere before he regains consciousness"

"This is the key alright," Courtney enthused, as he came back to the room. "What's the matter?"

"We're wondering where to take Neville so he won't make any trouble when he comes to," Alfred said.

"Janet's room," Frieda suggested.

"Good idea," Courtney agreed, and Harvey nodded in a puzzled, half-convinced way. "We better get the windows or shutters nailed up. I'll tell Cowpers . . . ." He was off toward the kitchen again.

"I wonder," Harvey was saying, "whether we ought perhaps to be worried about Neville's condition. Being outside in this weather after the exposure he had earlier . . . ."

"Seems to be his own lookout," Frieda said shortly.

"I must see that room where Janet . . ." Harvey began in a nervous sort of excitement of which he had given no evidence earlier in the night. He got up easily and deliberately in spite of Alfred's gesture of remonstrance. Cowpers and Courtney could be heard going along the upper hallway.

"Well, Cowpers," Courtney was saying indulgently, "you see, you were wrong. Not that I blame you exactly. You were fond of him, I know. But you were wrong, you see." Cowpers was apparently acknowledging this with a few low monosyllables.

"If you and Mrs. Trevor," Harvey was saying to Alfred, "would come upstairs with me and show me exactly how you found things." They followed him up the stairs. "Please," he said to Frieda, "if Neville shows any sign of recovering—call to us!" Frieda nodded and looked uncertainly at Neville.

"And so," Harvey concluded, when Ethel had given her version of the episode, "when you heard Janet and someone else going along the hallway it was Janet and Neville, presumably, and Neville was luring her into Henry's room to strangle her."

"I don't see," Alfred objected, "why Neville should take her in there—or how, granted he had a reason, he ever persuaded her to leave her room. She was acutely suspicious of everybody when she came downstairs to tell us about the letters being gone."

"But you were in your room, Mrs. Trevor?" Ethel nodded. "Then," Harvey continued, "Neville probably wanted to get her as far away as possible. But, of course, there was Mrs. Larnard . . . ."

"She wasn't in her room," Alfred explained. "She admits she was in Courtney's room, on the other corridor, talking."

"Oh, that's different. But you were in your room, Doctor."

"Yes. I came up, after leaving you in the dining room. I wanted to speak with Ethel. But her light was out, so I didn't bother her. Thought she was asleep."

"Was the light on in Miss Larnard's room then?"

"Yes."

"Was anyone in her room with her then?"

"No, as far as I know. I couldn't hear anyone."

"After you went to your room did you hear anyone in the corridor?"

"In about ten minutes, I heard someone go by my door. I distinctly heard a door closing, and voices. They stopped for perhaps half a minute. Then I heard them again. A door closed, and I heard apparently two people going along the corridor. One of them walked with scuffling sound—like Janet's slipper. And the other seemed like the tread of a man. I heard Janet talking, and a little later I heard someone come back down the corridor, and then nothing more, until Ethel came to my room. We must have been talking for about five or ten minutes—when we heard the buzzer ringing in Ethel's room. At least, we thought that's what it was but the wind was making quite a commotion, and we couldn't tell. I opened the door and called out. There was no light in Henry's room and nobody answered me. It was rather weird. We left the door open and in a minute or so we distinctly heard the buzzer again. We went to Henry's room. It was very cold and we thought the window was open. I spoke. Nobody answered. I went in and turned on the light—and found Janet on the bed strangled. I made certain of her condition, and then thought of the window. It was still pretty dark, but the snow was beginning to let up. I could see tracks, when I got to the window, from the window to the edge of the roof. I got out the window and went over to the edge, saw someone lying just below in a drift."

Harvey nodded and hauled his pipe out of a pocket. "Does that correspond with your recollection, Mrs. Trevor?"

"Yes," she said, "except that after I heard people going down the corridor—I went to my own door and looked out. Janet was just going into Mr. Larnard's room. She was talking with someone who was already in the room. I couldn't tell who it was. She said. 'Where did you say they were,' and I heard the other person say, 'Shhh.' That was all. I wanted to speak to Alfred, but I didn't want Janet to see me go into his room. So I waited until I heard someone come quietly down the corridor. I listened to hear Janet's door close, but it didn't. After a few minutes I went out. The light was out in Janet's room. At least there was no light showing under the door. And the light had been put out in Mr. Larnard's room. I went right in to see Alfred."

They were standing at the head of the stairs. Harvey methodically lighted his pipe and dropped the match onto a tray resting on the telephone table. Cowpers came silently out of Janet's room, followed by Courtney, and passed them to go downstairs. Harvey stopped Courtney.

"How long was Mrs. Larnard in your room with you?"

"From," Courtney frowned, "about twenty minutes to a half hour before we heard—Mrs. Trevor calling downstairs."

Harvey shot little wisps of smoke from his lips parallel with the pipe stem. "You and Cowpers better bring Neville up here before he wakes up." He turned to Alfred. "Now, I want to discover Janet exactly the way you did. You were . . . ."

"In here," Alfred led the way into his room. "Mrs. Trevor was . . . ."

"Sitting there," Alfred said, and Ethel sat in the chair by the chest of drawers.

"You heard the buzzer," Harvey said, "or thought you did—and went to the door?"

"I was sitting here on the bed," Alfred explained. "I go to the door like this, look out. Nothing wrong. Come back . . . ."

"Leaving the door open?"

"Yes, that way." Alfred came back from the door and sat on the bed again.

"You had a view of Henry's door from where you were sitting?"

"Yes."

"And you saw nothing."

"The room was dark."

"Were the lights," Harvey inquired, "turned off in the hall."

"Yes, but I could just see the door from the firelight downstairs."

"And you're sure no one came out?"

"Certain of it."

"Was Henry's door open?"

"Halfway," Alfred said, "just about the way it is now."

Harvey stood beside Alfred and looked through the open door along the hall. "You—didn't hear the window open?"

"No. It must have been open before we looked out. The hall was very drafty."

"Now, then," Harvey said, "you heard the buzzer again?"

"Yes," Alfred replied, getting up and going through the door. Ethel followed him.

"Wait," Harvey murmured, and took Alfred's place in the hall. "Now—tell me what you did."

"Go to the door," Alfred said. Harvey moved a few steps down the corridor, Ethel following. "Speak—get no answer. Realize window is open. Turn on the light—" Harvey had entered the room. His hand went out to the lamp by the foot of the bed. "Then—catch sight of Janet."

Harvey stared composedly at Janet's ungainly dead figure sprawled under the folds of her bathrobe.

"Was that," he asked, "just the way you found her?"

"No," Alfred said, "the collar was wadded up around her neck—so you couldn't see at first that she'd been strangled. I felt for a pulse in this wrist. The right arm was just as you see it now—stretched out toward the buzzer. I listened for a heartbeat, and in pulling the collar aside . . . ."

Harvey turned to Ethel. "That—is just the position you found Mr. Larnard in?"

"Not quite," she told him. "He was entirely on the bed."

"Yes," Harvey acknowledged. "But . . . ." He bent over Janet's body and carefully lifted the right arm, examining the fingers which flopped inertly against his hand, "the arm was like this reaching toward the buzzer."

"Yes."

"And that, Doctor," he said to Alfred, "is exactly the position Elizabeth's arm was in—when we found her reaching to the button there on the wall."

"Yes." Alfred said eagerly. "—you mean . . . ."

Harvey let the limp arm fall back on the sheet.

"Don't touch anything," he said, and went through the door to Neville's room. Ethel and Alfred stood in the door. They saw Harvey reach over Henry Larnard's corpse, which was stretched out on the floor at the foot of Neville's bed, and lift the rigid right arm. The shoulders lifted up slightly as he did so. He squinted through the smoke of his pipe and scrutinized the tips of the fingers. Courtney and Cowpers went along the corridor carrying Neville to Janet's room. Harvey's curious expression of concentration did not change as he let the arm of the corpse gently down to the floor and came back to stand by the bed, gazing down at Janet. He lifted her body to one side, and knelt on the bed looking closely at the button of the buzzer. The button itself was dark, made of polished wood, about a quarter of an inch wide, set in a round, raised frame, about an inch and a half wide, which was fastened to the wall with three small screws. Harvey took the pipe from his mouth and pressed the small stem end against the button, looking at it closely. The buzzer sounded from Ethel's room.

He stood up, took a large nail file from the bureau, and went back to unfasten the screws in the frame. He pulled it from the wall fastened to the two wires, which he yanked out of the fixture. He touched the bare copper ends of the wires together. The buzzer sounded again. He carried the little fixture over to the bright light of the window and looked into the hollow back of it. He pressed the button against the spring again with the stem of his pipe, then pressed it with his finger.

"No," he said, and threw the contraption listlessly onto the bureau, "I was wrong."

"You said . . ." he began, as his eyes snapped alert, and went back to the window to peer through the frost-patterned glass at the snow-covered roof. "Ha!" he shrugged philosophically, "Wind is a bit too fast for me." Whatever traces there might have been of footprints had been drifted even with the white smoothness that extended the length of the roof. Occasional long curls of powdery snow lifted into the gale and swirled out of sight toward the tall columns of the snow-frosted pines that swayed above the tiny peaked roof of the boathouse. A steady, hard-driving wind, close on the flank of the blizzard, had torn through the gray-lined clouds above the far mountains that lined the shore. Through this riven, ragged section the sun slid abruptly with a flood of dazzling brilliance. The slender needles gleamed on the nearby pine tops. The roof of the boathouse sparkled into a sheet of quartz. The snow on the piazza roof twinkled in a million pinpoint gems. The unevenly pale reaches of the congealed lake were blended into spots of treacherous, dark-bluish water. These spots thickened and lost themselves entirely in a slender, dark line that marked the current from a river brook that poured into the lake around a bend three miles upshore. The sun struck fire from the two minute crystals of the windows in the distant shore boathouse. Otherwise, the world outside was infinitely white.

"Apparently," Harvey said to the window, "we'll have to take over the functions of coroner, undertaker, and jailer—for quite a while to come. Let's hope," he added, fastening his teeth doggedly onto the stem of the underslung pipe, "that we won't be obliged to play executioner."

Courtney was standing in the doorway looking flabbily haggard in the sunlight. He held up a key. His voice, unsoothed by sleep, was roughly catarrhal. "He's secure in there now," he said, and cleared his throat. "What shall we do with this?"

Harvey took the key without seeming to notice it, and it clinked against the revolver in his right-hand coat pocket. Courtney's mouth loosened as he got his first glimpse of Janet's livid face scratched with brownish wrinkles. Her eyes were like dull agate in the glare of the sun that streamed ruthlessly through the window and left a shadow from the wooden framing straight across the discolored bruises about the lean, hawser-like neck. Courtney turned his head away, his eyes blank and out of focus, his face a sickly white beneath the unshaven gray stubble of his beard. His bulbous Adam's apple bulged and contracted above his collar as he swallowed and his breath made a catching noise in his throat as he exhaled. His pudgy left hand moved in a vague circle and clenched over the bed post steadyingly. Cowpers' face gleamed in the sunlight like polished mahogany as he passed the corridor door and his footsteps clopped evenly down the stairs.

Courtney's eyes fixed as if they had been instantaneously petrified in their sockets and whitened about the edges as he glimpsed the button fixture on the bureau. His neck bent forward from his shoulders. His eyes switched to Harvey, then Alfred, and met Ethel's glance. He pointed a thick forefinger at the bureau.

"What's the matter with that?" he said in coagulated syllables.

"Nothing." Harvey's lips closed firmly over his pipe. Courtney went over curiously, picked up the circle of wood, fingered it over like an expensive ornament in his splotchy pink hands, looked over at Janet's body, then replaced the article on the clean white of the bureau scarf.

"I see," he said. "Was it right here when you found it?"

"No. I took it off the wall."

"Oh," Courtney nodded in a relieved tone. "A good idea."

"Maybe," Harvey agreed. "But there's nothing wrong with the thing. I was mistaken."

"It's a good idea all the same," Courtney said.

Harvey was prodding his straightly-cut under-lip with the tip of his pipe, his eyes reduced to slim lozenges by narrowing lids, gazing upward at the career pineapple-top of the bed post.

"Mrs. Trevor," he began without looking at her, "you overheard Miss Larnard saying something as she came into this room. 'Where did you say *they* were?' Am I right?"

"Yes."

"Was that said casually, or did she seem interested in where *they* were?"

"She was excited about it."

"Well," Harvey decided, "I can think of only one thing she was keen about finding at the time. Her collection of letters."

"That's very plausible," Courtney told him.

"My inference is," Harvey said, "that she was persuaded to come in here under the pretext that they were hidden in this room." His gaze fastened on Courtney. "You searched Neville thoroughly?"

"Nothing on him but that key we discovered downstairs."

"Well," Harvey murmured dubiously, "perhaps he can explain it all when he comes to."

Courtney was looking at the small object on the bureau again, and the jaw muscles protruded under his lower cheeks clenching the flabbiness into momentary rigor. "Wait a minute," he said to Harvey. "You were alone downstairs just before this happened."

"Yes?" Harvey seemed interested. "After Dr. Trevor left me, I was alone for about—well, ten minutes—until I was slugged over the head."

"You went down cellar. Did you go directly from the dining room, or did you go into the living room first?"

"I stepped into the living room to look at Neville. He was asleep and seemed alright."

Courtney's eyes faltered, but flashed back keenly. "Did you go down quietly?"

"Just ordinarily—" Harvey replied, "as anyone would walk around. I didn't think there was any need for caution or silence. Neville was sleeping very soundly. Everyone else was upstairs."

"But—if Neville *hadn't* been asleep, he might easily have heard you go out to the kitchen, open the cellar door, and even go down the stairway."

"That's quite possible. But he was very much asleep." Harvey had stopped listening to Courtney, and the reply was automatic. His eyes were scanning the rug.

"Those spots," he said, pointing out the wet patches that led from the door to the window, "were they here when you came in?"

"I didn't notice any snow on the floor," Alfred said. "It's very probable I made those myself after I went through the window onto the roof."

"But there was nothing when you came in. That means the person certainly didn't come into this room from the roof. Must have come in with Janet. Whoever it was Mrs. Trevor overheard Janet talking to. I don't understand it at all. If it had happened almost immediately after you saw them enter the room . . . . But you say you heard someone come back down the hall. It might have been Janet, but you didn't hear her door close. Yet when you went out the lights were off in here and in Janet's room. While you were in your husband's room—neither you nor he heard anyone pass. If you hadn't heard Janet in the hallway the first time—that would be alright. But I can't understand how, having once been in this room openly, she could be persuaded to come back again in absolute silence. Unless—you don't think, Mrs. Trevor, that they overheard you when you opened your door and saw them?"

"There was nothing to indicate they heard me."

"But you did hear the other person in here try to silence Janet"

"Yes."

"You closed your door right away."

"Immediately. But I could still hear them talking in very low voices."

"Then there's a very strong chance," Harvey brooded, resting his weight on his left leg and prodding the green rug in front of him with the toe of his right boot, "that they did hear you, that they put the light out, thinking you were coming down the hall. When no one appeared— one of them came back down the hall. You heard that."

"Yes."

"Went quietly into Janet's room, extinguished the light, and closed the door very softly coming out. Then they waited until you had gone into your husband's room. What they waited for I can't conceive. Presumably Janet thought the person she was with could be trusted, and thought she was being taken in on some secret. It may have had to do with Henry's corpse in the next room. Or, as I said, it may have been something connected with the letters."

Frieda appeared in the doorway. Her eyes were hard and bright, gazing at Harvey.

"Of course," Harvey continued in a level tone, "Janet may—actually—have gone back to her room, as you thought, and may have sneaked along the corridor later, trying to surprise the other person, whereupon she was throttled, and rang for help in the struggle. Anyone who was choking her wouldn't have been able to hold her neck and arms at the same time. But that's pure conjecture."

"Presuming," Alfred began, "that she was brought in here by someone who definitely had in mind the idea of making away with her I can't see why she should be brought *here*. The person had no way of knowing Frieda was not in her room, and even if she was out of her room—no method of telling when she might return. Ethel was in her room; I was in mine. It seems to me a pretty risky place to deliberately plan a killing.

"It seems to have worked," Harvey said dryly.

"Certainly," Alfred agreed, "but I don't see how it can have been planned. I think your last theory is the one to count on—that Janet came in here, surprised the person at something incriminating; and was strangled when she threatened to show him up. I've no doubt it was something to do with the body in the next room."

"In other words," Harvey questioned, "Janet found out who killed Henry, and the murderer killed her to keep her from telling?"

"Remember," Courtney hurried to say, "that Neville was the one who transferred the body to his own room."

"If Janet's murder had been planned," Alfred went on, the pupils of his eyes almost point-like in the glaring sun, as he faced Harvey and spoke with a metallic insistence, "and if, as you say, the letters were used as a bait—certainly this room wouldn't have been selected. She'd have been persuaded to go downstairs. The coast was absolutely clear down there. Everything points to Neville's having been the one. Let's take that for granted. He pretends to be asleep until everyone's gone upstairs but you. He sees you come in, take a look at him, and, as you admitted was possible, hears you go into the cellar. He gets you with the fire poker when you're coming back, drags you down to the cellar, puts Hodges near you, locks you in for the time being, knowing you won't come to for ten minutes to half an hour, planning possibly to unlock the door later so that when you do come to—you'll naturally wander about and fall under suspicion yourself, with that bruise on the head.

"At this point, the natural thing for him to do if he wants to kill Janet is to persuade her to come downstairs, using the letters perhaps as a ruse, strangle her, and put her in the cellar with the fire poker nearby, indicating that *you* were hit while struggling with her—and collapsed after you'd finished the strangling."

"What are you driving it?" Harvey growled genially.

"That this thing was *not* planned. That if it had been—there'd have been better ways of doing it."

"You forget," Harvey assured him, "that this room remains the ideal place—the roof outside onto which all the rooms on the corridor open, the wind ready to cover up footprints in the snow, and the most essential thing—the door into Neville's room—so that there is an escape into the hall—even at the very second someone is discovering the body in here. And if it *weren't* planned, why should I be disposed of beforehand?"

Alfred nodded, his eyes narrowed to little glittering triangles gleaming at Harvey. "Yes," he said, "that *does* make me wonder a great deal. How do you know you were disposed of beforehand?"

"But," Courtney broke in, "Neville was just getting away from this room when he fell. The key was in his pocket. He wouldn't have had a chance . . . ."

"No," Alfred said in a straining whisper, his lower jaw sliding aggressively forward, his words cutting the air like a knife-blade drawn jerkily through a sheet of silk, "*Neville wouldn't* have had a chance!" The first and second fingers of his right hand prodded into the air just in front of Harvey's chest. "But we don't have to take for granted that Neville was the one until we know a little more about this."

Smoke wafted from Harvey's straight lips into the sun-filled air just in front of Alfred's face. The deep lines dropping from the leathery sides of his nose on either side of the dull, terse mouth drew themselves a trifle deeper.

"Did you see Neville, doctor," he asked, "jumping from the edge of the roof?"

"No," Alfred said quietly, his eyelids quirking up, "and there was no reason why I should have. Neville had been out in that snowdrift for a good deal longer than we're expected to suppose he had. His body was almost drifted over. And he was *extremely* cold when I brought him in here. He must have been out there for at least ten minutes."

"Ten minutes!" Harvey said in polite surprise.

"Plenty of time," Alfred reminded him, "for anyone to dispose of Hodges, come upstairs, strangle Janet, and go out over the roof, leaving Neville to cover the trail, and get into the cellar through the bulkhead out back, dry one's clothing in front of the open furnace door, gouge one's head slightly by hitting one's self with a piece of kindling, and lie on the floor till discovered."

"But the key . . . ." Courtney began aghast.

"Already in Neville's pocket," Alfred said, "and the cellar door already locked, the bulkhead opened in advance, and then locked from inside after you've gotten in."

"It will be quite illuminating," Harvey smiled easily over his pipe, "to see what Neville has to say." He took the round fixture from the bureau in one of his large, muscular, tan-backed hands, the nail file in the other—and knelt across the bed to reaffix it to the wall. He poked the nail file at one of the small screws on the back of it from which he had ripped the wires. The file was too blunt for the minute head of the screw. He ran his free hand into his trouser pocket, and turned to Alfred.

"Have you a knife, Doctor?"

Alfred slipped a slender, green-gold penknife from the pocket of his vest, pried a blade open with the thick nail of his thumb and passed it, handle first, to Harvey. In pressing the tip of the blade against the brassy screwhead, Harvey's hand slid suddenly forward, and the blade snapped close, scraping a tiny white scratch on the dull polish of his forefinger nail. He made an irritated click with his lips and tongue, tossed the file onto the bureau, dropped the fixture on the sheet beside Janet's wooden head, and reopened the knife, prying out a larger blade.

"I'm afraid my boyish enthusiasm for intricate criminal methods carried me away as far as this thing goes," he said, and rapidly loosened the screws with the large blade, hooked the shiny ends of the wires about them, eased the fixture against its socket on the wall, and turned the outside screws until they were fast. He stood up from the bed, tapped his pipe into a tray on the bureau, and scraped the inside of the sooty pipe bowl with the blade of the knife, tapped the little fragments of burned crust onto the tray, replaced the curved stem in his mouth and blew cleanly through it as he wiped the soot from the blade on a clean handkerchief from the upper pocket of his coat. He closed the knife with a sharp click, said "Thank you, Doctor," as he handed it back to Alfred, and began neatly refolding the large handkerchief. He tucked it back in the pocket so that the wide lavender band about it was hidden—and only the white edges showed against his coat.

"There'll be breakfast," Frieda said from her vigil in the doorway, "in about ten minutes—for anyone who wants it."

# CHAPTER XI

Ethel drew herself out of the comforting warmth of a bathtub nine inches deep with hot water and pressed the rough surface of a large towel against her face. She threw the towel about her firm shoulders and drew it scratchingly back and forth across them, and down her shoulder blades back and forth against the small of her back. She dried her thighs and legs with a quick vigor derived from the bath, and slipped into the wool of her kimono. As she tucked her toothbrush into a blue-leather toilet case, she saw her face pale and fatigued-lined in the white-framed mirror. The bath had made the beginnings of color in each cheek. Several tiny red veins showed against the whites near the inner corners of her eyes.

Alfred's face was an opaque, pale gray when she passed him in the hall. His hair gleamed wetly and was freshly parted in the center and combed against his wide head. His jaw and neck were a dull red beneath the freshly shaven pepper of his beard. He let one hand rest on her shoulder and kissed her silently on the forehead. She was too tired to object. She tried to smile. Her face seemed stiff. Alfred sighed. His dull, metally eyes had a weary, half-buried, longing expression. He started heavily down the stairs when she turned away.

"I'll be down in a minute," she murmured, as she hurried past the glare of sunlight from Henry Larnard's doorway. She paused for a few seconds of listening outside Janet's door, thought she could hear Neville breathing deeply, and spoke his name quietly. Receiving no answer, she went into her own room.

The crumpled white of her uniform lay across the pink pattern of the silk puff rolled at the foot of her bed. She hung the uniform in a small closet that jogged out of a corner against the outside wall, and took down a plain brown Jersey coat and skirt. When she pulled the dark coat over a tan waist and fastened the oval silver buckle of the wide belt she assured herself again, before the mirror, that the dark costume gave her hair an illusion of brilliance, even in the daylight, by contrast. But the newly-washed pinkness of the tip of her straight nose made it seem shorter and more snubbed than usual, and she patted it into becoming paleness with a powder puff.

When she stepped into the hall a shadow was outlined in the sunlight that lay rectangularly in front of Henry's door. It gave place to Harvey's figure, the sun glistening on the bristles of his unshaven face. Something gleamed minutely in his hand before he tucked it into the pocket of his vest. He was coming toward her, his eyes looking down and ahead of him in preoccupation. He looked up, saw her, and smiled easily.

"Hear anything from the patient?" he asked.

"I listened," she said. "I think he's still asleep."

Harvey drew the key from the bulging right hand pocket of his coat and unlocked the door to Janet's room. The closed shutters were keeping it in dull gloom except for slender bars of sunlight extending slantwise through the three holes, each the size of a quarter, triangularly spaced in the center of each shutter. The shutters were held together by boards nailed against them from outside. One three-cornered beam of light struck the pillow just to the left of Neville's face, which lay sidewise on the pillow facing them. He stirred in his sleep as they opened the door, threw his right arm across the other half of the pillow, and turned hitchingly over to face the wall. His breathing resumed its regularity. The gauze showed white beneath the tousled locks of his black hair. Bits of dust, moving fitfully in the momentary draft from the opening door, drifted into sight along the straight rods of light and away again into the gloom.

"Let him sleep it out," Harvey whispered kindly, and closed the door. As he turned from relocking the door Ethel looked straight into his gray, candid eyes. They seemed larger than the average and sagged down into traces of amused wrinkles at the outer corners.

"Excuse me," she said, "but you were in that room just now." Her hand waved vaguely down the corridor.

"Yes," was all he said.

"When you came out you were putting something bright and shiny in your vest pocket . . . ." She saw his hand move to the left-hand lower pocket. "No," she said, "it was the other one—your right-hand—what was it?"

A smile drew his long face together. "Are you trying to figure this out, too?"

"You object to telling me?" she insisted.

"Certainly not." He drew his right hand from the pocket of his vest and held out to her a slender, gold plated penknife. Her eyes rested on it for a second and returned to his large, drooping, pleasantly smiling eyes. "Would you like it?" he asked, as if her age were six and a half. "I'll make you a present of it." He looked down at the tiny scroll work on one flat, gold surface and pointed to it with the key. "It has my monogram to be sure—but that could be taken off."

"What were you doing in there?" she said.

He glanced down at the penknife, then dropped it back in his pocket. His rock-gray eyes were seriously meeting her own. "I'm sorry, Mrs. Trevor," he replied, "I'd like to trust you. I think I could. But I don't dare to trust anybody yet." His voice was low and easy, almost a drawl, but the muscles about his mouth had pushed his lips into two hard lines. "Shall we go down to breakfast?" The key clinked against the gun in his pocket. His right hand indicated suavely that he would follow her.

As she preceded him around the landing on the polished stairway into the living room, where a newly-built fire showed pale flames in the sunlight that fell plentifully through the tall windows, she could hear Frieda, whose voice had become jinglingly musical again, chattering to Alfred in the dining room, and Alfred saying "yes," "no," and occasionally "that's right, Frieda. You're right about that," in a gruffly impolite voice. Cowpers stood over the table behind the lounge wiping away the stain made by a nearby empty whiskey glass from the shining dark surface. He turned the cloth limply over, rubbed the spot dry, dropped the cloth onto a tray. He nodded demurely to Ethel.

"Mawnin', Miss," and his eyes smiled over her shoulder. "Mawin', Doctah!" He placed the dull cylinder of the glass on the tray alongside the squat crystal cube of the bottle with its inch and a half of amber whiskey, took up the tray and went into the dining room. Ethel clutched Harvey's arm beside her as she looked at a small rectangular parcel resting on the table about a foot from where the tray had been, about two dozen letters tied together with a slim piece of green cord, the top letter showing its post-marked stamp, faded pink in the sunlight.

"The letters!" she whispered to Harvey. His hand held her own firmly against his arm for a second.

"Ssh! Don't—say anything about them. You haven't seen them. You don't know anything about them. We'll see what happens."

A door closed upstairs. Ethel was poised in front of the fire, wondering if Harvey was right, or if he were in some way involved. He was taking the pipe from his pocket, wandering casually back of the table, his eyes on the packet of envelopes. His eyes were raised to hers. He nodded. His lips and teeth formed the scarcely whispered word— "Janet"—and he indicated the parcel with the tip of the pipe.

A tread echoed from the upper stairway. Ethel glanced upward to her right and saw Courtney's figure immaculately fitted into a neatly pressed suit of heavy gray tweed coming over the stairs with his usual morning dignity. He gave her a gracious smile. His hair was brushed and roughened up slightly above the ears, suggesting the man of letters, and the uneven gray of it fell back thickly and gracefully over his head. The lower part of his full face was a whitish gray, where powder had smoothed over the traces of his quick shaving, splotching into the babyish pink of his cheeks. The closely trimmed white of his fingernail tips slid with a hint of affected grace along the glassy finish of the bannister rail. Cuffs of a soft shirt showed full and white beneath the wrists of his coat, and a black tie with white polka dots was snugly, but amply, tied against the closely fitting soft white collar.

Harvey's stance was like stone where he stood behind the table, left hand in trouser pocket, right hand with pipe halfway to mouth, neck thrust alertly forward, his eyes watching Courtney. His head bent grimly, just a trifle, in response to Courtney's smile. He shoved the pipe into his mouth and drew in a whistling breath through the stem, removed it and dipped it elaborately into the canister of tobacco on the table beside the letters.

"I've demolished this supply of smoking material," Harvey said, and threw an apologetic smile in Courtney's direction.

"Plenty more upstairs in my room," Courtney smiled back. "I'll get it after breakfast if you can't . . . ." Instantly the whites of his eyes gleamed wider as he glimpsed the packet of letters. His mouth opened and resolutely closed. He bent across the lounge, took the canister, and said offhand, "Or I'll get it for you now. Aren't you eating?"

Ethel saw his eyes slide sideways toward the packet, and looked at Harvey's face. Harvey's expression was fixed and calm. He was not looking at the letters or at Courtney. He was levelling his eyes straight over Courtney's eyes, through the passageway under the stairs that gave onto the dining room. Frieda's voice came tinnily from the table: "Doctor, aren't you coming to breakfast?"

Harvey's mouth twitched into an amused upward curve as Courtney set the canister down with a thud on the rug that covered the middle of the table and faced about standing up, looking toward Frieda.

"Right away," Harvey said, with a polite nod. He walked around the lounge, stood beside Courtney. "After you," he said with a wave of the hand.

Courtney turned from a direct look into Harvey's eyes to bow slightly in Ethel's direction. "After *you*," he said, with a gracious sweep of the white-cuffed hand, "Mrs. Trevor." And his laugh was the essence of dulcet composure.

Ethel walked into the dining room to confront Frieda's blank eyes surrounded by her breakfast smile, reigning with fragile-handed delicacy over silver coffee urns and silver platters of poached and scrambled eggs and crisp, brown bacon at the head of the table. The huge chair at the opposite end, with its back to the wide, high bay window looking over the frozen lake, was empty as it had been for more than six weeks. Courtney took his place at a side chair on Frieda's left, from which he had an excellent view of the living room. Ethel sat between Courtney and Alfred, who was trying to eat an egg with obvious distaste, and resorting with a sigh to his cup of black coffee. Ethel could see only one side of the living room. The lounge and table were far to the left and hidden by the left wall of the passageway. Harvey was waved into Neville's vacant chair on Frieda's right, with his back to the living room. He glanced at Janet's empty chair beside him, frowned, shook the folds of a napkin into his lap, and swallowed off a large tumbler of orange juice in one draught.

"You must excuse me," he said pointedly to Frieda, glancing at Courtney's consciously austere and well-groomed facade, "for not completing the niceties of shaving. In my excitement last night I left my suitcase in the motorboat. Er—unpardonable of me." He smiled as Frieda handed him a cup of coffee. His hard-ended fingers plucked a lump of sugar from an urn-like silver bowl. Frieda's slim arm fluttered out to scoop up a silver spoonful of scrambled egg. She handed a plate to Harvey with a pardoning smile and dropped her napkin daintily into the lap of her white dress which was covered with the print of enormous black poinsettias. The drooping edge of one sleeve swung precariously over her half-filled cup of coffee.

Harvey's hand shot quickly out, held up the edge of her sleeve, and smiled with an iron gallantry.

"Thank you," Frieda's voice tinkled, "thank you so much."

Courtney blinked fussily at his glass of orange juice, but as he raised it to his oratorial lips his eyes crept up slowly under their lids to look at Harvey. Harvey's somber gray eyes turned from his cup to look through the window at the salt-white spread of the lake.

"I find a certain consolation," his voice rumbled easily, "in the fact that the sun continues manifestly to shine." Frieda looked as if certain he was out of his mind. He continued: "Just as it shines through the—ominous foliage of the jungle while one animal feeds and derives his life from the carcass of another." Frieda dropped a spoon back into the saucer of her cup and took a mouthful of coffee without stirring it. Cowpers came fortunately in with a platter of steaming eggs.

A dull insistent pounding sounded from upstairs.

"Neville!" Harvey exclaimed, dropping his napkin carelessly across his plate as he left the table. Alfred and Courtney got up simultaneously and followed him from the room. "He may want something to eat," Harvey called back from the stairs. The three pairs of footsteps went hurriedly, jumbledly along the upper corridor. Then Neville's voice could be heard in excited crescendos. Frieda had started from the table but came back.

"Get a tray of fried eggs and coffee for Mr. Neville, Cowpers, please," she said with cool efficiency, "and—a half grapefruit, if there is any." When Cowpers had faded into the kitchen, she leaned her elbows carelessly on the table in front of her and folded her hands beneath her small, creamy-white chin to look with what passed for an attempt at honesty into Ethel's eyes.

"I'm genuinely sorry," she said in a level, soothing voice, "for all that may have upset you here, and particularly for what I said to you in the course of the night. I hope you'll understand—it was only the harrowing—excitement. Nothing I really meant. I—I'm afraid I lose my head—too easily."

Ethel could only look back at her, unable to hide her own amazement, and say: "Why, of course. Quite alright—I . . . . Well, it doesn't matter. Naturally you thought . . . ."

Frieda leaned toward her. "I hope you haven't been given a mistaken idea of me."

Ethel laughed with uneasy embarrassment. "I don't see quite what you mean."

"Well—" Frieda began gracefully pouring herself another cup of coffee, "I thought you might have been embittered against me." Ethel simply looked at her. "I don't know really what Neville thinks about me. Of course, he's very rude and inconsiderate on the surface, but that's his manner." Frieda smiled with martyrish tolerance that disposed of Neville as an impolite boy. "But he doesn't—mean anything by it. He's not . . . ." She looked wistfully down. "He's not himself, you know—always. It's in the family. His grandfather, my—" she drew in a strengthening breath, "husband's father was a terribly—*eccentric* man, and I understand it goes further back than that. *His* father was an inventor of some sort—and quite unbalanced, I'm afraid. I should have given all those things much more thought, of course, before I—married. But when you want to do a thing very much it's so easy to gloss over the obstacles. I—" Her voice dropped to a grieved whisper. "I'm afraid it was a great mistake."

"I don't think there's anything the matter with Neville," Ethel told her, trying to keep her voice steadily impersonal. "He has a certain amount of temperament—that's all."

Frieda smiled gratefully and sweetly. "You haven't known him long enough to tell, Mrs. Trevor. You're not able to distinguish between—his real self and what he is now." Ethel's answering stare was unyielding. She felt her cheeks growing hot with resentment. Frieda toyed with a spoon. "Janet, of course, was fond of Neville. We all are, but Janet—was very strange herself, and Neville's—eccentricities didn't offend her so much. Two—of a kind, so to speak. She was more than eager to defend him. I—I don't know what sort of things she said about me to other people. But I do know she was apt to be so—unreasonable and almost—vicious. Of course, I don't know whether she pretended to take you into her confidence or not, but I'm sure you're penetrating enough to see that most of what she said was simply the delusion of a—with all respect—jealous old maid., One couldn't help being fond of Janet, but she was so unreasonable! Did she—try to turn you against me?"

Ethel found it difficult to meet Frieda's gaze. "Why, I wouldn't say that, Mrs. Larnard. She—that is, I did gather that she wasn't over fond of you." Cowpers came from the kitchen with a tray and went upstairs. Someone spoke to him on the stairway, and Alfred appeared in the passage.

"Is—Neville alright?" Frieda asked him.

Alfred's eyebrows were drawn together with concern. "Must have had a bad blow on the head—worse than I thought. Seems almost—stupid. It'll wear off, I suppose. Complains of a frightful headache. Could I have another cup of coffee, please?"

Ethel passed his cup to Frieda, as Frieda asked, "What did he say about . . . ?"

"Says he doesn't remember anything after he spoke to you until just a few minutes ago. Says it's an absolute blank. When did he speak to you?"

"Oh," Frieda said, "while you and Dr. Harvey were talking in the library. I came downstairs and asked where Mrs. Trevor was. Neville told me she'd gone upstairs. He seemed very sleepy then. Scarcely able to keep his eyes open."

Alfred glanced at Ethel. "Were you upstairs?"

"Of course. Why?"

"Because Frieda said something last night about your suddenly appearing in the living room—was that the time?"

"Oh, I was nervous," Frieda laughed. "I didn't see her when I came through the room, that was all. She was just going through the alcove into the library to get a book."

"Oh," was Alfred's answer. He drained his cup of coffee, and looked at Ethel again as he wiped a napkin over his dourly-set mouth. His voice was gruff, "Says he wants to see you."

Frieda pushed her chair back hurriedly, and started through the living room. "I'll run up, too."

Alfred held Ethel by the arm until Frieda was well up the stairs. "That was true," he inquired "about what Neville said and where you were?"

"Why, of course. What makes you think . . . ?"

"I just hope," he said as he followed her into the living room, "that you weren't letting Neville make a fool of you."

She stopped by the stairway as she noticed that the packet of letters had vanished from the table. A darkened, rectangular pile of crisps were sending thin black flakes along with a stream of smoke up the chimney. They were resting, completely burned, between two blazing logs, and fell through, as she watched them, with a slight flurry of soot onto the orange embers below.

"What's the matter?" Alfred was saying.

"Nothing. I—I'll tell you later. Something Frieda said." She ran up the stairs.

Courtney's bickering voice was opposing Neville's. A white-frosted light burned on the ceiling of Janet's room. Neville was sitting up in bed, his back supported by two pillows, stuffing forksful of egg into his mouth with ravenous haste, his eyes dark and malevolent never leaving Courtney's face. Harvey sat, his face twitching with amusement, over in the corner in a small chair by the desk. Frieda sat on the foot of the bed, reaching over with prim care to take an empty plate from the tray on Neville's lap.

"I want to talk to Janet," he was clamoring through a very full mouth, pointing his fork vindictively at Courtney, "and I want to talk to Miss—Ethel! I want to know what's been going on. I won't lie here and be cross-examined! As if I'd been stealing jam. And I want two aspirin tablets and an ice pack for this damned head. Oh, hello." His voice modulated politely as he saw Ethel standing in the door.

"Janet," Harvey told him, "has been strangled."

Neville lowered the fork. "You mean she's—dead?" Courtney nodded. Neville's face went limp for a second and then contorted. He tossed the tray to the foot of the bed, sending a small pitcher of cream onto Frieda's skirt, and swung his legs over the side.

"*Do* be careful, Neville," Frieda was saying. Harvey took a step over to the foot of the bed. Courtney dropped back a pace.

"Where? How?" Neville was asking rampantly. "I want to see the place."

"Don't start trouble, Neville," Courtney advised him.

Neville sat on the edge of the bed glaring at him defiantly. "Are you making me stay in this room? Is that what you mean?"

"Yes." Harvey drew the revolver from his pocket and levelled it over the foot of the bed at Neville, who looked more shocked than scared.

He shrugged and drew himself back into the bed. "You'll have it your own way I suppose. I'd like more coffee, please." Frieda picked up the tray, to which she had restored the empty cream pitcher, and left the room in aggrieved silence. Ethel remained in the doorway as Harvey tucked the gun back in his pocket. Alfred went in and sat on the bed.

"They seem to think," Alfred began, "that it will be best to keep you under lock and key for the present. *I'm* not altogether satisfied with the conclusion. There are a lot of things to be cleared up yet as I see it. But I seem to be in a minority." He looked over his shoulder at Harvey's face, drawn wryly down on one side by the pipe, then back at Neville. "You're sure you haven't anything else to say—outside the fact that you don't remember anything from the time you fell asleep till just now?"

"I went to sleep on the lounge downstairs," Neville said glumly, "and I woke up here."

"Why," Alfred wanted to know, "did you particularly ask to talk with my wife?"

"I want to talk to someone," Neville exploded, "who'll tell me what happened and how!"

"Well," Alfred began quietly, "*I* can tell you what happened. I was with Ethel when we heard the ring from Janet." He gave Neville the details chronologically, with a frequent glance at Ethel for confirmation as to time. "Your mother," he concluded, "was apparently discussing the previous happenings with Courtney in his room"—Courtney was looking placidly at the frosted globe of the light above his head—"for about half an hour before the—incident. I found you in a drift just below the piazza roof. Your head had *apparently* been cut open when you jumped from the roof . . . ."

"But that's all rot!" Neville broke in.

"And . . . ." Alfred monotoned on, "and fell against the piazza railing. The cellar door was locked. Courtney found the key in your pocket. Dr. Harvey was found lying at the foot of the cellar stairs—unconscious, with a good sized bruise on his head. Hodges' body, stripped and hacked with an axe, was found nearby. The fire-poker from the living room was discovered by Courtney on the kitchen floor. Harvey says he was knocked out just as he was passing from cellarway to kitchen. The bulkhead entrance to the cellar was locked and bolted on the inside." Neville's heavy-lidded eyes went on staring at Alfred's profile for several seconds after he had finished speaking.

"And so?" Neville said finally.

"And so," Alfred repeated, standing up to confront Harvey, "we'll keep Neville locked up for the time being. But I suggest we go out right now and see how reliable that ice is for walking ashore to notify the police. Personally, I think this whole business is becoming more than amateurs can easily handle. Ethel, you might see if anything's happened to the telephone in the meantime . . . ."

While Ethel was at the 'phone table near the bannisters, Frieda came up with another steaming pot of coffee for Neville, left it in his room, and came immediately away. "Courtney," she called back, "I'd like to speak to you for a minute."

Courtney followed her along the hall, past Ethel, and into the guest corridor. Ethel could hear nothing but a dead silence in the receiver. She replaced it gently on the stand, listened to make sure Alfred and Harvey were still talking with Neville, and slipped across the intervening stairs to the other corridor. She saw Courtney's door close and went softly down the hallway to stand outside it. Frieda was talking in a low, hurried voice:

"I left them on the table in the living room."

"You should have asked me first," Courtney told her.

"But we had to get rid of them. Don't you see how it might have looked if anyone had found out I took them?" Her voice became raggedly insistent. "I thought if I left them there someone would be sure to find them, nobody would find out who took them, and if they *did* happen to have anything to do with what's been done—we wouldn't be worried about concealing them. Don't you see?"

"I don't see when they can have been taken away," Courtney's voice answered with irritation. "They were there when I went in to breakfast. I'm sure Harvey saw them then. So did the nurse. But they didn't say anything. They were watching to see what *I'd* say."

"Were they still on the table when you came upstairs to see Neville?"

"I don't remember," Courtney said. "I was hurrying."

"Good Lord," Frieda exclaimed in a louder voice, "you might keep your wits about you."

"*I* wasn't the one who left them on that table," Courtney expostulated, "and I wasn't the one who took them in the first place. *That* was certainly a fool idea . . . ."

"Don't be pompous!" Frieda was saying, her voice threateningly near the door. The handle turned as she showered a few contemptuous epithets on Courtney, and Ethel ran quietly back to the telephone. She was holding the receiver when a door slammed down the corridor, and Frieda stalked mincingly over the stairs to shut herself in her own room. Alfred came out of Janet's room and stopped in front of his own door.

"Nothing doing?"

"Nothing," Ethel replied, and dropped the receiver onto the hook.

"We're going to get into some togs and try the lake," he said, and went into his room.

Harvey was trying to appease Neville with his horse-sensible voice. "No good raving around," he was saying. "I'm not throwing up the sponge. I'm just waiting and watching and doing a little prowling around on the side. You stop acting like a monkey and pretend you've got a little patience."

"I can't even do anything to protect myself," Neville complained gutturally, when Ethel stood in the doorway, "locked up like this."

"What else can I do?" Harvey demanded lazily, and got up from a sitting position on the bed.

"Nothing, I suppose," Neville grumbled and yanked the wrinkles out of the bedding over him. A small wad of paper, the size of a bantam's egg, rolled out of a fold in the blanket and dropped lightly onto the furry gray of the rug.

"What's that?" Harvey murmured, as he picked it up, and pulled out the crumpled edges until they took the shape of an envelope, with a faded, postmarked stamp in one corner. "That corresponds to the one I saw downstairs," he said to Ethel, eyeing her piercingly as he handed over the wrinkled paper. The post-mark read "1902," and the envelope was addressed to Janet. Ethel slid her fingers inside, but the envelope was empty. She passed it to Neville.

"Are you sure you've never seen that before?" Harvey asked him.

"I certainly have not. It just dropped out of the bedding."

Harvey took the envelope back, shoved it into his pocket, and puffed steadily on his pipe as he studied Ethel's eyes. Then, without another word, he waved her off the threshold, patted Neville on the shoulder, and stood in the hallway with Ethel, as he locked the door.

# CHAPTER XII

Harvey's eyes brooded through the arched window at the end of the corridor, smoke clouding about his speckly-gray head. As Ethel went into her own room, he half turned as if to speak, then shoved his hands into the pockets of his baggy trousers and continued staring over the northern end of the island. When she turned from closing her closet door, he was facing her, shoulders sagging slightly, from the threshold. His eyes were focused on the bureau beside her.

"Mrs. Trevor, why did you steal those letters from Miss Larnard's desk?"

"I didn't."

"Where were you when Mrs. Larnard came downstairs looking for you last night?"

"I had just started through the passageway into the library."

"I see," he said, "I'm sorry." He seemed satisfied, and with a few casual looks about the room, he turned and went to knock on Frieda's door. Ethel stood in the hallway watching him. He pulled the crumpled envelope from his pocket and held it in his hand. When Frieda opened the door he shoved it with a quick motion within six inches of her face.

"Ever seen this before?"

Frieda stammered a denial. Harvey went into the room. The door closed. In two minutes the door opened and Harvey came out with a three-inch piece of glittery metal in his hand.

"You were the only one who came upstairs after I did," he was explaining to a silent, pale Frieda. "You'd heard Janet and me talking about the letters. You knew where they were, and you probably knew that Janet was down cellar. You'd already taken the letter from your husband's drawer—the letter he wrote to me. You knew you were the

**169**

only one who'd been upstairs, besides myself, and you tried to make us suspect Mrs. Trevor. You forced the lock on Janet's desk with this bent shoehorn. Now what I want to know is why did you tuck this envelope onto the bed beside Neville?"

"I didn't," she protested. "Oh, I didn't!"

"I suppose you think he isn't deeply enough involved already. Is that it?"

Frieda closed the door in his face.

"I beg your pardon," Harvey said to Ethel, "for thinking it was you. It was Mrs. Larnard. She won't admit it but . . . ." He held up the gleaming shoehorn, "I have this."

"Those letters had disappeared from the table," Ethel told him, "when I came upstairs just now. Someone had thrown them into the fire."

Courtney blustered from his corridor. His thighs swelled carrot-like in corduroy trousers that tucked into high, laced, oiled boots. His bright green Llama's wool ski-jacket was a flash of Intervale in season. The white collar of it rose and fell in an elaborate curve beneath a black teamster's cap faced on three sides with brown fur, which he was pulling down over his ears. He dangled a pair of huge, paw-like mittens from one hand. Altogether he suggested a thoroughly barbered Santa Claus.

"Did you search Neville," Harvey inquired, hiding a wide grin behind a barrage of smoke, "before you put him in Janet's room?"

"Certainly," said Courtney.

"Thoroughly?"

"Well, all his pockets."

"And you didn't," Harvey began, as he unfolded the envelope beneath Courtney's nose, "notice this? Tucked into his boots perhaps?—or concealed in the mouth?" Courtney looked at the envelope with genuine amazement, then into Harvey's eyes with even more amazement. He shook his head weightily.

"No," he managed to say; and, "No, I certainly didn't."

"Mrs. Larnard," Harvey said, nodding toward Frieda's door, "took the letters from Janet's desk, you know." Courtney's face took on fantastic incredulity. "Oh, yes," Harvey went on, "she forced the lock with a shoehorn. It's quite alright. Quite understandable. I was anxious to get a look at the letters myself."

"When did she tell you that?" Courtney demanded.

"We were talking about them just now."

"Well," Courtney said in a somewhat relieved tone, "I hope she gave you to understand that neither of us *read* the letters."

"Oh, you didn't? Why not?"

"Well, there was no excuse for it really—reading other people's letters. Frieda was going to turn them over to you in case they had any bearing on what occurred. Then when Janet was found—like that—things happening so fast, Frieda was afraid someone would suspect her so she left the letters downstairs on the table."

"Who threw them into the fire?"

"Is *that* where they went?"

"You knew—" Harvey insinuated casually, "that they had disappeared."

"Oh, yes. She told me . . . ."

Frieda appeared from her doorway. She was looking at Courtney. It seemed that she saw nothing else, that Harvey was not within miles of her vision, and that when her disgust had withered Courtney to the minute proportions which the expression on his face began to apprehend—she would be left alone with her scorn. Courtney was visibly sagging inside his bolstery clothes, but Frieda did not wait for him to diminish completely. She simply passed by him as if he had been the shoddiest of gateposts and went downstairs. There was deep relish in Harvey's smile behind the curling smoke.

"And you have no explanation for this?" Harvey wanted to know, as he tapped the wrinkled envelope in his hand.

"That?—No!" was the curt reply.

"It wasn't on Janet's bed when you took Neville in there."

"No. I'm sure of that. I spread the covers over him myself, and there was nothing on the bed."

"Did you look at her desk?"

"Yes. Carefully."

"At the drawer that had been broken open?"

"Yes. It was empty."

"Well," Harvey turned vaguely away to go down the stairs; "we know *something* anyway—more than we knew before."

From the great-paned bay window of the dining room Ethel could see Courtney's monstrous glaring figure hulking from the boathouse with the stiff skeins of a heavy rope writhing along the snow behind him. He plodded off the foot-printed pathway, passed behind a clump of shivering saplings, and waded laboriously over a waist-high drift, stumbled down a boulder-rounded embankment to join Alfred and Harvey on a stony tip of the island looking toward the boathouse on shore. The three of them made their way over a slaty stretch of rock, swept clean by the wind, and stood crouched against the gale where the ice began in a clean, dark, polished streak that jutted in a ragged triangle into the roughened white that masked the lake. Loose eddies of hurrying snow lashed about them. The dusky patch of Harvey's slouch hat suddenly lifted from his head and was carried bounding and scudding out of sight down the blanched reaches of ice. His head shone silvery in the sun. He tied the fold of a scarf over it and hauled his collar high about his ears.

Harvey fastened a noose of the rope under Courtney's shoulders, and held the loose end with Alfred. Courtney eased the noose about until it was taut over the chest of his parrot-colored jacket and the knot stood out at the back between his shoulder blades. He stepped testingly down onto the sheer surface of the ice and started out, cautious, foot by foot, ten feet, twenty, thirty, Alfred and Harvey paying out the stretch of loose rope after him. He reached the edge of clear ice and edged his way into the white area of snow. Harvey followed along the tested pathway on the ice, Alfred about seven feet behind him. Courtney's arms flew suddenly up. The other two braced themselves against the taut rope. A hoarse cry came smothered through the wind. Courtney's legs sank into the white surface. He floundered backwards, clutching the chunks of snow beside him as his waist was buried. Alfred and Harvey leaned back on the rope; Courtney's body was hauled a few feet onto the clean layer of snow, a black patch showing where he had slipped through. Then he went downwards again, covered except for his head and one arm, which waved frantically, grabbing at the empty air. Harvey's voice shouted something. Courtney's arms folded over his face protectingly, and they heaved him swiftly through a track of breaking snow and ice until his figure slid limply along the glassy stretch. Alfred pulled him swaying onto his feet. Harvey yanked off the coil of rope, and they ran him, Alfred grabbing one arm, Harvey the other, up over the stone slope, through the drift, around the reed-like saplings toward the pathway.

Courtney looked very stupid, bloated, blotchy and proud when they pushed him through the door into the living room and rushed him upstairs, hauling the wilted, soaked jacket from his back. Courtney protested in a pleased, gruff voice that he was all right, and gave several gusty sneezes. Frieda clattered downstairs and pattered up again with whiskey. Water roared in Courtney's bath. Steam filled Courtney's corridor. Frieda hung his dripping clothing over the andirons, where it gave off the aroma of burning horsehide. An armful of blankets were thrust into Ethel's arms, and she was breathlessly told to "roast them before the fire." Harvey and Alfred could be heard plodding professionally about Courtney's room. Courtney's bathrobe was hurled over the bannisters at Ethel, already feeling like a full-rigged ship with stretching blankets before the hearth, to be thoroughly warmed. Courtney's protesting figure was rubbed with towels until he groaned for help, slapped, pummeled, and smothered in hot woolen. The prescription was that he should remain framed in these woolens in his bed for most of the day. An early and enormous lunch was served to him, and, between hissing mouthfuls of soup, he told Ethel and Frieda, who had been watching him from windows, every detail of the catastrophe. His loquacity was tripled by the whiskey. Harvey proposed solemnly that he should be awarded a medal cast in pure, white ice. Frieda looked reproachfully at Harvey. Alfred rubbed his own nose and ears until they looked very red and he looked very silly. Courtney was plied with additional whiskey, and sank into a comfortable stupor with the luncheon tray still on his knees. Frieda's tenderness was quite lost on him. Ethel decided that she herself was exhausted, and went to her room to sleep when two cups of coffee had revived Courtney to the extent of giving a second version of the near tragedy.

Physically tired, but nervously wide awake, she slipped on overshoes, a woolen beret, and a fur-collared coat, went quietly downstairs and out the front door to plod through snow-filled pathways that led windingly along the shore of the island. The wind was veering, and drifts that had piled against the shrubbery during the night were being leveled away and sifting off in flurries of snow, leaving patches of bare ground uncovered. About twenty yards from the boathouse she saw what seemed to be the curve of a large boulder half covered by snow. Familiar enough with the pathway to know that a stone of that size had never been there before—she gave it a slight prod with the toe of her boot.

The feel of it was not like stone but resembled firm rubber, and she realized immediately that it was the haired flank of a frozen animal. Before she had entirely cleared the snow away she knew that the body was that of a dog—and could tell from the brass-studded collar about the neck that it was Hansel. In pushing the snow away from one foreleg her glove struck a sharp surface—which proved to be the irregular blade of a slender saw, the type used for cutting a curve in wood, a small metal handle at the larger end. The saw tapered to a point at the other extremity and had apparently been used to wound the animal just behind the neck—where a jagged cut gaped between the parted hair.

The saw was not more than a foot and a half in length, an inch and a half wide near the handle. Excepting the handle it was not more than a sixteenth of an inch thick—surely thin enough, minus the handle, to slip—under Neville's door. And, if Neville could work with sufficient patience and silence, it might easily be used to saw between the two shutters and sever the boards which were nailed on from the outside holding them together.

In the boathouse she fumbled along a work bench, found a rusty screwdriver, with which she removed two screws that fastened the blade to the handle. With the slim blade tucked up the sleeve of her coat she hurried back to the house. In her own room she scribbled a note for Neville—describing where and how she had found Hansel's body. She folded the note flat about the saw blade—and, after she had heard footsteps going downstairs, went quietly out to slide the saw under Neville's door. She waited in her own room with the door open. In about ten minutes another slip of paper poked from beneath the opposite door.

"Thanks," it read, "but I can only work slowly to avoid noise. It will take hours. Leave your window unlocked. When I do get through the shutters—I will come 'round over the roof to your room. N."

She undressed, threw herself limply on the bed and was suddenly asleep.

When she awoke her room was half obscured in the dusk. One of the window curtains was moving sleepily in a slender draft of air through a crack by the hinges of the casement. The horizon above the white mounds of the western mountains was strewn with ruddy gold clouds, drawn thin by the wind and paling into a transparent amber mist. High over them a solitary star hung silverly in the luminous blue. A pine tree beyond the window shook its dark tassels stiffly in the wind. A pale blue pall of half-light covered the frozen lake that lost itself in the inky groves of pines lining the far shore. The casement rattled in its fastenings under a stunning buffet from the wind, and the white curtain lifted and fell silently like the hand of a dying woman.

The gloom of the hallway ended in the red glow from the hearth downstairs. She listened at Janet's door, and heard the intermittent purring scratch of the saw on wood.

As she went softly down the hall she heard Frieda's rippling laugh from Courtney's corridor, and Courtney's deep, rounded tones rumbling steadily, punctuated frequently by the clink of a tea cup and the ring of a spoon against saucer. From the living room beneath she could discern a dull grating noise, repeating itself regularly, as of a piece of heavy metal being drawn back and forth over stone. She rested her hands on the smooth wood of the bannister rail and looked down.

Harvey was kneeling on the hearthstone, his face a hearty bronze in the steady flare from the fire, his hair shining like strands of fine platinum wire interspersed with thin dark on top. He had the black iron fire shovel in his wide, square hand and was making a little heap of ashes, flecked with glow-worm embers, on the hearth beside him. He spread them into a thin surface with the flat of the shovel, and began combing carefully through them with a tinny looking kitchen fork. The fork would catch a lump, and he would lift it to one side on the hearth and meticulously prod it to small bits—till it proved to be nothing but a partly burned bit of wood or a compact pellet of ashes. Then the eager combing would begin again, and another lump would be subjected to the same poking scrutiny.

The fork plunged again and again into and through the two-inch layer of dusty gray on the hearthstone, until it unearthed a sooty little sphere about the size of a marble. The fork dropped, and Harvey's fingers plucked the small sphere out of the ash flakes. He placed it on the palm of his left hand and smoothed away the soot with the fore-finger and thumb of his right. He wiped his blackened finger tips absently on the leg of his trouser and took the gleaming penknife from his vest pocket, placed the tiny lump on the hearthstone, flicked open a steel-shining blade, and cut precisely through the center of the marbly lump. The two minute halves fell aside, showing a pale brownish center about the shade of a walnut shell. Harvey placed these peculiar fragments in his clean handkerchief, rolled it into a wad and shoved it into the left hand pocket of his saggy coat. He shoveled out another heap of ashes and began searching through them with the fork again.

A door latch clicked down the corridor, and Ethel turned to face Alfred. He smiled and was about to speak. She placed her forefinger quickly against her lips and pointed over the bannisters. Alfred walked quietly over to stand beside her. When he looked down his eyebrows slid together in a puzzled fashion. He turned to her, his eyes questioning.

His lips moved almost inaudibly. "The letters?" She shrugged and they both leaned over to watch Harvey panning through the ashes like a nugget miner.

As the fork plunged again there was a barely audible crunching click, and he drew the fork slowly to the edge, rake fashion, pulling out a flat, blackened fragment about the size of a half dollar, but lop-sided. He bent over to blow the particles of ash from it, and when his fingers tenderly picked it up, most of it crumbled away in black dust. But he held the remaining portion close to the light of the flames. As his hand moved the fragment gleamed like a glossy piece of smoothly hewn coal. Harvey stood up quickly and walked to one side of the room out of sight. The sound of tearing paper could be heard and he came into sight again wrapping the bit of shiny black preciously in the print-covered leaf from a magazine. He took a wallet from his inner coat pocket, placed the folded paper between two bills, and stowed the wallet away again. Bending to his knees, he shoveled the ashes back under the blazing logs, and with a pair of bellows blew away all the minutest traces. He let himself sit relaxingly in the wing chair, filled and lighted his pipe, and watched the sprawling smoke trace gew-gaw patterns against the firelight. When he seemed to have settled himself into a lasting mood of contemplation, his eyes parted quickly in a wide flash out of their narrow staring. He took the pipe from his parted lips and smiled with a paradoxically soft-lined grimness at the shrouding smoke. As he stood up the fire crackled unevenly and tossed several sparks toward his shoes. He turned and walked beneath them.

They could hear his soft footsteps, one shoe squeaking slightly, on the thick carpet, and then on the floor at the other end of the living room. The sound of chair legs moved against the polished hardwood, then the pipe tapping against an ash tray, and then, harmoniously, notes slipping into chords, chords slipping into a swaying melody from the piano, like gentle waves washing against gentle waves, the tones of the "Liebestraum," gathering strength until it welled through the entire house and the shadows became softly vibrant.

Alfred's hands slid from the bannister rail and fell at his sides. He had half raised his eyes from the fire and was staring through the chimney in front of him. His expression was that of a person who has just dug, unawares, into a grave. The music melted to a finish and began again.

"God!" he murmured chokingly.

"What's the matter?" she asked.

He closed his eyes firmly and opened them again. "Elizabeth," he said in a weak, flat voice, "used to play that often. It was the only piece she could ever remember."

His hand touched vaguely against her arm as he turned and walked dazedly back to his room.

Wind hounded whiningly through the outer darkness as she turned up the lamp in her own room and drew down the shade. In a baffled fear that made her aware of hidden presences that she knew could not be real she was even afraid to go downstairs and wait in the firelight to hear Cowpers striking the dinner chime. She tried to pretend to herself that she had come back to her room to give an additional smoothing to her hair, but when she looked at its crinkling gold in the mirror she knew that it needed no further fussing. She sat rigidly on the edge of her bed, clasping her hands in a tight grip, trying to force herself into a resolute tranquility, trying to ignore a childish impulse to look under the bed, in the closet, and lock her door. For a moment she forgot herself in an effort to devise some quicker way of getting Neville out of Janet's room, but realized that Harvey had a loaded revolver in his pocket with the key and knew that he was quite beyond any wheedling. She stared at the outline of the arched frame surrounding the mirror. She watched the white curtain stirring feebly in the draft of air.

The rasping whir of the buzzer suddenly seemed to tear its way through her. For a second she was unable to move. Then the sound of it flickered again, more lightly. When she opened her door Alfred was standing in the corridor outside his own doorway.

"Did you hear that?" she asked.

"The buzzer? Yes." He snapped on the light switch beside Henry's door frame, and the iron sconces flooded the hallway with parchment-tinted light. They stood together outside Henry's door, which was half open. Alfred looked between the door and the frame, his eyes on a level with the upper hinge.

"No one there," he said, and went in to turn on the lamp. She followed him. He walked close to the window and tugged against it. "This is locked," he murmured, "from the inside." He pulled aside the door into Neville's room, peered in, then walked over the threshold and turned the switch of a lamp on the bureau. Except for an irregular dark stain on the faded blue rug there was no sign of Henry's body. Alfred was trying the door to the roof, which was securely locked.

"It's gone!" she said.

"Oh," he said, "yes. It's in the spare room on the other corridor. Harvey and I were doing an informal autopsy this afternoon. He thinks Henry was poisoned—but no traces of anything in the stomach."

Footsteps were coming up the stairs with a harsh, scraping regularity. They went back through the door to Henry's room. Harvey stood in the hallway.

"Was that the buzzer ringing?" he asked.

"Yes," Alfred said.

"I thought so." He turned away, and then said over his shoulder. "Oh, by the way, Cowpers tells me dinner will be ready in about half an hour." He crossed the stairs to the other corridor, and a door was heard closing. In a few minutes he came back, smiled at them, went downstairs and returned, slightly out of breath, with a suitcase, which he carried into the other corridor.

"Now that's damned strange!" Alfred pondered, as he watched Harvey distrustfully from the doorway, and then, dismissingly, "Well, I suppose Frieda will dress for dinner and expect the rest of us . . . ." He wandered puzzle-eyed down the hall to his room. Ethel could hear him muttering to himself as he took down a dinner jacket from the hanger in his closet, threw it lackadaisically across his bed, and closed the door.

The curtain in her own room was waltzing fitfully in the draft from the crack beside the window. She raised the shade to see if the casement could be more tightly fastened. The lighted windows along the other corridor were sharply cut against the blackness of the outside walls. She could see Frieda, seated on the edge of the bed in Courtney's room, dutifully lighting Courtney's cigarette, and Courtney very wise-eyed blowing a thin stream of smoke speculatively toward the ceiling. She saw Harvey pacing back and forth before the window in the next room, nearer to her, rumpling his gray hair with his box-like left hand, and then dropping into a chair in front of a table desk, one corner of which showed beside the window, to scribble with schoolboy fierceness on a sheet of paper. He arose, performed several more caged paces, placed his pipe on the table, and let himself tiredly out of the arms of his coat to hang it over the back of a chair which stood just in front of the window facing into the room. He disappeared to one side for an instant, reappeared with a toilet case in his hand and moved out of sight to the right.

It suddenly occurred to Ethel that this was her chance to get the key to Janet's room. She knew that a bathroom adjoined the room Harvey occupied. He was still unshaven. The business of erasing a two days' growth of bristly beard might take him ten minutes. The guest corridor was the coldest portion of the house. There was an efficient radiator in the bathroom. He would probably have the door closed. He might— he undoubtedly would—indulge himself in a bath or shower before dinner. That would mean another five minutes. She locked her door softly from the inside. She tucked a coat about herself and slipped on a pair of light overshoes, opened the casement, drew herself onto the roof of the porch, and swung the casement to behind her. Wind had carried all but an icy sheet of frozen snow off the roof. She kept to the wall of the house. Alfred's shade was drawn. There was no light coming from the window of Frieda's room. The bathroom window was high and she crouched under it, still safely in darkness. She turned the corner of the wall and started off at right angles to her own corridor. She clung to the blind of a dark uncurtained window. Beyond it a dull light came from the guest hallway through an open door. The light outlined a sheet-covered figure stretched straight and motionless on a table in the center of the room. She imagined Henry Larnard's ivory profile beneath the lumpy, head-like portion at one extremity of the sheet. This window was open several inches and a waft of formaldehyde singed her nostrils as a zephyr of warm air struck across her hand.

She heard water tumbling full force into a tub as she reached the bright window of Harvey's room. She could see a somewhat wrinkled dinner coat limp on a hanger through the open door of his closet, then the bars of a brass bedstead, and a bulky pig skin suitcase thrown open on the white spread. On the green blotter of the table immediately to the left of the window, the curved pipe took a polished gleaming from the parchment-shaded lamp just above it. The red tubing of a stethoscope stretched along the circle of lamplight, and beside it a much-scribbled sheet of stationery. Nearby was the crumpled letter envelope with the faded pink stamp addressed to Miss Janet Larnard, partly covered by the white handkerchief, streaked with smooches of soot. On top of the handkerchief—she supposed they were the fragments he had cut from the lump yielded up by the fire ashes—the two rough semi-spheres with the brownish, cut faces. With a bit of stretching she assured herself that the bathroom door, far to the right, was almost shut. She looked at the dark lumps again. They rested lightly on a fold of the handker-chief—apparently the weight of charcoal, but the pale brown faces were almost patterned with tiny criss-cross lines. Then she recognized what they were—bits of cork—burned on the outside—longer than they were wide. When placed face to face, and unburned on the outside, they might very easily have formed the stopper of a wide-necked bottle.

Then—on the leaf of magazine paper—she saw the other coal-like fragments removed from the ashes, dark and glassy, somewhat like butterscotch dropped on a flat pan, but black instead of brown. She noticed that they were not entirely black, but only dark because of soot fragments congealed into their centers, and that about the edges the fragments were clear and transparent.

from something originally of glass, melted into their present lack of shape by the fire.

She tried to read the scribbling on the sheet of paper, but it was quite illegible. Harvey's coat hung, back to her, over the chair, within six inches of the window. Water was still thundering in the tub off to the right. She knelt on the hard crust of snow, placed her fingers on the frame of the window just above the lower panes of glass, and pushed as hard as she could upward. The window would not give. It was either frozen or locked. The tips of her fingers tingled and hurt in the cold. Her knee slipped against the roof as she tried to push again. She could hear the dinner chime striking distantly. The bathroom door swung open and a rush of brighter light fell from the right of the room. She shrank back along the wall, turned the corner of the roof outside her own corridor. There was a light in Frieda's room now, but the shade was drawn. Alfred's window was dark, and as she went by she could see his door open into the lighted hallway.

She drew out the casement opening to her room, and realized, when she had drawn herself halfway through it, that someone was standing near the closet beyond the bureau. She turned her head slowly till her eyes faced the figure. It was Neville. He came toward her laughing silently, placed his hands firmly beneath her armpits, drew her through the window, and kissed her on the mouth for many seconds.

"I was trying," she explained, quite sure that he would not believe her, "to pick the key to your room out of Harvey's pocket. But his window was locked. I thought, while he was in the bath I might . . . ."

She outlined everything that had transpired since she had left him lying on the lounge the previous evening to overhear Harvey and Alfred chatting in the library. She was just finishing a description of the curiosities Harvey had hauled out of the fireplace, when Neville's slender fingers tightened about the bedpost.

"Shhh!" he said. They could head a scraping sound along the roof outside, then a light crunching, then silence. "Put out the light," Neville whispered. She stepped to the table by the bed and switched the room into darkness. "Now unlock the door," Neville said, "and pretend to open it and close it." She went over to turn the key and pulled the door a foot out from the frame to send it back with a faint, woodeny thump. "Good," Neville muttered, his back outlined against the deep night color of the sky beyond the casement, which he pushed slowly and silently open to thrust his head through just far enough to survey the length of roof to the right.

"Someone," he said, "has just gone through the window into Alfred's room."

She crowded to one side of him till she could see over his head the window lighted length of the other wing. "See those curtains waving back and forth over there," she said. "That window's open. It was locked a few minutes ago. That's Harvey's room." They could hear the slightly grating slide of a window being shut, and a light shone dimly through a drawn shade from Alfred's room. Neville started from the window.

"I'm going in there and see what's happening."

"No." She held his arm. "You don't want to give away the fact you're out. If it's Harvey he'll either shoot you or lock you up somewhere else."

"That's true," he admitted.

"I'll go in," she told him quickly. "You see—I'll call Alfred's name and walk in. Perfectly natural."

"He'll shoot you."

"No he won't. And while I'm talking to him—you go across the roof and see if you can find any of those things on his table, and that paper with the writing."

"Alright." Neville was sliding out the window.

"He'll come out with me," she said, "through the corridor. That'll give you just enough time to come back over the roof." She went into the corridor and closed the door silently after her, holding it firmly against the draft of air from the open casement. Alfred's door was shut. She could see a thin bar of light just above the threshold. "Alfred," she called, knocked, and turned the handle of the door. When it opened— the light had gone out. "Oh," she said, as if surprised. She was, not quite knowing what to do. Then she said, as if entirely to herself, feeling acutely self-conscious. "Oh, thought he was here." She heard a brief brushing sound, no louder than the flick of a duster over a roughly finished table. She went over to the lamp by the bed and turned it on. Without actually looking at it she could see that the closet door was nearly closed. She leaned over beside the window, picked up Alfred's medicine satchel, and planted it with an obvious thud on the runner of the bureau. She rustled through the contents for several seconds, took out a bottle of iodine, carried it over to the lamp, which was clearly visible from the two-inch opening of the closet door. She examined an imaginary hangnail on the second finger of her left hand, and daubed it elaborately with iodine, surveyed it anxiously under the lamplight again, and replaced the bottle in the satchel with leisurely nonchalance. When the satchel had been carefully lowered to the floor beside the window, she took unnecessary time in switching off the light, and left the room.

When she opened the door of her room the dinner chime was ringing again with loud insistence. She heard a crunching footstep on the roof, and Neville's head and shoulders pushed their way through the window. His lips were compressed and his eyes shone dark and hard like oynx. "Nothing there," he said shortly, as his feet reached the floor and he brought the casement to a quick close, drawing the shade in front of it. "Of course—he wouldn't leave that stuff stringing around. Got it in his pockets."

"I'd better go down to dinner," she said.

"Yes. I'll go back to my room over the roof when he's had time to get out of the way. I want to be in there when they come up with my supper tray."

When she went into the hall Harvey was just starting down the stairs, his dinner jacket hanging not quite trimly with the weight in the right hand pocket. She closed her door loudly. He turned, smiled, and waved to her, and continued down the stairs. She opened her door, slipped inside, and whispered, "He's just gone downstairs," and left the room to follow Harvey. Voices were mingling over the dinner table. Harvey stood on the hearthstone waiting for her.

"Tell me," he said in a confidential voice, "did you give Mr. Larnard any medicine before you left him last night?"

"Yes," she said, "a triple-bromide."

"You gave it to him yourself?"

"Yes."

"That—and nothing else?"

"That was all. He'd had some whiskey. It excited him. He couldn't sleep, or said he couldn't. So I gave him that."

"Thank you," he said, and with a polite inclination of the head and a wave of his square hand, sent her into the dinning room ahead of him.

Frieda was chattering about the quality of the clear night sky after the storm clouds had cleared away, and Courtney had a few blithe words to say about the phosphorescent green of the northern lights— particularly in June.

# CHAPTER XIII

With Janet thoroughly out of the way and Neville safely niched upstairs, Frieda had openly recovered from a suitable and not unbecoming interval, alternating between pathetic panic and a studied wanness, and was carrying out her own notions of propriety with a high, if slightly nervous, hand. Now that Janet's quick and flexible tongue had been choked into silence, Frieda felt free to ensconce Courtney in Henry Larnard's patriarchal throne at the head of the table with its massive back to the inclusive windows, now protectively curtained against the ruthless blue of the winter night. Courtney, feeling his right to succession undisputed with the obvious heir under lock and key, let the substantial shapeliness of his pink hands loll magisterially, even a bit fatuously, on the ornate lion's paws carven roundly at the ends of the chair arms. As the figure of Cowpers, trim in a white serving jacket, deposited a plate of steaming consommé before the master's place, Courtney indulged him a curt nod of approval.

Other dispositions had been juggled about, and Frieda's deliberate innocence proved beyond question that she had thought the changes mincingly out beforehand. Alfred, sullenly pale behind the quick gestures of raising his soup spoon, his deep-set eyes constantly edging toward Ethel as she sat on his left, had been placed on Frieda's left. Opposite him Harvey, with a business-like smile of complete self-possession, was being dismissed into a chair on Frieda's right. Neville's chair and place had been retained at the table, one felt as a mere matter of form, but Janet's chair had been utterly banished to a shadowy corner beside the cut glass cabinet, where rows of lustry sherbet glasses glittered brightly and remoter rows of champagne, sherry, and port

185

glasses glittered with a dim reminiscence, and batches of thick, deeply-cut water tumblers looked intricately crystalline, yet frozenly solid.

The consommé was dispatched amid a scattered flurry of banalities and monosyllables, the banalities flaunting from Courtney and Frieda, the monosyllables, when they occurred at all, being returned from Harvey and Alfred. Ethel said nothing except to thank Alfred—twice, on the events of his considerately passing her the celery when Cowpers was kept bickering in the kitchen with Sophie over some culinary formality and the celery was not properly circulated. But when Courtney had fallen to slicing a ponderous, red-centered roast of beef, Harvey wiped his mouth elaborately with his napkin, planted his elbows on the table, and let his hands sprawl formidably across the frosty looking cloth.

"I may as well explain now," he began, "to all of you, as I already have to Dr. Trevor, why I came here, since it seems to have nothing to do with the cases in hand. Henry thought it was very strange that Elizabeth should take her own life when she had left the disposition of part of her fortune hanging in the air." He went on with methodical indifference to outline the details she had overhead him confiding to Alfred in the library on the previous night. "She had promised the London banking firm that she would arrange about the further disposition of this secret trust fund when the contingency of the man's death should occur. She never made that arrangement, and when the party for whom the trust was made passed away, the bankers wrote to Henry . . . ."

"Who was this man," Courtney inquired sharply, with a glance divided between Harvey and Alfred, "for whom the trust was established?"

"That's another strange thing," Harvey told them. "Nobody seems to know who he was or, rather, what he was. Alfred has never heard of him. I'd think, of course, that he might be involved in all of this—but he's dead. His name . . . ." He fumbled a hand to the inside pocket of his packet and drew out a long envelop, slid a typewritten letter from it. "Yes . . . . This is the letter Henry received and forwarded to me." He let his finger run down the lines of typing, his spectacles shaking with tiny reflections of the lighted candle-tips. "Yes, here we are. His name was—Geoffrey Seaburne."

Frieda was just reaching to clasp a tumbler of water in her slender fingers. Her hand remained gauchely stretched out, and then fell limply to the tablecloth, jangling a silver knife against a silver spoon at the right of her plate. Her round, amazed eyes were on Harvey. Something seemed to stiffen in her throat. Then her eyebrows fell and her eyes narrowed to an ordinary curiosity, but her voice was husky when she managed to speak.

"Who," she said, "who was the man?"

"Geoffrey Seaburne," Harvey repeated. "Know anything about him?"

"Oh! Geoffrey *Seaburne*. No," she gave a weak little laugh. "No—I guess, I thought . . . . I didn't understand. Thought you said another name. Now isn't that strange," as her voice grew stronger, sinking to its hostess contralto. She looked at Alfred, "and you never heard of him?"

"No," Alfred said, in glum embarrassment. "Complete riddle to me."

"Under the circumstances," Harvey finished, "I presume the trust, not of any great size to be sure, will revert to Elizabeth's heirs—as would the money of anyone who has not made a will—and be divided according to the usual legal stipulations."

"Remember," Frieda said to Courtney, as he drew the carving knife through the roast, "that Dr. Harvey likes it quite rare." She turned her beguiling smile on Harvey. "Am I right?" He nodded politely, and tucked the folded letter into the envelope to restore it to his inner coat pocket. Cowpers was filling glasses with a grapey looking beverage—his own version of Italian red wine. He wielded the glass decanter with an almost cocky gracefulness—and lifted it from the rim of each glass with a successful flourish. Frieda took a dutiful sip with an upward smile at Cowpers. Alfred mouthed a bit of his with a wry face and followed it almost immediately with half a glass of water. This only prompted Cowpers, who was standing behind him at the moment, to refill Alfred's glass. He found it impossible not to smile at Cowpers, who answered with a deferential inclination of his head, placed the decanter in temporary repose on the high sideboard, and went silently into the kitchen to start haggling with Sophie again.

"By the way, Doctor," Alfred began, giving his slice of beef a meticulous salting, "You remember that we placed the dagger in the closet of that—spare room where Henry is now?"

"Yes?"

"Well, I went in just before coming down. The closet door was wide open and the dagger was gone."

Harvey's eyes distended with polite interest. "You don't say so!"

After dinner Cowpers bore a tray of demitasses to the living room. Alfred finished his coffee quickly, standing at one end of the lounge. Frieda took dainty sip after sip between regal puffs on a long, ivory cigarette holder. Courtney placed himself like a section of dinner-clad masonry on the lounge a few feet from Ethel, slipped the gilt ring from a slender cigar, and said that he thought it would not be altogether irrelevant to discuss Henry's will, since it might have considerable bearing on what had happened. Harvey, sniffing one of Courtney's cigars appreciatively, took the chair on the other side of the hearth and said Courtney was probably quite right. Alfred touched the flame of a match to his cigarette, and flicked the match into the fire. He asked Courtney if the change effecting Neville's inheritance would be effective. Courtney said that Henry had, unfortunately, not signed the revised will, but that it was distinctly a matter for the courts, if anyone wanted to break the existing will, since it was certainly not an actual representation of Henry's sincerest wishes, as they could all stand to witness. Courtney managed to break his cemented comfort on the lounge to arise and declare he would get both wills—the signed and the unsigned, tucked his cigar vaguely between his teeth, and went in all dignity upstairs.

Cowpers appeared with Neville's dinner tray. Harvey said, "Oh, yes; of course," and led Cowpers upstairs to unlock Neville's room. Neville's voice racketed indignantly as the door was heard opening in the corridor above them. Alfred, cigarette poised between the two yellowed tips of his fingers, his other hand resting with its thumb in his trouser pocket, paced back and forth just beyond the table. He strolled to the window, narrowed his eyes at the thermometer outside, said the temperature was still falling—and that they should be able to walk ashore the next day without any mishap. Frieda said a meaningless "That's right," gazing dreamily into the smoke curvetting from her extended cigarette. The clock in the library gave forth nine deep-toned strokes. Cowpers came downstairs and passed into the dining room. The occasional chink of silver and the ring of an empty tumbler was all that could be heard of his clearing the table. Harvey's chuckling laugh sounded long and heartily from Neville's room. Alfred wandered aimlessly to the piano at the far end of the room, shuffled through several sheets of music. He moved 'round behind it and his stocky shoulders and dark, carefully combed head sank behind the oriental rug that covered the upright back of the piano. Notes poised themselves roundly on the air and sank into slow obscurity among the shadows. Alfred's playing was slow, listless, easy.

Ethel moved over to the end of the lounge near Frieda. A sharp movement of Frieda's eyes to one side was all that betrayed any interest in Ethel, and the cigarette holder was languidly raised to the petulantly-cut, very red mouth.

"There's just one thing," Ethel began, "that worries me." Frieda's eyes were considerately attentive. Ethel felt that Frieda was hearing her as she would hear the ungrammatical protests and threats of a discharged cook. "Something Janet confided to me last night," she went on, conscious of malicious eagerness to see Frieda's composure begin to crack. "Of course, if she were still alive, I'd have to rely on her judgment about not telling anyone, because it *was* her secret—hers and *yours*." The ivory holder dropped several inches from the freshly red lips, and a splotch of ashes fell on the silver curve of the evening gown rounded by Frieda's knee. The needle ends of her lashes made lacy little frames around the fixed ovals of her eyes. Ethel spoke quietly against the pattering of soft notes from the piano. "She told me Neville was not Henry Larnard's son. Is that—true?"

Frieda's mouth jerked open. Her whisper was brutally intense. "Of course it isn't true. I told you this morning—about Janet. Her jealousy— she was out of her mind. I thought she'd been filling you up with a lot of vicious nonsense . . . ."

Ethel shrugged. "I have no way of knowing," she said, "but I thought I should tell you before I tell—the others. I certainly can't be expected to keep quiet about it. You'd say it wasn't true, of course . . . ."

"Please!" Frieda said, her eyes frenzied, leaning toward Ethel, "Please don't. You mustn't say anything. It's— It hasn't anything to do with this." Her anger had broken into desperate entreaty. "It can't have. I promise you that."

"Then it *is* true," Ethel said.

Frieda glanced apprehensively toward the stairs, then leaned closer to Ethel. Her head shook—strivingly, as if she could not find words. Her outstretched hand contracted helplessly. "Yes," she whispered on top of a long, indrawn breath. "But it . . . ."

"Well, I can't see," Ethel told her, "why it might not have a great deal to do with your husband's—death."

"But he *can't* have had anything to do with it," Frieda insisted, her voice more hysterical.

"Who can't?"

"The man I—the one who really is Neville's father. He— He's dead."

"How am I to know that?"

"He was the one—Elizabeth made the trust for, Geoffrey Seaburne."

"Oh," Ethel said, "then it *must* have something to do with it."

"No, no, no!" Frieda protested wildly. "It was just—coincidence, and Elizabeth's hatred for me. He—Seaburne—he and Elizabeth met each other somewhere—I don't know when it was in Europe—long after everything was finished as far as I was concerned. And Elizabeth must have—" her voice caught in little breaths of effort "—I don't know— been in love with him or maybe just out of spite . . . . You see, Neville's very much like him. Anyway, Elizabeth and Geoffrey were very intimate. He was completely down and out. She gave him money. They were *very* intimate, I guess. And he must have told her about Neville and about me. That gave her—well, she always had that hold over me. She knew she could threaten to tell Henry about—that, and force me to do anything she wanted. It was horrible. I couldn't—almost couldn't breathe without making sure first that she'd approve."

"Is that—why you poisoned her?"

Frieda's hands clutched at her. "I didn't. I didn't even know anything about it until Harvey . . . ." Footsteps sounded from Courtney's corridor. "Please," Frieda almost cried, "don't say anything. Wait, anyway—and then, later, if you *have* to tell—to protect yourself—I'll admit it. even tell them myself. But there's no need . . . . That's why I took those letters. I thought—" She shrank back against the tall upholstery of the chair as Courtney came over the stairs with sheaves of paper in both hands. His brow was wrinkled with a solid consciousness of his own importance.

Courtney stretched himself permanently back against the lounge, drew his right hand caressingly the length of a black ribbon that looped about his trunk-like neck, beneath the coat collar, and lifted a shiny pince-nez to the wide bridge of his nose. Knife-like reflections flickered across the glasses as his eyes scanned the documents loosely folded on his knees. He placed them in order and sat back patiently as Harvey descended, the stairs holding Neville's plate-piled tray gingerly in front of him. He stood for a second on the last step.

"Neville says," he announced, "that the crumpled envelope must have appeared on the bed in Janet's room at some time during his breakfast, when we were all in the room, because he swears it wasn't there on the bed when he first woke up."

"That," Courtney replied, "is approximately what I'd expect Neville to say under the circumstances." Harvey took the tray into the dining room and came back to relight his cigar. Alfred was called over from the piano, and sat dutifully between Ethel and Courtney during the hour and a half which Courtney required to read and explain the several wills, five in all, which gave an index of Henry Larnard's fluctuating mind during the six weeks of his illness. Courtney spieled off the legal terminology with mouthy emphasis, pausing to render each fragment in the translation of his own cluttery phrases.

Since Courtney had already given away the fact of Henry's having left the secret bequest, which he assumed would go to Hodges—now, of course, to Hodges' heirs—there was nothing astonishing about the recent wills.

When Courtney refolded the documents at quarter of eleven everyone knew exactly just as much as had been known before Courtney began—since Henry had never altered any of his bequests without formally summoning the household to his bedside and informing each member of the family of any loss he was about to suffer in the inheritance—and why. If the loser had displayed sufficient contrition—the bequest had usually been restored within the space of three days. Everyone but Janet had been summarily cut from the will at one time or another, and everyone but Janet had eventually been awarded more than Henry, before being stricken, had planned to bequeath. The extra was always subtracted from a fund to establish a non-fiction library or libraries for woolen-mill operatives in Massachusetts, the details and handling of the fund to be taken over by the board of directors of which Henry had at one time been president.

Harvey excused himself politely during the tag end of Courtney's explanations and said he was going upstairs to complete the autopsy on Henry's body. Alfred wandered over to the piano again and began playing languid chord after chord in various minor keys. Frieda shuddered a trifle when Harvey mentioned Henry's body, and said she was going to bed. Courtney lumbered up the stairs after her, patting the documents into a uniform packet in his hands, and slipping a large rubber band over them. Ethel was about to go upstairs herself, but realized she would not sleep immediately, having slept till five in the afternoon, and went to the library to look along the high, closely-filled shelves for some book that Henry Larnard's bibliophile taste might have connived at to divert his light-minded guests or family.

The lamplight struck softly along the worn backs of large volumes, the paper backs of French novels, and gleamed on the red leather backs of Henry's made-to-order bindings. Here in his island refuge Henry had assembled his library—weighty tomes of reference, stiff-backed histories, legal works at one end of the room, worn first editions, sets of classics, and shelves devoted to political pamphlets at the other end. When in the city he had read very little, never hurrying—so Janet had once told her—always punctual, finding time only for his bankers and brokers, his time-measured walks in the park, his directors' meetings, and the small formality of entertaining dinner guests. But here on the island, which he had made an escape from the world which irritated his finicking and hesitant tastes, he had devoted himself to prolonged reading and correspondence, interspersed with gentlemanly fishing on the lake, and very occasional excursions in a high-powered launch with Neville. If guests had broken into this remoteness—they were treated to a traveling survey of the shore in the launch with Henry. If they had been welcome enough to remain long—they had sometimes been included in the dignified but unprofitable fishing. If they had, as rarely happened, been acquaintances who were graced with Henry's conservative respect—they had even been permitted to read with him in the shadowy library. Otherwise the library had always been a section of the house sacred to Henry, and, until his illness, no one, except Cowpers, who went stealthily in for dusting and sweeping, had trespassed there except by special permission.

On the long wall, opposite a row of haughty windows, gloomily draped, the length of shelves was cut in the middle by a large square of dull green wall, extending down to a bookcase that rose only five feet from the floor. This space held a life-size portrait of Elizabeth, her plentiful hair glowing auburnly in the lamplight, her languorously slim, long hands drooping across the arms of the chair in which she had once, apparently, been seated in this very room. The polished top of the chair curved ornately outward on each side, a chosen dark backing for the coppery coiffure. The original chair stood facing a desk that was backed against the wall beneath the windows on the other side of the room. Ethel looked at the face that Henry had once, when verging on delirium, confided to her was the "handsomest, loveliest, and proudest face" he had ever known, adding the regretful comment that "Elizabeth should have been a man—too fierce a creature, much too fierce, to be content with womanhood!"

Elizabeth's low-lidded eyes shone deeply cobalt, crystal-hard beneath clinging dark lashes. The light smoldered into their glamorous width. They were rimmed with melting white that finished in abrupt, sharp corners. The high forehead curved whitely in at the temples, and the temples rounded into the slightly high cheekbones that would have been prominent but for the eyes, which made the whole pale face seem unusually slender. The nose was long and perfectly straight, finishing in delicate, wide nostrils. The mouth, full and deeply cleft beneath the nose, darted out on either side to very slim points. And the cheeks sloped sharply, almost gauntly, to a pointed chin. The face—luminously pale, and eyes, fascinatingly, liquidly brilliant—had been caught looking slightly to one side with an arrested musing expression that might have hidden anything from tenderness to the subtlest guile.

Watching the gleamily russet hair that curved airly out in contrast to the firm brow below it, and the tartar slenderness of the confidently tilted face, Ethel recognized a small shadow of resemblance to Henry's emaciated, ascetic jaw and mouth—but the firmness about Elizabeth's lips was not the sparse shrewdness of self-denial; it was the full, primitive strength of unslakable want. All of Elizabeth's calculating qualities, all of whatever restraint she might have had, all the instant perception, lurked in her eyes—wide enough to be oriental. The rest of her face might have been an adroitly taken death mask for all the traces it showed of what might be the impressions and wishes behind it. Ethel realized that if she herself still cared for Alfred she would hate and fear Elizabeth more than any other force, human or elemental, and that if Elizabeth were alive and desired Alfred she herself might just as well consider Alfred as immediately lost, and save herself the trouble and humiliation of fighting desperately against Elizabeth only to see the faint smile of facile winning flicker through Elizabeth's eyes.

She was suddenly aware that the scattered groupings of chords Alfred was touching on the piano had given way to a perceptible, rippling, to-and-fro melody, and the "Liebestraum" lilted through the book-walled room. Granted the several "ifs" about Elizabeth, Alfred, and herself, the music would have made her feel unbearably wretched, because it was not the sort of music that could make her angry. But Elizabeth being wholly dead, and she herself being irresistibly in love with Neville, the music only made her feel tenderly sorry for Alfred. She wondered if the trouble was that Alfred had really always loved Elizabeth, had never whole-heartedly given himself to his second marriage, and that was why Neville had been able to catch her own affection so easily in his cobwebby charm. The music halted abruptly, halfway through a bar. The bottom dropped suddenly out of the basket of sentimentality her thoughts were weaving. She realized that Alfred was a morose and broken middle-aged man, that he cared for nothing in the world but herself, and that there was no reason for making excuses for her meanness to him. But she knew she would be mean, and even downright cruel, because she could never rest without Neville, and because she was not yet thirty she was aware that she could not bring herself to tolerate a halfhearted existence devoted to coaxing happiness into Alfred's frustrated wreckage. Had she been ten, or even five, years older . . . .

She vaguely hauled out a bright-backed novel, presumably one of the pieces of bizarre fiction Frieda had smuggled in during Henry's illness, but she glanced through several pages only to realize that there were no capitals, no marks of punctuation, and unwilling to be confused by it, she was reaching it between two like-backed volumes when she sensed that the "Liebestraum" had ceased. Hesitant footsteps came from the living room, and Alfred stood framed in the low archway. His gloomy, resenting eyes bored into hers accusingly. An artificial smile refused to hide her face. He continued staring at her as if she had unjustly whipped him. She stood back from the shelf and brought herself to speak.

"What's the trouble—Alfred?"

A fleeting smile dimmed the gaze of his disappointed eyes. His puffy white lids blinked down over their staring shadows, and his eyes opened wider, as if with an effort to seem bright. He came slowly toward her, and took her arms in his white, sharp-knuckled hands, which felt moist and warm through her thin sleeves.

"You've hardly spoken to me all day," he said. His voice was low, pleading, and kind.

"I've been—asleep, Alfred." She thought her own voice sounded flimsy.

His eyes ignored the shrinking reserve in her eyes and his look probed slowly and strongly into her until she was afraid. "You don't need," he said, as if he knew the futility of saying it, "to avoid me now—now that they all know who—you are."

"I thought," she smiled feebly, "we talked this all over last night." He said nothing. He seemed to be looking at her hair, the edge of her temple, and then into her eyes again. She tried once more. "You don't seem to take what I said seriously."

"No," he answered patiently, "I've been trying not to take it seriously—all day." His colorless face, with the sagging shadows beneath his eyes and the lines graven down about his resigned mouth, was drawing close to her own. She shook her head a little, and looked away. She stared at the portrait, it's gilt frame shiny between the looming bookcases.

"You don't really love me, Alfred. You can't after having her." Alfred's head turned with a quick distrust to look at Elizabeth's slim, white face. "You just wanted someone to help you forget her, and I'm not capable of that." His fingers tightened on her arms. "Or, perhaps, I reminded you of her. My hair is a little like that—not as lovely . . . ." His fingers clutched painfully into her arms.

"Stop," he said gruffly. "You don't know—what you're saying." His eyes were fierce and demanding. Then, as they met hers once more, they wilted. The puffy lids dropped palely. His fingers loosened, and his hands dropped to his sides. He turned away and went slowly through the doorway without looking back. The piano playing began again with hushed, lingering notes. They were not of the "Liebestraum." They were meanderingly melancholy—no tune holding them together. She took a book, any book, went through other door and upstairs. She opened her door expecting to discover Neville sitting on the edge of the bed, but he was not there. The piano playing continued from downstairs. It was louder. There were definite tunes. Some she recognized. After she had brushed her teeth in the bathroom at the other end of the corridor, she came back, again expecting Neville. But, again, he was not there. She undressed, creamed her face, wrapped the kimono over her night dress, and crawled into bed to smoke a cigarette and read. The novel dealt with a prurient shoe salesman who was bullied by his wife and wanted his son to become a Senator. Between chapters, or even pages, she stopped a few seconds to let the piano music absorb her, think with pitying aloofness of Alfred and his pathetic, dog-like face. The idea of Alfred became too depressing and she was unable to change her own feelings even if she had wanted to. She let herself mull through page after page of the vicissitudes that befell the aspiring shoe salesman, with the distant notes of the piano constantly striking dully into her. She tried not to be foolishly intrigued by the hope that Neville would, sooner or later, come to the window and at least say good night to her.

Once she fancied she heard a faint noise against the window pane or on the sill outside. She turned off the lamp, raised the shade, pushed open the casement. No one was there. She listened in the absolute silence of the night air, only made more absolute by the dim rippling of piano notes which were smothered in the quiet, chill darkness. The burnished points of the stars were scintillant up and down the vast inky-blue sky. The silhouettes of the pines were motionless. From somewhere on the lake came the low, crackling noises of the ice.

She saw a shadow pass across the lighted, drawn shade of Courtney's window. There was no light in Harvey's room, but she could see Harvey through the bright window opening from the room where Henry's body was, standing over the table on which the body lay, busy with silvery instruments. He paused to light his pipe and draw the shade. There was no light, as far as Ethel could see, in Frieda's window. She closed her own casement, drew the curtain, relighted the lamp, and eased herself back to the unglamorous shoe clerk with another cigarette. She was beginning to wonder if Alfred would go on with his melancholy piano playing all night. The noise was not enough to keep her awake, but she feared that without the book to burrow in she would be kept from sinking into sleep by a quantity of tawdry sentiment that threatened to engulf her. The piano continued and she went on reading.

# CHAPTER XIV

A quarter of an hour later she heard a distinct tapping on the pane of the window. The uninterrupted music had risen into the triumphing strength of the "Tannhauser Overture." She twisted the button on the lamp and stepped over to raise the shade to the middle bar of the window. Neville was crouched in the darkness outside. He raised his hand. She pushed open the window. His hands were strong and cold as they clasped her own. His lips were insistent and warm when he kissed her quickly.

"Juliet mustn't get bronchitis," he said. "Let me come in." She went over to turn the key in her door as he climbed through the window, shut it behind him, and pulled down the curtain. She turned on the lamp. He took a key and a small sheet of paper from his trouser pocket, and handed her the paper. "What do you make of this? It was pushed through the crack under my door with the key to the room less than a minute ago." Scrawled in ink across the scrap of paper were the words. "Neville, come to the room where your father's body is in about two minutes. Don't let anyone see you. Be sure. Harvey."

"Did you go?"

"No," he said. "I wouldn't open the door. I thought it was some kind of trap. I thought I'd come 'round this way. Damned strange." He went over to unlock her door and look cautiously into the dim hallway outside. The music thundered louder from downstairs, careening through rapid crescendos, "Who's at the piano?"

"Alfred," she said. "He's been playing steadily for almost an hour. I definitely told him—that I'm—fond of you." He turned, smiling, and embraced her, then went to the door.

"I'm going to creep around to that room," he said. "Stay here." He disappeared into the hallway, leaving the door ajar behind him.

He had been gone about fifteen interminable seconds. The notes of the music were dancing noisily, madly, with increasing swiftness. She heard a throaty, terrified shout, which finished when a loud shot banged through the corridors, and the shock of it left her motionless for several seconds. The music stopped on a suspended chord. She went into the hallway. Frieda's door was flung open and Frieda darted out, and over the stairs to the other corridor. Ethel hurried after her and heard Frieda give a terrified little shriek.

"Neville," she was saying, "Neville—what have you done?"

As she hurried up the five stairs to the other corridor she could see Neville standing in a lighted doorway looking into the room where Harvey had been working on the body. Frieda was bent sobbing over a prone figure on its side just in front of the doorway. She went to look over Frieda's heaving shoulders. Courtney's wide open, startled, dead eyes gazed hideously up at her. There was a small, round hole bored darkly into his right temple, from which a glistening trickle fell over his gray hair to a tiny dark pool on the carpet. Frieda was making little whimpering sounds through her sobs as she feverishly chafed one of Courtney's limp wrists.

Ethel followed Neville's gaze into the room. Beside a long wooden table, on which a sheet covered all but Henry's left arm and shoulder, Harvey lay on the floor face down, his left arm crumpled underneath him, his right sprawled out angularly from the shoulder, the missing dagger plunged into the back of his white shirt just to one side of the left shoulder blade. Not two feet from the outstretched right hand the revolver glittered on the bare floor.

"Was that a shot?" Ethel turned and saw Alfred coming up from the stairs.

"It was," Neville said tersely, walked into the room, and stooped to pick up the revolver beside Harvey. He broke it open and took out one discharged shell. The rest of the chambers were empty.

Alfred's incredulous eyes wavered from Courtney's figure to the bulky outlines of Harvey and back again. "My God," he murmured, "they certainly got each other." He leaned down to take Frieda's shaking shoulders between his hands and lifted her gently to her feet. She was completely, passively hysterical. "Come," he said, "you'll go all to pieces if you stay here." She allowed herself to be half led, half carried, along the corridor to the stairs, and across to her own room. Alfred came quietly back along the hall. "Well," he said to Neville, "what shall we do?"

"Let's leave everything the way it is," Neville replied, "go downstairs and see if we can figure it out." He pocketed the revolver. Ethel followed Alfred along the hallway. Neville pushed her quickly aside to walk just behind Alfred. As they started over the stairs Neville reached for Ethel's arm, and held his mouth close to her ear to whisper a hurried "Bullets—my room—bureau," and went down after Alfred.

"I'll be down," Ethel said, "in just a second." She pretended to go into the bathroom. When they were ought of sight below she hurried through the dark room where Janet's body lay among the shadows on the bed, and in through the door to Neville's room. Hastily turning the lamp button, she opened the two small upper drawers of Neville's bureau. In the right-hand one, among rows of folded neckties, she glimpsed a worn pasteboard box. She poured half a dozen cartridges into the palm of one hand, put out the light, and went downstairs.

Alfred sat on the lounge staring into the fire. Neville sat in the wing chair beside the chimney, the empty revolver in his hands. "I can't understand," he was saying, "when or why Harvey took the rest of these cartridges from the chamber. The thing was full when I had it last night, and it hasn't been used since then, except for the one bullet which went into Courtney."

"I can't understand any of it," Alfred said. "I suppose one or both of them might be able to tell us what was what. But with both of them dead we're even further away from knowing what's back of it than we were before. I suppose we never will know,"

"That's possible," Neville said, "but we can try to find out—at least until we can get the police out here."

Ethel went 'round to the table behind the lounge and opened a box of cigarettes with her free right hand. She was standing just back of Alfred's head. Her eyes met Neville's. She let the cartridges slip from her left hand onto the soft surface of the oriental rug just behind the box on the table, lighted her cigarette, and went over to sit in the chair opposite Neville.

"It's a little item," Neville went on, "like this empty gun chamber, which may lead us to puzzle out which one was the criminal . . . ." He rose inconsequentially, getting up to go 'round back of the table. Alfred's eyes swerved to follow him until Neville tucked a cigarette between his lips and handed the box far over the table to Alfred, letting his elbow hide the bullets. Alfred took a cigarette. His eyes were squarely on Ethel as he lighted it and Neville was tucking cartridges with swift fingers into the chamber of the revolver. He slid the revolver into his pocket, touched a match to his own cigarette, and wandered back, puffing heavily, to sprawl into the wing chair, his booted legs stretched out before him, his brilliant eyes studying Alfred between half closed lashes. A door slammed above them and Frieda appeared on the stairway. She had stopped crying, but her eyes were red and glaring. Her small hand shook as it slid along the bannister. She spoke—not to, but at, Neville as she came down to him stair by stair.

"You did it—Neville." Her voice was rasping weakly. "I saw you."

"You did not," Neville replied in a matter-of-fact tone.

"I saw you there in the hall," she babbled, beginning to sob again in a trembling hysteria. "I saw you there the first thing—when I came out."

"I saw Courtney shot," Neville said, "but I didn't do it. The shot came from the room where Harvey was."

"Did you see Harvey fire the shot?" Alfred asked him.

"No," Neville admitted, "I saw Courtney backing out of the room with a ghastly look on his face. Then he screamed. The shot was fired and he fell dead."

"You went right into the room? Was Harvey still alive?"

"I did *not* go right into the room. I didn't want to get drilled. The trap was set for me in the first place. Courtney blundered into it."

A blank surprise had come over Frieda's convulsing face. Her voice stuck when she tried to speak. "What—makes you—think a *trap*—was set for you?"

Neville plucked the note and key from his pocket and passed them to Alfred. "These were passed under my door about two minutes before the shot was fired." Neville drew the revolver deftly from his pocket as he sat down and made a sweeping gesture toward the lounge. "Do sit down—Mother. You'll be interested in what I have to say." Frieda started back slightly when the wave of the gun included her. Then, as she shrank over to the lounge, Alfred placed the note and key on the arm beside him, folded his arms, and sat back in a bored fashion.

"The gun is empty, Frieda." His voice was reassuring.

Neville pointed the revolver at the ceiling. His fingers contracted. A flashing explosion deafened them. Frieda screamed. Neville lowered the gun and his eyes twinkled at Alfred, whose eyes were horrified and unbelieving. "I—thought you said it was empty!" he exclaimed.

"It was," Neville told him, "when I found it."

Alfred swallowed his surprise. "After you saw Courtney shot, how long did you wait before looking into the room?"

"I heard something fall and saw the revolver slide along the floor from where I was standing. I went in. Harvey was dead by the time I got to him."

"You were in the hallway," Frieda insisted, "when I saw you."

"Yes. I was making sure that Courtney was dead."

"I can't understand," Alfred muttered, "why Courtney should have stabbed him."

"Courtney didn't stab him," Neville laughed.

Alfred leaned forward. "How do you know so much about this."

"I know," Neville admitted, "only what Harvey told me at supper time. I was locked up then and I couldn't do anything about it." A terrified wonder began to grip Ethel, watching Neville speaking so calmly and tersely. "Harvey explained the whole thing to me. He had the revolver and I was helpless. It was his business anyhow, not mine." Neville turned his gaze to Ethel. "Elizabeth and my father were killed by the same person. You heard the buzzer ring from that room this afternoon when Harvey was downstairs. He had spliced the wires on the button fixture in father's room so that they made a connection, and he had severed the wires in the cellar near the electrical transformer. When he touched those wires in the cellar together—the buzzer rang. It was very simple. That's why no one was ever discovered in the room immediately after the murders. In the case of father it was a bit difficult—because I was to be made the goat.

"Tracks were made across the room with my rubbers. Windows and doors were adjusted to indicate that I'd done it and slipped away over the roof. After the buzzer had been rung from outside the room was watched. When Ethel didn't appear there was a danger she might sleep through it and I might return before the thing was discovered. And the murderer took a chance that made everything seem more convincing, pushed the actual button in father's room, and slipped into my room . . . ."

"But," Alfred objected, "you say the wires on the button were spliced. That would render the button useless."

"Yes," Neville conceded it would, "but I haven't finished."

"Why was I locked in the room?" Ethel asked.

"Because," said Neville, "the getaway—really—was not onto the roof but through the house. The door slamming, the footprints, the whole thing was a hoax, and you had to be kept in that room. Whoever did it must have known you pretty well to be sure you wouldn't scream right away, to be certain you'd be curious enough to follow down those noises and not get panic stricken first thing."

"How," Alfred wanted to know, "was Elizabeth ever persuaded to drink poison?"

"Probably given to her in coffee or tea or some such thing, and then the glass with the traces of poison in it planted on the table after she was dead. People *will* drink things, you know, if they have no reason to suspect. I was drugged last night. I couldn't have slept through the fracas in any other way. I was made the goat again. Slugged over the head and tossed into the drift from the downstairs piazza. I couldn't possibly have gotten that bump even by diving head first into a drift. And as for the piazza railing—it's several feet in under the edge of the roof. I couldn't have fallen anywhere near it. I was probably given a harmless but nasty looking bruise by the poker that Courtney found in the kitchen, just after Harvey said he was knocked out."

"Wait a minute," Alfred said. "You're trying to tell us that he strangled Janet, went downstairs and threw you into the drift, then locked himself in the cellar, made a connection on the wires to ring the buzzer, gave himself a fake blow on the head and then let things happen?"

"Well," Neville said, "doesn't it sound reasonable?"

"But the key to the cellar door was found in your pocket."

"That's true." Neville's eyelids dropped as he studied the worn toes of his boots. Then he looked up. "Perhaps he locked the door first, put the key in my pocket, and went in through the bulkhead."

"That seems more probable. But how about Courtney? Why should Harvey shoot him?"

"I told you Courtney blundered into that. Harvey had given me all this information. But with a bullet through me—everything was set. He was clear. He'd locked me up—because of evidence incriminating me in the murders of my father and Janet. Elizabeth's poisoning was a matter of some question. But he had the goods on me for a stabbing and a strangling, and I was shot when I escaped from the room and threatened him. The dagger was right there. And when he got Courtney by mistake . . . ." Neville gave a conclusive wave of the gun.

"You think," Alfred said incredulously, "that he stabbed himself when he realized he'd shot Courtney?"

"There was nothing else to do," Neville answered, "with only one cartridge in the gun."

Alfred stared gloomily into the fire. Then his head jerked up toward Neville. "How could Harvey ever have gotten in through the window and persuaded Henry that there was nothing out of the way."

"Father might have been asleep; and, besides, he didn't go in the window."

"But the dagger miscarried the first time—that slash on the arm. Surely there would have been some outcry."

"That stabbing was a hoax, too," Neville told him. "Harvey himself said father must have been poisoned. Something about the pupils of the eyes proved that."

"I know," Alfred said, "but we found no traces of poison in the stomach."

"He wasn't poisoned the way Elizabeth was," Neville said. "Poison was injected through the arm with a hypodermic needle. That slash with the dagger was to cover up the pin prick made by the injection. The little glass tube and the cork stopper that held the poison with which the hypodermic was filled were thrown into the fireplace. Harvey got the melted pieces out this afternoon when he was alone down there."

"Good God!" Alfred murmured, and turned to Ethel, "That's what he was doing when we watched him from upstairs."

"How about the letters?" Ethel wanted to know. "They were here on the table when Harvey and I came downstairs this morning, and when I went upstairs they were almost burned up in the fire."

"That was very simple," Neville explained. "There were only three people who could have taken those—you, Mother, and Harvey. You disappeared when you started into the library. Harvey had already been upstairs. Mother was upstairs at the time."

"Had he taken them from Janet's desk," Alfred asked, "before he talked with her about them?"

"He didn't take them. Mother did. Harvey proved that today—when he got Mother confused about a shoehorn, and Courtney made the usual blunders. Taking them was a bad move in the first place, but once you had them—" his eyes arched slightly at Frieda, "you should have read them."

"I didn't have time," Frieda fluttered. "Janet found out too soon. I was afraid I'd get caught with them. I thought they must have some bearing on the thing. Then I wanted to give them to Harvey, but Courtney wouldn't let me. We'd just decided to read them when Janet was killed. After that I just wanted to get rid of them. So I left them on the table."

"And by doing that," Neville reminded her, "you made it very easy for someone to toss them into the fire—and plant the crumpled envelope on my bed."

"And the 'phone call—last night," Alfred said out of a deep musing, "*was* a fake."

"Not from my end," Neville replied, "I was on shore alright."

"And the wires were tapped in the cellar."

"The wires were *scraped* in the cellar—more hoaxing." Neville corrected him. "There's no proof that any instrument was fastened on. That was a point that almost gave things completely away. Harvey was quite pleased with himself for getting around it. Told it to me as a great joke. The wires had been scraped with a penknife. It left little specks of sticky black insulation on the blade. When he was fooling with the button fixture this morning he almost forgot himself and used his own knife. Perhaps no one would have noticed. But he used yours instead."

"What was he doing in Alfred's room just before dinner?" Ethel demanded.

"I suppose he'd taken the hypodermic originally from Alfred's medicine satchel and was returning it."

"Why was he probing into Henry's corpse?" Alfred inquired.

"The hypodermic needle had broken off about a quarter of an inch from the tip. He wanted to get it out."

"You're trying to make us believe," Alfred said sharply, "that Harvey stabbed himself after he shot Courtney. He couldn't have. He was stabbed in the back."

"That's right," Neville laughed, "I hadn't thought of that."

"And then Hodges . . . ." Alfred persisted, "are you trying to tell me the whiskey was poisoned when it was left down cellar?"

"Who says the whiskey was poisoned?" Neville demanded. "I drank a glassful—and it didn't kill me."

"That means," Alfred said tersely, "that you were the only one who could have put poison into the liquor that killed him."

"Yes," Neville repeated in a dry voice, "I was the only one who *could* have . . . . We mustn't forget about Hodges, either—those cheques—his sister who left our employ to get married two years ago. Only five people knew the explanation of that—Hodges, his sister, my father, you, and Harvey."

"What did Harvey tell you about it?"

"That Hodges' sister had been my father's mistress—and had a child by him." Ethel was watching Frieda's blanched amazement at being thus paid in her own coin. "You and Harvey were the doctors who supervised the child's birth two years ago in Syracuse. There—among strangers—Hodges masqueraded as the woman's husband, and has since acted as go-between for any transfers of money, which occurred regularly. He was, I suppose, to serve as beneficiary in the will—bound to turn the funds over to his sister. It was a thoroughly confidential matter and need never have been raked up. But the man whom Hodges saw tampering with wires in the cellar must have been someone who knew the story. He may even have spoken to Hodges and warned him not to tell—or the story about the sister would be told in return. This was quite a hold over Hodges and kept him quiet until we began to nag him about the cheque. Then, when he saw the sister's story was coming out anyway, he was on the point of identifying the man in the cellar—only to be killed. He was not poisoned, however, by what he drank at the table. The whiskey bottle disappeared; so did the glasses. What's more—there was no evidence of poison in Hodges' stomach when Harvey performed an autopsy. He was killed with a hypodermic—just as father was, and his body was defaced to conceal any trace of the small needle wound."

"We're taking your word for all of this," Alfred snapped, "when, as a matter of fact, you're in an even worse position now than you were after the first three murders. It's pretty incredible that Harvey should tell you all these things if he did the killings himself—even if he did plan to shoot you. He was no idiot."

"I've been telling you how it was done," Neville said more sharply. "I haven't told you who did it. Harvey said he wasn't sure himself."

"But you've been implying that he . . . ."

"Maybe I have," Neville barked, standing up in his excitement. "But Harvey wasn't the one. He had no motive at all for doing all this. He did have a motive for trying to get to the bottom of it. He wanted to acquit me. Everything that's happened here for the past twenty-four hours has been foisted onto me. I suppose there wasn't any reason for that! Harvey suspected *you*, Alfred, when he first arrived and found father looking as if he'd been poisoned. He wondered why your professional smartness hadn't noticed that and said something about it. He was thrown off when the letters disappeared, because he was with you at the time. He said you were obviously worried about those letters. And Janet made some reference to you in connection with them. The minute Janet found out Ethel was your wife—she knew immediately that you'd not only killed father and Hodges, but Elizabeth as well. You strangled Janet to keep her from telling. I don't know exactly why you killed Elizabeth, but we all know you hated her, and I'll admit she made life miserable for you. For all I know you may have met Ethel—and knew you could never have her unless you got rid of Elizabeth." The dull smile on Alfred's face was fading into a stare of total blankness. Neville's words pounded on.

"No one ever suspected about Elizabeth, until those bankers wrote from London. You knew where she did her banking, and recognized the postmark. Father may have questioned you about that trust. You knew where he kept his letters, and you could have gotten a look at them damned. easily. You probably read the letter from Harvey, and you realized things were beginning to get ragged for you. Father was dying, although you tried to hide it from us, and you knew I was in love with your wife. So you got both birds with one stone when you put father out of the way and thought you'd planted it on me. You figured Ethel probably wouldn't become deeply infatuated with a murderer—

and you were right. It was all planned—and pretty well planned, even to scraping those wires to make them look as if they'd been tapped. But Harvey had you on that when he used your knife this morning.

"You knew Hodges would keep quiet about seeing you in the cellar because of his sister. I was unconsciously playing into your hands when I tried to get him drunk to make him talk. You knew I'd taken my glass of whiskey. You threw your own onto the table—and snatched Hodges' glass away when it was almost gone. At the same second you were holding him by the left shoulder with your right hand. I didn't see what you did, and I don't suppose anyone else noticed either. We didn't see it—because you kept us watching the glasses you threw down and the change of expression on Hodges' face. But I presume you plunged the hypodermic into the back just beneath the left shoulder blade—and drew it away in the palm of your hand when he flopped forward onto the table. With two or three violent motions you were able to cover up the one essential gesture near his shoulder. I think you almost fooled Hodges himself—but you remember he muttered something about a 'sharp pain' just before he went unconscious. It seemed to me at the time that he died altogether too quickly to have been poisoned by what he drank. But poison going directly into the blood stream is quite another thing.

"You tried out the hypodermic method on Hansel some time late yesterday afternoon, and covered up any traces there might have been of the needle by gouging him with a saw. From Hansel's reaction you had a way of figuring how long it would take to overcome a human being. In that way you knew exactly what you were doing when you went after Hodges.

"You saw those letters on the table at breakfast time. That envelope you hid on my bed was dated 1902. That was the year you were engaged to Janet. I suppose those were love letters you'd written to her, and when they disappeared she had another reason for supposing you were up to something. That was all Mother's fault for taking the letters. When you saw them on the table this morning, you threw all but one envelope in the fire. You remember—Harvey and Courtney were upstairs with me—and you went down alone to speak to Mother. You had a chance to fix them when you went through the living room. When you came up—you slipped the envelope onto my bed.

"Harvey suspected you because of the knife, but that wasn't much to go on. He played a few tricks with the buzzer, but it hadn't been tampered with when he first opened up the button socket. So it couldn't have been rung from the cellar. It must have been rung by independent batteries and a switch tapped on somewhere between Father's room and the buzzer itself. I knew where the wires ran. I put them in myself—under the flooring across the hall, under the floor of Mother's room, and yours—and up the far wall of Ethel's room to the buzzer itself. Harvey was hunting for some such arrangement when Ethel surprised him in there before dinner. He also found a hypodermic in your medicine kit—with the tip of the needle broken off. He couldn't locate any electrical fixture—and decided he'd have to get you by discovering the tip of the needle in the arm of the corpse. I found the electrical stuff myself while you were downstairs at the piano—about an hour ago. I didn't need a key to get out of my room. That was one thing you didn't figure on.

"That electrical switch, by the way, is very neat—so you can press a button on the floor with the toe of your shoe just behind the leg of the table beside the bed. I pulled up a loose floorboard and found two dry cell batteries and the tap, as I suspected, onto the wiring. It worked when you were sitting in there with Harvey and signaled Elizabeth's death. You tried it again for Father—only Ethel didn't appear soon enough and you got caught sneaking back to Father's room to rearrange a clue, and you had to do some door locking. It worked all right for Janet when you were sitting in the same place talking to Ethel.

"As for Harvey—he thought you were at the piano tonight, and figured he was safe as long as you stayed there. I thought you were at the piano myself until I heard the middle of that 'Tannhauser Overture.' You happened to put the one roll on the player part of the piano that I know almost by heart. No one can play it the way it's played on that roll. I've tried hundreds of times. You unlocked a window by the piano, started the roll, came upstairs, stabbed Harvey quietly in the back while he was looking for the tip of the needle, placed him on the floor with his right arm stretched out, slipped the note and key under my door, went back to the room where Harvey was and waited. You were going to hold me at the point of the gun until the proper place in the music for the break—I suppose you'd cut the roll off at that point—shoot me just before you knew the music would stop, duck out the window, drop to the ground and get in to the piano over the downstairs piazza through the unlocked window. You did exactly that—but you had to shoot Courtney instead of me. You took the cartridges out of the revolver just after you stabbed Harvey—in case anyone got the gun and suspected you. It almost worked. If you'd gotten me—I would have been the goat and no one else would ever have been suspected. It was 'Tannhauser,' Courtney's blessed stupidity, and Harvey's intelligence . . . ."

The telephone bell rattled insistently through the silent room.

"Wires along shore must have been repaired," Neville murmured, as Frieda hurried into the library.

"A hospital in Syracuse calling for Dr. Harvey," Frieda was saying with a baffled expression.

"Tell them he's been murdered," Neville replied, "and then call the police. The lake must be solid enough now. They can get across with a team and sleigh." Frieda went dumbly back to the library and spoke softly into the telephone with a tired, dreary voice.

"All right," Alfred's face worked into the dull, beaten smile again. "All right, Neville, I give up." His white hand flashed from the right hand pocket of his coat with a short, needle-tipped tube of glass. As Neville started forward the needle buried itself in Alfred's left arm—just below the shoulder. Neville let the revolver fall to his side, watching Alfred's right hand relaxing away from the hypodermic. Alfred's shoulders drew up sharply and he fell back against the lounge. His mad, beseeching eyes turned to Ethel. They were changing slowly into a fixed stare. His loosening lips moved weakly. His voice was deep in his throat.

"It was because—of you," he murmured. "That's why I had to . . . ." His voice dropped into a sigh. His head fell back over one shoulder. His eyelids drooped. He seemed asleep.

**COACHWHIP PUBLICATIONS**
**COACHWHIPBOOKS.COM**

# THE
# RUMBLE
# MURDERS

Henry Ware Eliot, Jr.

MURDER
A LA
MODE

ELEANORE
KELLY
SELLARS

CLASSIC RED BADGE PRIZE MYSTERY

**COACHWHIP PUBLICATIONS**
**COACHWHIPBOOKS.COM**

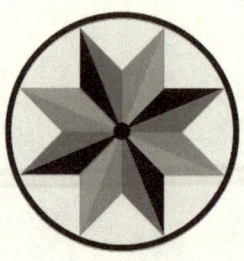

# THE HEX MURDER

## Alexander Williams

COACHWHIP PUBLICATIONS
COACHWHIPBOOKS.COM

THE
DARTMOUTH
MURDERS

THE
WAILING ROCK
MURDERS

CLIFFORD
ORR

**COACHWHIP PUBLICATIONS**
**COACHWHIPBOOKS.COM**

LOUIS F. BOOTH

THE BANK VAULT MYSTERY
BROKERS' END

COACHWHIP PUBLICATIONS
COACHWHIPBOOKS.COM

CRIME IN
CORN-WEATHER

MARY MEIGS ATWATER